For my sons, Glyn and Warren.

THE RISE AND FALL OF BARTLE FRERE

Colonial Rule in India and South Africa

Roy Digby Thomas

authorHOUSE®

AuthorHouse™ UK Ltd.
500 Avebury Boulevard
Central Milton Keynes, MK9 2BE
www.authorhouse.co.uk
Phone: 08001974150

First published by AuthorHouse 10/20/2009

ISBN: 978-1-4490-3043-8 (sc)

Library of Congress Control Number: 2009910259

This book is printed on acid-free paper.

Other Books by the Author

Digby: The Gunpowder Plotter's Legacy

George Digby: Hero and Villain

Outram in India

CONTENTS

Acknowledgements

As with previous books, I am indebted to my two sons, Glyn and Warren, for their ideas, suggestions and advice. They both lead very busy lives, and I am grateful for the time and effort they have devoted to my cause.

A number of other people have contributed significantly to this book. Joe Roberts polished up my prose and shaped my ideas. Jim Young applied his sharp mind to the broad historical sweep and offered good advice. Anthony Coleman, a guide to the Natal battlefields, gave me fresh information and helped me put the Anglo-Zulu War into an appropriate perspective. Norman Leveridge, the archivist at Talana Museum in Dundee, Natal, assisted considerably by not only locating the files I needed but earmarking the passages that were of value to me. I enjoyed talking over some of the more controversial issues of the Anglo-Zulu war with him.

I am grateful to the Army Museum in London for giving me permission to use an image of the painting in their possession, "The Last Stand of the 24ᵗʰ" by C.E.Fripp for the front cover of this book.

The portrait of Bartle Frere at the front of the book is reproduced by kind permission of the National Portrait Gallery, London.

The maps in the book, which are so important to an understanding of the action, were laboured over by Caroline and Bob Markham (the South African ones) and Alan Bridges (the Indian ones), to whom I tender my heartfelt thanks for a job well done.

Finally, no acknowledgement would be complete without my gratitude to my dear wife, Eileen, who not only supported, encouraged and helped me throughout the writing of this book, but conscientiously read the drafts (several times) to correct errors and suggest improvements.

R.D.T.

PORTRAIT OF BARTLE FRERE.

Maps.

Introduction

This book charts the life and career of Bartle Frere. He spent his entire working life in public service to the British Empire, first in India and latterly in South Africa. He was awarded high honours for his achievements in India. He served as Governor of Bombay and on the Governor-General's Council in Calcutta. On returning to London he was appointed to the Indian Council advising the Secretary of State for India. He was regarded as one of the leading experts on India.

Further commissions came his way. He succeeded in bringing a halt to the slave trade in East Africa emanating from Zanzibar, returning from his visit there to great acclaim. He received a baronetcy for his services. The Colonial Secretary saw in him the ideal person to bring together into a confederated state the disparate factions in South Africa, and he was appointed Governor of the Cape Colony with a wide brief and considerable authority to implement policies and edicts.

Within three years his career was destroyed, his name reviled in England. Politicians criticised him openly in

Parliament and the press was vitriolic. The Spectator referred to him as a man with "no influence but for evil" and "fanatically blind as to the fundamental laws of political responsibility."[1] Even recently the noted historian Norman Etherington wrote of him:

"When a bully with a black hat and a moustache is
caught with a smoking gun in
his hand, posses and juries don't ask very
penetrating questions. Neither, it is
embarrassing to admit, do historians. Frere was the
sort of villain cinema audiences
love to hate, a sanctimonious, pig-headed, officious,
self-righteous, ambitious city
slicker from out of town."[2]

How did it come about that a man so feted, so devoted to public service that his private life and ambitions always remained subservient to his work, went from hero to villain in three short years? How could a leading administrator, renowned for his judgement, knowledge and steady leadership, have got it all so wrong in South Africa?

Frere's decision to declare war on the Zulus led to his downfall. The disastrous defeat at Isandlwana, in which almost all the British soldiers were killed, came as a huge shock in Britain. Doubtless Frere suffered from being the British Government's scapegoat for the defeat, and from attempts by desperate politicians to spin an account of culpability that took the opprobrium off their shoulders. That could not explain the full extent of his disgrace. His decisions and actions in South Africa were open to criticism, and the consequences disastrous. What caused him to act as he did, given his previous exemplary record?

This book will attempt to examine the causes and provide answers. It will show that some of the seeds of the disasters that were to follow could be seen in the mindset and actions of Frere himself during his days in India.

RDT.

Chapter 1

ORIGINS.

The name Frere was familiar in England well before Bartle Frere made it famous. Originally le Frere, it occurs in deeds and documents in Norfolk and Suffolk before the thirteenth century, the earliest mention being that of Henry le Frere in 1212. The coat of arms – two leopards with the motto "Frere ayme Frere" - can be seen in many parish churches in the eastern counties of England. John Frere, the earliest recorded member of the family, lived at Thetford in Suffolk in 1628, and the family owned estates in other parts of Suffolk and Norfolk until the twentieth century. John married into the Thurston family and is consequently often referred to erroneously as living in Thurston. The Thurston family seem never to have been connected with the place of that name.[3] The family came to greater prominence in the eighteenth century when another John Frere sat as Member of Parliament for Norwich and was High Sheriff of Suffolk. One of his seven sons, the poet John Hookham Frere, took centre stage in a prominent group of statesmen and scholars, and succeeded Lord Canning as Under-Secretary for Foreign Affairs. In 1800 John Hookham's brother Edward (1770-1844) married Mary Anne Greene, eldest daughter of James Greene of Llansanfraed in Monmouth, the Member of Parliament for Arundel in 1759. She bore him nine sons and five daughters, one of whom, Henry Bartle Edward, is the subject of this book.

There was nothing in his early days to suggest what Bartle Frere (the "Henry" was hardly ever used) would achieve in life, or how his name would become familiar to a whole nation, and to the generations that followed, although tracing his ancestry back in time discloses that he was directly descended from both Charlemagne and Alfred the Great. His father Edward was educated at Eton and studied metallurgy at St Quentin, in France. Edward's first job was in the infamous Albion Mills at Blackfriars Bridge in London, an engineering works of some renown with the first steam-driven corn mill in Britain. It was described by William Blake, who lived nearby, as "the satanic mill." Edward's father, John, was a large shareholder.

When the mill was destroyed by fire in 1791 Edward moved to Clydach, five miles from Abergavenny in Wales, and set up as an ironmaster. His father invested the huge sum in those days of £20,000 in the ironworks there, which Edward ran. Edward quickly gained a reputation for introducing worker benefit schemes well in advance of the age. He also attracted notice in 1811 for building an iron barge to ply on the canal at Clydach. This event caused quite a stir, as few local people believed it would float, and the entire population turned out to witness the launch. (It did float). Canals were blossoming across the industrial landscape of Britain, and this was cutting-edge technology. Edward was not the first to build an iron ship but it seems that this was the first iron barge in Wales. His knowledge of metallurgy also led to improvements in the fabric of coke iron, which in turn led to cable chains and iron suspension bridges. The ironworks gained a reputation for producing some of the best quality iron in Britain.

Bartle's parents appear to have possessed many attractive qualities. Edward was a good rider and dancer, and an ardent horticulturist. His granddaughter recalled that he had a "sweet and sunny temper, a great power of attracting others, a wonderful memory, and much inventive genius."[4] He collected books and was able to recite long tracts of poetry from memory. Bartle's mother was described as a quiet, gentle woman who also excelled in riding and dancing. It was she who provided the base values for the family, and quiet common sense. She was quoted as liking "the old-world idea of good breeding, hospitality, religion."[5] Both parents were deeply religious.

Bartle was born the sixth son at Clydach House on March 29, 1815. He was described as "a very pretty child, small, but beautifully formed, with a brown complexion, high colour, and very bright, expressive eyes."[6] He inherited his name from his uncle, also Bartle. The unusual name appears to have been an abbreviation of Bartholomew. The family was close and loving, and Bartle was to grow up in a stable, sympathetic environment. When he was three extensive riots broke out among the workers in South Wales campaigning for better conditions. Gangs, often several hundred strong, roamed the countryside compelling those who had not joined the cause to blow out their furnaces. Edward Frere, whose men were prepared to work on, was aware of the dangers and ensured the furnaces were out when the rioters appeared. On one occasion when he confronted them, he learnt that for days they had not enjoyed a square meal. He and his wife provided bread and cheese, prompting the response: "Oh, Sir, if our Masters had treated us as you do, we'd never have turned out."[7] Bartle, three years old, witnessed the scene and helped hand out the food, taking a little nibble on the way. The pretty child and his charming manners softened the hearts of the strikers even more. They raised a hearty cheer to him before moving on.

War with France caused the price of iron to fluctuate, and Edward proved to be a poor commercial manager, with an inadequate grasp of accountancy and cost control. Recurring labour problems among the workers in Wales added to his woes. Despite the Works' reputation for producing high-quality iron, the foundry was not profitable. Edward's brother, John Hookham Frere, who had inherited the bulk of the original capital from his father, (and therefore the majority ownership of the Works) was forced to make repeated loans.

Good quality education was not available in the rather remote district of Clydach. Bartle was seven years old before he could read, when he was rewarded with a prayer book of his own. Two years later it was common to find him so absorbed in what he was reading that he was oblivious to everything around him. Edward could not afford to send his sons to boarding school, so in 1822 the family moved to Bath. Edward placed the Clydach

Ironworks in the hands of an agent, and only visited it occasionally. The house they took was a small cottage near Prior Park.

Bartle and his brother Richard, two years younger, with whom he had close ties throughout his life, were sent to Edward VI's Foundation School as day scholars. Their cottage proved to be inconveniently far from the school, so in 1827 the family moved closer, to Sydenham Cottage on the banks of the Avon. The two boys crossed the Avon four times daily by ferry, which was worked by a ferryman hauling on a rope. In a letter written much later to his younger brother Arthur, Frere was to reminisce with some pleasure on summer days spent swimming in the Avon.[8] At the age of twelve Bartle and Richard were sent to Bath Grammar School as day boarders. The annual cost was £16, a large sum in those days. This school had a high reputation, boasting as former pupils Sir Sydney Smith and Sir Edward Parry. Bartle was later to describe the headmaster, the Reverend James Pears, (who was a friend of William Wilberforce) as a great scholar. It is possible that the link with Wilberforce was to influence Bartle's later active involvement in the anti-slave trade. Bartle's education at this stage could be described as rudimentary: he had learnt no Greek, rather modest skills in the three R's, a little Latin and French, and a considerable store of folklore from South Wales. He was an avid reader, and this stood him in good stead, for at the entrance examination the Headmaster remarked that he was "so well grounded in what he did know" that if all boys were as well taught at home he "would not wish them sent to school till the same age." [twelve].[9] Bartle particularly enjoyed travel books, and in later life could remember an impressive list of books which he had read before he was twelve, including Robinson Crusoe, Gulliver's Travels, Arabian Nights and several travelogues on Europe, America and the Far East.

Both at school and at home religion occupied an important place. Bartle was particularly influenced by Dr Jeremie, the Dean of Lincoln who was a junior fellow of Trinity College, Cambridge. An inspirational man with a keen intellect, he was able to harness passionate religious beliefs to muscular intellectuality. Bartle was to carry his firm religious beliefs into his public life, but his schooling also equipped him with an enquiring mind, a willingness to listen and a thirst for knowledge. Home life was happy. His cousin and early companion testified to his even temper, and his modest, unselfish personality made him very easy company. His father's interests in science and botany were passed on to his children.[10] The combination of a grammar school education and his father's encouragement to open his mind and broaden his interests had an important effect on Bartle's approach to life.

Bartle's wish was to be a soldier, missionary, doctor or "anything which would ensure his being a Traveller,"[11] but in 1832 his future career was determined by a stroke of good fortune. In order to place this in context, it is necessary to sketch in some background information. For those aspiring students who did not have the necessary connections, wealth or social position to move into the upper echelons of public service in Britain, India offered a glittering alternative. The English East India Company, founded in 1602 to explore trade with the Far East, had developed into an influential force in India, but only after a long struggle to establish itself. Known colloquially as "John Company" or simply as "The Company," in the first century of its existence it traded with the Indians in silk, cotton, spices, sugar, indigo dye and saltpetre in return for silver bullion, other metals, tapestries and mechanical novelties. It encountered stiff competition from the Dutch, Portuguese and French. Britain's dominance of the sea proved vital in prevailing over the French and Dutch, and confining the Portuguese to the area of Goa in the south-west of India.

A growing demand for tea led to a burgeoning trade in that commodity which eventually became the largest import into England. It had first been imported as a medicine and "digestif" in the 1660's. Samuel Pepys approved of it and by 1685 it was a fashionable drink at court. There was a significant increase in demand in the 1720's, thought to be linked to the import of sugar from the West Indies, and prices fell to a level that the ordinary citizens of Britain could afford. By 1770 tea was the single most important commodity in the Company's portfolio, and Company trade represented over ten percent of Britain's entire public revenue. In order to secure this trade, the Company was anxious to cement its position in India. This meant establishing warehouses and factories. The local population quite reasonably suspected creeping colonisation, and resisted these moves, but the Mughal rule, which had united India, was decaying, and by the mid-eighteenth century large, semi-independent states with their own rulers had emerged in the regions of Mysore, Hyderabad, Oudh, Bengal and Deccan. Whilst paying lip-service to the Mughal rulers in Delhi these new princes saw themselves as the legitimate successors to the Mughals.

These rulers, hitherto content to allow the Company to establish warehouses and factories close to ports, felt that the Company was impinging upon their sovereignty as it expanded inland. As the Mughal empire crumbled, its rulers felt increasingly vulnerable to interlopers, and offered resistance to the Company's expansion. However local armies, lacking support from outside their territory, were no match for the Company's army, comprising professional European officers and trained Indians, well-drilled and organised, equipped with modern weapons, Local rulers were forced to sign trading agreements that often involved the Company administering their territory in return for protection against intruders.

By the beginning of the nineteenth century India was largely under the control of the Company, although many states were still ruled nominally by Nawabs (princes, or deputies under the Moghul Empire). Direct management of the Company was in the hands of the Court of Directors in London, operating out of palatial offices in Leadenhall Street. As the Company became more involved in the direct administration of India, the British Government became interested, and not a little alarmed at the freedom of a private enterprise to control such a huge country. There was pressure in Parliament to abolish the Company and assume direct rule, but instead it was decided to establish a Board of Control to monitor the Court of Directors by a system of close scrutiny, consultation and accountability. Governors-General were to be appointed by the Board, almost always from outside the Company.

India was seen as offering young men unrivalled opportunities to make their reputation and fortune. Frequently they were placed in positions of great authority at an early age. In order to prepare these young men for their role, the East India Company established a training college, Haileybury in Hertfordshire, to provide a solid grounding in the civil and military disciplines necessary for colonial service in India. For many sons of middle class parents such a career offered the best option for advancement. Boys were normally admitted there at the age of fifteen and spent three years studying mathematics, natural philosophy, classical and general literature, and law, history and political economy as well as Oriental languages. Victorian Britain was still a country of privilege and class, where who you knew and where you came from was more important than what you knew, or what you could do. Indeed Haileybury itself was a college of class differentiation: most of the pupils were the offspring of senior officials in the East India Company, or the sons of the aristocracy.

Fortunately for Frere and three of his brothers, William, Richard and Arthur, their father enjoyed patronage through his brother, John Hookham Frere, who had been an envoy to Spain during the Peninsula War, and was a friend of Lord Canning, the Foreign Secretary. Their uncle promised to pay the cost of Bartle's education there, as he was the boy's godfather. In addition Frere's grandfather had been a Member of Parliament and his mother the daughter of a politician. Through a connection with the Chairman of the Court of Directors of the East India Company the boys were able to gain entry to Haileybury.

The college proved an ideal finishing school for Frere. There he learnt Indian languages, political economics and was introduced to evangelism. Dr Jeremie, the Dean of Lincoln, taught there. There were only thirty young men at the college, one of the aims being to develop close bonds between the scholars that would carry through to their service in India. Bartle remained there for a year and a half, excelling at all subjects, gaining medals and prizes and passing out top of his year in 1834 at the age of nineteen. This enabled him to choose from several options available to him in India. He elected to serve in the Bombay Presidency, probably because his elder brother William was already there. Although the East India Company organisation in India was presided over by a Governor-General resident in Calcutta, for historical reasons Bombay and a large area of the country surrounding it was run from Bombay. The Bombay Governor was answerable to the Governor-General in Calcutta, but enjoyed considerable latitude in governing his province. This included having his own army.

Recruits to the East India Company were expected to bear a considerable proportion of their expenses themselves. The usual method of reaching India in those days was by ship around the Cape of Good Hope, which took up to four months. This was a great inconvenience, as the ships were cramped and young recruits had to pay around £95 for their passage, a sum many (including Frere) could ill afford. Once again John Hookham Frere came to the rescue, paying Bartle's initial expenses in preparation for his journey to India. At the time Frere started for India, steamboats were radically changing the manner and speed of the journey, and the Governor-

General of India, Lord William Bentinck, was exploring feasible overland routes. He planned to send a steamer from Bombay to Suez to "meet any adventurous persons coming from England."[12] When Frere suggested to his employers that he try out this route, they refused to countenance such a risky venture. Frere pointed out that Egypt was at that time peaceful, that such a trip would test the feasibility of the overland route and that he was bound to pick up companions along the way. Finally the Company gave way, on condition that the journey was his own responsibility as no one would come looking for him if he went missing.

Frere left England on May 3, 1834. He sailed from Falmouth on the packet *Firefly* to Malta, where he stayed with his uncle, John Hookham Frere for a month. This was as far as any steamer from Britain went. Whilst waiting for an onward connection he set himself to learn Arabic, and by the time he left, his teacher pronounced him capable of "scolding his way through Egypt."[13] He sailed for Alexandria on July 7 in the Greek brigantine *Corriere*. There he met three army officers and a midshipman all set on the same goal as he. They went on together to Cairo, taking the opportunity to sightsee at a time when European visitors were still not very plentiful. No news of the steamer had been received, so from Cairo, after visiting Carnac, Luxor and Thebes they crossed the desert on camels to Kossier, a port on the Red Sea about 350 miles from Suez, which they reached on August 12. There they learnt that the steamer had not progressed past Ceylon (Sri Lanka).

The only alternative to returning to England was to find a boat to take them down the coast to Mocha, in the

Yemen, more than 900 miles away, where they hoped they might obtain a passage to India. With the help of the local British Consul, an Arab, they chartered a ship's longboat, open to the elements, which was being used as a fishing boat, and without shade in the middle of summer set out for Mocha. They crossed to the east coast, threading their way through the many coral islands, sandbanks and reefs. They landed at night to cook and sleep. A violent storm one night blew them out to sea and nearly swamped the boat, but they finally reached Mocha on August 31. There the midshipman left them, taking ship for Madras (now called Chennai), while the rest boarded an Arab dhow crowded with pilgrims from Mecca bound for Bombay, two thousand miles away. Conditions were far from easy. Bad weather induced by the tail end of the south-west monsoon drove the dhow from its course. The captain had no direction-finding equipment, and navigated by Frere's pocket compass. Instead of taking two weeks the voyage lasted three weeks, causing a shortage of food. Nevertheless Frere and his companions, half-starved and ragged, reached Bombay safely on September 23. When he went to his bankers to draw some money and find out where his brother lived he was treated with great suspicion, as no British ship had docked. Nor did his brother recognise the tall, sunburnt figure of Bartle.

INDIA IN THE 19th CENTURY

Chapter 2.

BOMBAY.

Bartle's brother William worked as a civil officer in the judicial branch of the Company in Bombay. Bartle moved in with him and set about passing the stringent language exams that all new civil officials were obliged to take to be eligible for an appointment. This aim he achieved in three months. By December, duly qualified in Hindi, Maharatta and Gujerati, he was ready to take up his post, and was appointed a junior revenue officer in the important city of Pune, one hundred miles south of Bombay, in the heart of Maharatta country. The most noted Resident at Pune had been Mountstuart Elphinstone, one of a handful of senior East Indian officials who believed that India should be run by Indians. A well-read, thoughtful man, he took the trouble to learn local languages and understand local customs. Although not averse to handing out justice with a firm hand when required, he preferred to delegate authority to local officials rather than maintain an autocratic stance. He did not believe Britain's Indian Empire would be long-lived, and wrote: "The most desirable death for us to die of should be, the improvement of the natives reaching such a pitch as would render it impossible for a foreign nation to retain the government."[14] While in Pune he introduced a number of reforms and improvements that benefited local communities. Elphinstone was appointed Governor of Bombay in 1819, but his influence lingered on in Pune, and Frere was much influenced by him.

Frere used his time in Pune to make an exhaustive study of the history and customs of the Maharatta, showing the first signs of his interest in, and sympathy with, the indigenous peoples of India. "Young Frere was always seen sitting on the carpet by the side of old Narsopant Tatia, for whom he entertained the highest respect, and whom he used to call by the respectful name of Kakaji (elder uncle)."[15] Rapid progression was to follow. By October 1835 he was Acting Revenue Collector of Indapur and by 1838 Assistant Revenue Commissioner to Frederic Goldsmid, visiting almost every district of the Bombay Presidency and supervising the work of Revenue Collectors, an important source of finance for the Company. It should be remembered that at this time Frere was twenty-three years of age.

Goldsmid had an outstanding reputation with the local people, and Frere learnt much from him. The responsibility placed on the shoulders of the young men enlisted was heavy. Frequently alone in remote areas and without supervision among more or less hostile natives, they were expected to act as judge, tax collector, surveyor, accountant and militia commander, They spent a good deal of the year travelling by horse or camel, living in primitive conditions and eating unfamiliar food. Tax collecting was both onerous and difficult. The local populace, who resented taxes, used every dodge they could think up to minimise the amount they paid. It required considerable patience and tact to reach amicable settlements. It was the custom for the entire agricultural population of a district to assemble annually in front of the tax collector for what was called the Jummabundy Settlement, when individual liability was assessed. The collector had past records of assessments and payments, and was advised by local people of influence. These dignitaries were frequently corrupt, and the collector had to exercise care and judgement in his assessments.

Disease was rife and the climate inhospitable, but it cannot be denied that those who survived these rigours came through them battle-hardened, experienced and confident leaders of men. When Frere succeeded Goldsmid in October 1835 he came directly under the Revenue Commissioner, Thomas Williamson, for whom he worked for three years. He wrote:

"Since I have been working with Williamson, working himself, and making me work, as hard as well we could, he never once said or wrote a word to let me know he was master…It is true that this is the best way of getting work out of people."[16]

This sentiment was to be fundamental to Frere's career.

During these years on the road Frere participated in a reform of the methods of assessing and collecting revenue. The huge tract of arable land south-east of Bombay in the Deccan area was under cultivation, but the inhabitants were forced to pay onerous taxes that made no allowance for bad seasons, and left them severely impoverished. Many injustices arose through corruption and slack administration, and local tax collectors had at best a hazy notion of which landowners should pay tax, and how much. This led to friction, lengthy negotiation and inefficiency in optimising the collection of taxes. Without prompting from his superiors, Frere took it upon himself to make a new and careful survey of the district, mapping the countryside into divisions of fifteen acres and classifying the different qualities of soil. Every field was inspected and the cost of labour required to cultivate the soil calculated. This data provided the base for tax assessment, fixed for thirty years. The injustices prevalent in the system were eradicated by the reform, and the new measures brought in resulted in a dramatic improvement in the lot of the farmers. Frere's "Deccan system" was applied subsequently to other parts of the Bombay Presidency and also adopted in Mysore, Sind and Berar.

A local dignitary later recollected his impression of Frere:

> "He studied the Maharatta language, and so great was his mastery over it that he read all official papers himself... He used to rise early in the morning, take a walk for an hour or so, and then return home, after which he used to sit with his Munshi for learning Urdu and Persian... for a couple of hours.....In the office his gentle

17

and sweet disposition was highly remarkable, so much so that all the subordinates appreciated it extremely. When a clerk, or karkun, or peons asked him any question, Sir Bartle was ready with his reply, and that too with the utmost courtesy, so rare in modern office life. In the matter of promotion, he always had at heart the welfare of his own subordinates…..His private servants, even, were treated with the utmost consideration and civility."[17]

Frere's job provided ample time for other pursuits in his leisure time. He developed his skills at hunting, having a steady nerve and precise aim. Hunting big game was not merely a sport in the rural districts but a necessity in order to protect the villagers. Today we deplore the massacre of tigers that took place in the nineteenth century, but these huge beasts frequently terrorised villages and preyed at will on their livestock. One account of a hunt near Pune by an old Indian gentleman recorded Frere's bravery. A "full-built tiger, who was lying asleep in a thicket, furiously sprang [on the elephant], jumping over the trunk with full speed, and was about to pounce us in his jaws, so near he was, but Sir Bartle Frere at once aimed the pistol he had, and with one shot killed the tiger on the spot. If this would have missed…the result would have been disastrous. We three and the mahout were in tremendous terror during the conflict." [18]

The inhospitable climate and difficult terrain of India claimed many British lives. Frere's closest brother, Richard, had arrived with his regiment in Calcutta during May 1837. Although the two brothers were unable to meet, they corresponded regularly. In 1839, fearful that Russia was eyeing Afghanistan as a stepping-stone to advancing eastwards into India, the British moved to restore that country's deposed ruler, Shah Shuja, on the throne. Richard took part in the long march through the Sind (now Pakistan), across the treacherous Bolan Pass into Afghanistan. Having defeated the rebels who had deposed Shah Shuja, they entered the capital, Kabul, to a less than enthusiastic welcome from the local population. The Shah was not popular, and his reign was to be a short and disastrous one. The presence of the British was resented by the fiercely independent Afghanis. In October 1841 discontent boiled over. The Shah was deposed and the British garrison attacked. Penned in under the hills, there was no way of escaping. They were surrounded and massacred. Fortunately for Richard, his regiment had withdrawn from Kabul before the uprising in order to open a route to India in the north through the Khyber Pass. When he heard of the uprising the commander of this task force, General George Pollock, at once turned back at Jellalabad and recommenced the hazardous journey back through the Khyber Pass to relieve the garrison at Kabul, unaware that they had almost all been killed. Richard accompanied him, but at Rawalpindi suffered a pain in his right side that quickly incapacitated him. On 10th November he wrote to his brother that he had suffered a fit of what he thought was severe rheumatism. It seems that the affliction was much more than that – possibly a stroke – because his health deteriorated rapidly and on November 18 he died quietly, and was buried in Rawalpindi. It would be thirty-three years before Frere could visit his brother's grave.

The disastrous Afghan campaign placed a strain on the British throughout India. A large part of their success in controlling the territory was due to the local belief that their army was invincible. The massacre at Kabul showed them to be human and vulnerable. A significant motivation in the relief of Kabul by General Pollock, coming through the Khyber Pass, and General Nott approaching from the south, was to show that the British were not to be trifled with, and would seek redress. Nevertheless the Presidencies within India were placed on alert: they could only control their territory by making the local inhabitants believe in their dominance.

In 1842 a new Governor of Bombay was sent out from England to take over in the crisis. Sir George Arthur had a distinguished service record abroad, having seen action in the army in Egypt and Italy before becoming Lieutenant-Governor of Honduras. Thereafter he had been Governor of Tasmania (then called Van Dieman's Land) before being sent to Canada as Lieutenant Governor of Upper Canada, which was facing a rebellion in 1837. This he successfully suppressed, and remained in Canada until 1841. As he did not have any influential family connections, future promotion was by no means certain, but on the strength of his experience and achievements, Lord Ellenborough, the Governor-General of India at the time, chose him to fill the position of Governor of Bombay. On the way out to India by ship with his family and private secretary Arthur stopped at Aden, where he went ashore while the vessel was coaling. The climate in Aden was most inhospitable, sultry and hot. His secretary, Colonel Proctor suffered sunstroke and died before they reached Bombay. This left Arthur needing a private secretary. A previous Governor, Lord Clare, had prepared some notes for him in which he praised Frere as

> "an ornament to the service; his superior abilities are of a useful, practical kind, ever devoted to worthy objects. His views are at once correct and enlightened, and though he has not been many years in India, he has acquired a thorough knowledge of the languages, customs, tenures, manners, and resources of almost every province in the Bombay Presidency. He is competent to answer any questions on …. important subjects, and there is no person in the whole service who could be consulted on them with more advantage or confidence, he is so strictly conscientious and honourable."[19]

Arthur had no hesitation in taking him on as his new private secretary. This was a most fortunate opportunity for Frere. In June 1842 he had come close to forfeiting his career in India. He had suffered an attack of jungle fever so severe that the doctors advised him to return to England and never return thereafter. He had decided to stay in Bombay, and was able to recover there. Had he returned to England his life would have taken a decidedly different turn. The opportunity to learn from an able administrator and rise up the ranks in the Bombay Presidency would have been missed, and he would not have made the acquaintance of Arthur's daughter, Catherine. He was now twenty-seven years old.

Frere was an immediate success in his new post. He maintained a calm, even-tempered manner that took the sting out of even the most unpopular measures. His intellect was such that he could quickly analyse and advise on complex issues. Slow to arrive at decisions, he could be relied upon as a "safe pair of hands." G.T.Clark, an eminent Welsh archaeologist who visited Bombay at this time, noted:

"He was far more than a mere secretary.... His intellect was clear and acute; he was quick to apprehend, but in a general way slow to decide; very industrious and painstaking, seldom in a hurry, and anxious to be quite sure he understood the matter in hand before he gave an opinion on it."[20]

Early on he saw the significance of developing the railway system in such a huge country, and pressed for lines to be built. A plan for a rail system in India had first been put forward in 1832, but no action had been taken. In 1844 the Governor-General allowed private entrepreneurs to set up a rail system and the East India Company was asked to assist them. The British Government guaranteed the private companies an annual return of five per cent on their investment. Once established, the railways would be transferred to the government, but the privateers would retain operational control. Frere was enthusiastic about the initiative. Arthur was persuaded by him, and took up the cause. The first train in India ran on December 22, 1851, hauling construction material. The first passenger service was inaugurated on April 16, 1853, running between Bori Bunder, Bombay and Thane, a distance of 21 miles, using three locomotives. By 1875 British companies had invested £95 million in Indian railways, a vast sum in those days, and by 1880 9,000 miles of track had been laid, radiating out from the major cities of Bombay, Madras and Calcutta.

Frere's work brought him into contact with the Governor's family, and he came to know Arthur's second daughter, Catherine, who helped with correspondence. As a consequence of her father's career she had lived in Van Dieman's Land (Tasmania), Canada and England as well as India. This, and her experience as an aide to her father, had turned her into an accomplished and mature young woman, ideally suited to the life Frere was to lead. The two became close, and were married on October 10, 1844. Unfortunately Frere's father was not to know of his marriage, for he had died in the April of that year.

Prior to his marriage Frere suffered severe inflammation of his liver, and was ordered to return to England for treatment. He had delayed the trip because of his impending marriage, but now took the opportunity to combine his honeymoon with the return to England. On November 1 the newly wed couple sailed from Bombay. Frere appears to have been in no hurry to be treated, for the trip home was leisurely. It was thought inadvisable to return to England in midwinter, so at Suez they left the ship and travelled overland to Cairo where his wife saw the sights and he met the Pasha. Then it was on to Malta for the winter with his uncle, before meandering through Italy (where they spent three weeks in Rome) and France in a carriage, reaching England in the following summer.

His recuperation was prolonged, and he was not well enough to return to India until December 1846, two years later, by which time the couple had a baby daughter. His mother died while he was in England, and he was able to be with her at the end. His father-in-law, Sir George Arthur, was compelled by ill health to retire in April 1846 and return to England, so Frere's post as private secretary was no longer open. He thus accepted the position of Assistant Commissioner in the Customs Department in Bombay. This was always seen as a stopgap, and within six months the new Bombay Governor, Sir George Clerk, appointed him Resident at Satara, a state in the Deccan, south of Pune. This was a very responsible position, the political representative of the East India Company in the territory. Although ostensibly each district came under the rule of a local Rajah, the power and influence of the East India Company was such that the local Resident carried considerable authority over his territory, hearing complaints and law suits, dispensing justice, administering tax collection and advising the local ruler. Frere was just thirty-two years old.

Satara was a relatively peaceful and trouble-free area, ruled by a compliant Rajah, Appa Sahib. It also had a good climate and was within easy reach of Mahabuleshwar, a hill station popular with Europeans of the Bombay Presidency in the hot summer months. This was a good post for a new, young married civil officer in which to gain valuable experience. Mountstuart Elphinstone, the Governor of Bombay, had served there and was remembered with affection for his humane and liberal policies and his belief in promoting the interests of Indians. Frere succeeded a disciple of Elphinstone, Sir James Outram, who served with distinction as Resident there from 1845 to 1847. Thus the inhabitants of Satara had a favourable impression of British power, justice and goodwill. Like James Outram before him, Frere believed that government should be for the benefit of the governed and that corruption should be rooted out wherever it was encountered.

He developed affection for all classes of Indians, as his correspondence shows. There remained much to be done in organising the laws, police and public works, and Frere set about reforming the administration with youthful exuberance. Although offered troops as support, he refused them: he felt he could manage without them. He pressed ahead with economic development of the region with new irrigation schemes, bridges, roads and markets. Catherine, Frere's wife, was a great asset. Her experience of foreign countries made her adaptable and at ease with strangers, and accustomed to dealing with subordinates. Now she helped her husband with his administration. She was able to blossom. A visitor, Colonel Sir Herbert Sandford, wrote:

> "…I noticed also his (Frere's) lover-like devotion to his young wife, who, both then and in after years of hard work and many trials, proved herself so worthy of his attachment both as wife and, I may truly say, as coadjutor in his public and social duties."[21]

Like Outram before him, Frere believed there should be closer links between the British and the local Indians, who should be given executive authority and regarded as social equals. To this end he instituted a number of receptions at the Residency, although these were not always popular. When potential conflicts arose, his calm, friendly and sensible manner usually defused the situation. On one occasion a cow was slaughtered for reasons of hygiene and the Brahmin priests, conservative by nature and suspicious of Frere's innovations, cried "sacrilege." A huge, angry mob surrounded the Residency, but rather than suppress the protest with troops Frere invited spokesmen into the Residency. Far from yielding to them, he announced that each would be fined fifty rupees for their attempts at intimidation. He then chatted and joked with them, and accompanied them out into the garden. From there with quiet good humour he forced the crowd back from the gates and accompanied the spokesmen into the city, thus defusing the simmering anger.

The Rajah, Appa Sahib, was an intelligent and benevolent man with his subjects' interests at heart, and he and Frere became good friends. Frere's reforming zeal fell on fertile ground, and excellent progress was made over the following years. Frere suggested the distribution of New Orleans cotton seed and the introduction of the new model of a cotton gin. He supported agricultural development with plans for irrigation and sanitation, and tackled cholera. He kept meticulous records, and studied the causes of cholera in some details, suggesting the measures to be taken for its prevention. Trade was encouraged with a road improvement scheme.

It was not just the outdoor life that occupied Frere's leisure time. He read widely: Shakespeare, Voltaire, Malthus (the economist whose views prevailed at the time), Byron, Xenophon, Seneca and a number of religious works. He learned Urdu, Gujerati, Kanarese and Persian – the last of which was still spoken as the common language in many parts of India. His love of books led him to campaign for the preservation of the ancient library at Bijapur. An important old city of mosques, palaces and tombs within massive lava walls, it had been in decline for many years, and the important buildings were deteriorating rapidly. Frere persuaded the Bombay Government to provide a grant of five thousand two hundred rupees (approximately £500) for repairs, and was able to rescue from destruction the priceless manuscripts in the library.

In 1848 the Rajah fell gravely ill. He was descended from an old Mahratta dynasty that had established itself in the region two hundred years before. As he had no natural heir, succession was complicated. East India Company policy was to assume control in such circumstances so that firm leadership was provided. Local potentates facing such a situation frequently "adopted" heirs in order to preserve continuity, but in 1848 the Company did not approve of such a practice. The dying Rajah summoned Frere to his bedside and committed to his care a boy called Bulwant Rao Raj Adnega. Aware of British opposition to the practice of adopted sons inheriting the throne, Frere argued with the Rajah that the boy he had chosen was both a foundling and a stranger. He advised the Rajah to find a boy from a good family whom he knew well. The Rajah agreed, and mentioned the son of a well-known local family, the Bhonslays. He promised Frere that if he gained permission to adopt he would select this boy after due enquiry into the purity of his blood, his qualities and horoscope.

It was all too late. At the Rajah's request Frere travelled to the Governor at Mahabuleshwar to consult with him. Whilst there he received news that the Rajah was sinking fast. He hurried back but arrived after the Rajah had died. On his deathbed, with Frere out of town, the Rajah had persuaded the English doctor attending him to witness the adoption of his original choice. Faced with a fait accompli, Frere recommended that the adopted son be accepted as the new Rajah, but the new Governor-General in Calcutta, Lord Dalhousie, held the view that British rule was best, and wherever possible states should be brought under direct rule by the Company by annexation. This came to be known as "the doctrine of lapse." This policy ignored the fact that it was a long-held custom for Rajahs to adopt nominated heirs, and the decree created new animosity. For a year Frere fought this doctrine, pleading for local responsibility and authority. On April 12, 1848 he wrote an eloquent letter to the Governor of Bombay arguing the local case:

> "It is right I should inform Government that very great anxiety exists among all classes about the town as to the future….Government will not be surprised at this when it is considered that the bread of almost everyone in and about the city depends more or less on the decision….there are at least ten thousand individuals directly supported by salaries from the Court, and most of these have probably many persons dependent on them for subsistence."[22]

This was followed by his official report on September 23:

"The late Rajah having been a just and humane, a liberal and a popular ruler, any supposed want of equity in the appropriation of his dominions, whether by absorption into the Company's dominion or by transfer to a rival and inimical party, will lack the popularity which a similar measure, whatever the grounds, would always find among the industrious and peaceful inhabitants of a State delivered from anarchy and oppression."[23]

He was instructed to act as an interim Rajah until the final decision was made, and a detachment of troops was sent from Bombay to support him. Aghast, he instructed that they be recalled before they crossed into Satara, preferring to rely on moral force alone.

The decision was a long time coming, and all India had its eyes on Satara, for this was considered a crucial test case. Custom was that rulers were left alone to rule their own territories as long as they did not form alliances or wage war. There was criticism that shoring up the Rajah's power made him independent of his people and therefore less attendant to their needs. British dominance of India was complete: why, the argument went, should not the Company assume full responsibility for territories over which it had paramount influence? Dalhousie gave new impetus to this opinion. He was concerned about protecting India from outside invasion, and believed that those states within the borders of the country not fully controlled by the Company should be annexed to provide a cohesive, joined up country.

His opinion prevailed. Thirteen months after the death of the Rajah the Court of Directors in London agreed with his recommendation that the adoption be disallowed and Satara be annexed. It is instructive to read who opposed this decision: Mountstuat Elphinstone, a past Governor and major humane and liberal influence; Sir George Arthur, and Sir George Clerk, who was Governor of Bombay at the time of the Rajah's death. Frere, crestfallen, wrote to a friend: "It is an iniquitous business, and one of these days we shall have to pay the reckoning. However, everybody laughs at me for this."[24] Finally he was forced to accept the decision, which he did with a good grace.

The annexation changed Frere's role significantly. Satara became a British province, and as Resident he became Commissioner, ruler of the territory, with sole responsibility for its administration. Whilst he disagreed with the policy of annexation, at heart he believed that anywhere that the British exercised authority, whether annexed or not, should be ruled firmly and fairly, in a "civilized" manner. He thus felt that he could do most good by remaining in Satara. "Of course I shall do my best," he wrote, "but I well know the results must be disappointing, unless the Government will do many things to develop the resources of the country, which I well know they will not do. Hitherto I have kept the peace; whether I can continue to do so is, I think, doubtful."[25] In fact Satara was in future to prove one of the most troublesome states to manage, and observers put this down to the adoption issue.

There were advantages to the annexation, however. Frere used his new authority to further his ideas on improving the lot of the indigenous people. Armed gangs, sometimes twenty strong, who roamed the countryside terrorising local villagers and stealing from the rich, plagued Satara. Some local tribes made a living out of such activities. Frere used troops to reduce these activities as far as possible. The Rajah had seemed powerless to control these gangs, mainly due to an inept and corrupt police force and a reluctance among villagers to confront them. Frere reformed the police, imposed heavy sentences on gang ringleaders if and when they were caught, and reinstituted a system of "watch and ward" in the villages which was based on regular police rounds during the night and the participation of the villagers. He introduced the concept of municipality, the first in India, and maintained peace and order. Funds were provided for village roads, wells, bridges and public hygiene. Local committees that collected funds and kept the towns clean ran the new municipalities. They were partly elected, and within a couple of years every town and large village had an operating fund and showed the benefit of the improvements introduced. Trade blossomed. His fluency in the local languages enabled him to communicate with the local peasants and understand their needs. Although the civic improvement approach was not the conventional one of British Commissioners at the time, the new Governor of Bombay, Lord Falkland, noticed the evident benefits it brought Satara. He had something else in mind for Frere, a position that was to be of vital importance to the Company. Frere was thirty-five years old.

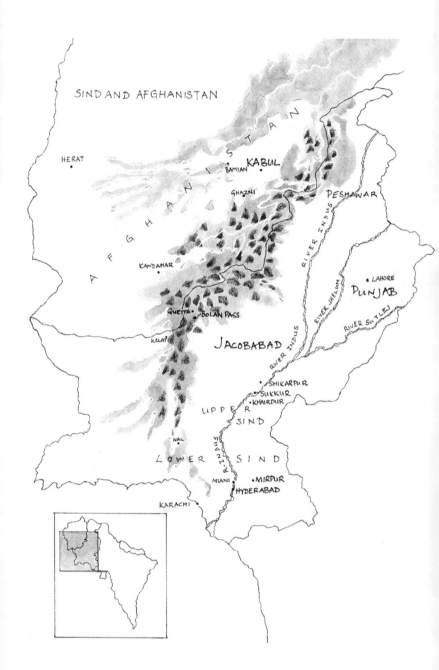

SIND AND AFGHANISTAN

HERAT

BAMIAN

KABUL

GHAZNI

PESHAWAR

A
F
G
H
A
N
I
S
T
A
N

KANDAHAR

RIVER INDUS

LAHORE

PUNJAB

RIVER JHELUM

QUETTA · BOLAN PASS

RIVER SUTLEJ

KELAT

JACOBABAD

RIVER INDUS

SHIKARPUR

SUKKUR

KHAIRPUR

U P P E R
S I N D

NAL

L O W E R   S I N D

RIVER INDUS

MIANI

MIRPUR

HYDERABAD

KARACHI

Chapter 3.

THE SIND.

Frere's next appointment was to the Sind, now Pakistan. Reference has been made previously to an attempt to reinstate the ruler of Afghanistan on his throne in Kabul, and the disaster that followed. The procession that took Shah Shuja back to his country commenced in Karachi, then a small fishing village on the coast of Sind, a province of India. The British had originally favoured approaching Kabul from the north through the Khyber Pass, but the ruler of the Punjab, Ranjit Singh, who had expansionist ambitions of his own, opposed the passage through his territory. Thus they were forced to transport the army from Bombay to Karachi and enter Afghanistan through the formidable Bolan Pass, fifty-nine miles in length across rugged mountains.

There was a sub-plot to British intentions. The Indus River flowed through the middle of the Sind, providing fertile fields on either side of the river. It was navigable for a great deal of its length, offering the possibility of trade with the north. To the Company, which had yet to penetrate far upstream, control of the river was a valuable prize. Land transportation to and from the interior was difficult and risky, and hitherto had not been profitable. There were valuable commodities, until now unexploited, to be bought and traded. The East India Company remained primarily a trading enterprise intent on making money, and the Sind represented an interesting commercial prospect.

The one million inhabitants of the Sind were mainly Muslims, ruled by Amirs of the Baluchi Talpur clan. The territory was divided into three areas, controlled from Khaipur in the north, Mirpur in the east and Hyderabad in the south. The East India Company had made several attempts in the past to establish factories in the Sind and to forge trading links, but the Amirs were fiercely independent, and resisted all British efforts. The people were mainly nomadic farmers, and many were warriors, given to marauding villages as a living. Establishing a presence in the Sind was not going to be easy. A series of treaties was signed, aimed at increasing British representation there in return for protection against outside influences. All of these treaties faltered either because they proved too onerous for the suspicious Baluchis or because the British sought to strengthen their grip by devising new treaties to supersede the existing ones.

James Outram, as a military officer participating in the march in 1838 through the Sind to Afghanistan in order to reinstate the Shah, was appointed political agent first to the Lower Sind and then to the Upper Sind when the resident agent there died. He formed a good relationship with the Amirs. Although he regarded them as rogues and recognised their marauding tendencies, he also understood their concerns and felt he could work with them. He also felt that through his dealings with them he could trust them, and when General Charles Napier, commanding the Company's army forces in Sind, showed warlike intentions he opposed the general, attempting to convince him that the Amirs were unwilling to take up arms against the British. Who was right in this regard is still argued about, and subsequently was the subject of heated debate in the Bombay and British press. Napier had a clear brief from Calcutta to assume control of Sind one way or another, and when he found the proud Baluchis resistant to British dominance by peaceful treaty, he concluded that armed conflict was inevitable. Outram struggled to interpose himself between the Amirs and Napier in an attempt to reach an agreeable compromise, but a combination of Napier's objectives and Baluchi suspicions led to both sides bypassing him. As a consequence of their differences, Outram fell out with Napier and left the Sind. By then the Amirs recognised that Outram held no influence over events, and lost all trust in British intentions. The uneasy relationship between the local Baluchis and the British finally broke down irrevocably in 1843 in all-out conflict which culminated in the Battle of Miani, convincingly won by the British under Napier. Five thousand Baluchis, including several chiefs, were slain at a cost of 19 British officers and 256 men. The Amirs immediately tendered their surrender, and Napier is famously reported to have telegrammed: "Peccavi (I have sinned)." It is highly dubious that he did: the quotation appears to have originated in Punch Magazine.

An experienced civil servant was required to succeed General Napier as supreme commander in the Sind. The country was effectively subdued; what was badly needed was a disciplined regime to bring law and order, efficient administration and revenue to the territory. Hitherto the Amirs had raised funds by simply plundering their people. The skills necessary to introduce law and order were not those of a soldier, and Lord Falkland, the Governor of the Bombay Presidency, initially chose the secretary to the Bombay Government, Pringle. However his experience was in a much more regulated, established environment, and he lacked the strength of personality to control such a wild and undisciplined territory. When he resigned in 1850 Falkland proposed Colonel Melville, military secretary to the Bombay Government, but his appointment was objected to by the Bombay Government, and the Governor-General in Calcutta supported their objections on the grounds that it had been decided that a civilian should hold the appointment.

Frere was thus offered the appointment of Chief Commissioner of Sind. The appointment was a controversial one: he was 35 years old, and members of the Bombay Council argued that there were sixty officers available with greater seniority than him. This was not a frivolous protest: officers in the Company normally advanced only when those senior to them died or retired and promotion was almost always on a length of service basis. Frere's appointment was very much out of the ordinary, and reflected the importance and difficulty of the post as well as the reputation he had built. Facing the

Bombay Council, who had blocked his previous proposal, Falkland intimated he would resign if the Council did not approve the appointment.

Frere duly moved to Karachi. Previously Hyderabad, the traditional seat of the Amirs, had been the capital of Lower Sind but after the annexation the British transferred authority to Karachi. With him went his wife and two young daughters, Mary (born 1849) and Georgina (born 1850). Karachi was an unprepossessing port, situated in a swampy area remote from any large conurbation. Until the British involvement it had been nothing more than a collection of mud dwellings and a fishing village. High humidity and intolerable summer temperatures made it an unpleasant place for Europeans. The family landed on January 12, 1851, in small boats dragged up through the mud to the shore as the steamer could not reach the jetty. Far from a magnificent ceremonious procession – which was the norm for arriving dignitaries in other parts of India – they rode and drove through deep sand on an ill-defined track to Government House, a long one-storied building with a broad verandah completely encircling the house. By a happy coincidence, on the same day General Napier arrived on his way back to Bombay at the termination of his position as Commander-in-Chief. He stayed with Frere for four days, giving the newcomer a priceless opportunity to learn as much as he could about his new territory. Napier made no secret of his contempt for civil servants, but said of Frere that there was no one so equal to the duties, or in whose hands he would sooner see the administration of the Province of Sind.[26]

Frere's brief was the development of Sind from a barren wasteland into an effective economic unit. It was roughly triangular in shape, 50,000 square miles in size, with the Indus, 2,000 miles long, flowing down its backbone from the north to the sea at Karachi. To the east were the unforgiving Rajputanja desert and the Rann of Kutch, sparsely inhabited mudflats extending over 9,000 square miles. To the west were the rugged Baluchi hills. Only close to the Indus was the soil sufficiently rich to support agriculture. The people remained resistant to outsiders: Napier and Outram had made some progress in subduing them and controlling their activities, but the vast territory remained difficult to police. Virtually nothing had been done to exploit the Indus in terms of irrigating farmlands, or to facilitate trade and shipping. Immediately upon arriving Frere initiated a series of fairs in Karachi and elsewhere in the Sind to which merchants from Afghanistan, Persia and Central Asia could bring their goods to meet traders from Bombay and southern India.

There was considerable concern in both Calcutta and London at the cost to the Company of the Sind campaign, both materially and politically. The Afghan adventure and the annexation of Sind had been very expensive, and it seemed that the administration of the Sind would cost more than the expected revenue derived from it. The Government of India had come under severe criticism from the Court of Directors over the cost of the Afghan war, which had burdened India with heavy debts. The annual deficit of the Company in India amounted to £1.25million, a fortune in those days. The cost of sustaining the unpopular Shah on his throne represented an ongoing drain on resources. The Bombay Government therefore considered its first priority was to save money, and resisted any proposed developments that involved additional investment.

Karachi was situated at the estuary of the Indus, and would clearly be the key to opening up the hinterland to trade. As Frere had experienced personally, it was in no way equipped to handle any trade at that time. Despite having natural shelter, it was hampered by a sand bar that prevented ships with a draft of more than fourteen and a half feet from entering the harbour. Such was the danger presented by this entrance that it was closed during the three or four months of the monsoon every year. The first task was to open the port up to larger ships. Frere requested a survey and a dredger to tackle the sand bar, but here he came up against the over-bureaucratic Company administration that was the blight of field officers such as Frere, and was to give them considerable trouble. The administrators in Bombay who had opposed his appointment now stalled, pending the report of a "competent geologist."[27] Such a person did not exist in the Sind, so Frere commissioned a report from the port officer at Karachi, Lieutenant Hopkins of the Indian Navy. He confirmed that the bar was not a major obstacle, and that there was no reason why a ship of five or six hundred tons should not have access to the harbour throughout the year, including the monsoon season. In fact in October 1852 the Duke of Argyle, a ship direct from England laden with troops, sailed over the bar safely, but for ships of more than 800 tons the depth of water was insufficient. Again and again Frere pleaded for his dredger. The Bombay Government referred the request to the Commander-in-Chief of the Indian Navy who replied, though he had never seen

Karachi, that a breakwater was what was required. It was not until December 1853, when Frere appealed directly to the Governor-General in Calcutta, Lord Dalhousie, that work actually started. It was still in progress in 1857 when access for supplies and troops to resist the Indian uprising was desperately needed. Nevertheless, between 1853 and 1858 the value of the sea-borne trade of Karachi grew from £8,850,000 to £21,500,000.[28] The port was to become of enormous strategic importance in later years: the British troops in Mesopotamia during the First World War drew their supplies from Karachi.[29]

Plans for a railway north from Karachi up the Indus as far as Hyderabad suffered similar delays from cost-conscious Bombay. Lord Dalhousie wrote to Frere in October 1854:

> "I have seen with great pleasure the many efforts towards progress and improvement which you have been making in Scinde. I should be better pleased if official questions took something less than a year or two before they reached this Government. It is a long road from Kurrachee to Calcutta via Bombay, and certainly the travel is very slow upon it for official business." [30]

The railway officials in charge of the work were instructed to take their orders from a department in Bombay instead of from Frere. In vain he argued that responsibility and authority must be borne locally, and could not function efficiently at such a distance, particularly given the poor communications. Work only started in 1858, four and a half years after Frere's correspondence with Dalhousie on the matter. It was at last opened in 1861, after Frere had left the Sind.

Frere also suffered frustration over the postal service. An offer by the Steam Navigation Company to run a fortnightly mail service between Bombay and Karachi was rejected by the Bombay Government on the advice of the Postmaster-General. Frere saw the service as not only a mail service, but a regular ferry for passengers, (often needing medical treatment), light goods, books and goods destined for the interior of the country.

Those activities within Frere's direct control moved forward with more success. Six thousand miles of roads, with bridges, were built during his stay in Sind and a canal system was introduced to bring irrigation to the fields. In 1854 the first postage stamps were printed and a postal service was established. Frere originally applied to Bombay for permission to open new post offices and improve the poor postal service, but was told that when the Government of India could afford money to spend on the Sind there were many things that were needed before post offices could be considered.[31] Without permission Frere had stamps printed and issued to every police officer and collector of land revenue and customs.

> "Thus every Government office in Sind became a district post office for stamped letters, and the first official who had a real post-office at hand sent to it all the stamped letters which he and his subordinates had collected."[32]

The first Sind postage stamps preceded any other stamps in India by two years.

Municipalities were established in all the main towns, providing a mechanism for local rule. Schools were founded, and for the first time a grammar and dictionary in the Sind tongue published. This was an essential requirement, for when Frere first arrived in the Sind he discovered that only two English officers were conversant in the tongue. The business of the courts was conducted in three languages: the Sindi parties were interpreted into Hindustani, which the officer understood, and written down in Persian. Frere could not see how adequate justice could be dispensed. He proposed that the official language should be Sindi, and that promotion in the civil service in the Sind should be conditional on at least a colloquial knowledge of Sindi, with two grades of examination.[33] In 1865 a museum and library, Frere Hall, was opened in Karachi.

Revenue raised by land taxes began to erode the extremely heavy debt carried by the Company as a result of its activities in Sind. Annual revenue in the Sind rose from £230,000 in 1850-51 to £430,000 in 1858-59.[34] Irrigation channels extending some 300 miles were built to carry water from the Indus to farmlands that grew indigo, sugar cane, rice, wheat and other grains. It was hoped that the local populace would appreciate these good works, and prefer British rule to their old feudal lords. Frere saw his position as that of a guardian, and the local people the true owners. Thus he encouraged his subordinates to take responsibility, setting high standards and treating them as individuals. This extended to giving them latitude to run affairs in their own way, and not according to some bureaucratic formula established in far-off Bombay or Calcutta.

Frere then turned his attention to the Sind's borders. The size of the province and its inhospitable terrain made the frontier virtually impossible to police properly, and lawlessness abounded on all sides. A remarkable cavalry officer who had achieved unusual success in making some of the borders secure came to the attention of Frere. His name was John Jacob. Three and a half years older than Frere, he had been in India since 1839 and had distinguished himself during the Afghan campaign of 1841. He was artilleryman, cavalry leader and rifleman in one. He was also a skilled engineer. He is credited with the development of the grooved rifle barrel, which improved its accuracy. Remarkably, he refused promotion to stay with his Irregular Horse, a disparate group of local horsemen whom he developed into a crack regiment by careful selection, rigorous training, unrelenting standards and a strong community bond. He distinguished himself during the Battle of Miani when the Baluchis were defeated, and accumulated unrivalled experience of the Sind. He established a camp in the desert at a small village called Kanghur (later to be renamed Jacobabad), twenty-five miles from Shikarpur, from which he could watch the northern borders.

This part of the country was wild and lawless. The tribes there paid allegiance neither to the Baluchis of Sind, the Amir of Kabul nor Khan of Kelat. They lived from raiding the plains of Sind, carrying off camels, cattle and goats. Jacob built houses, planted trees and developed a road network of 2,589 miles with 786 masonry bridges. His men, rigorously trained and disciplined, were extremely mobile and quick to react to threats. His ambition was to be so effective that all fighting and wars in his area would cease. He believed in forming local agreements and isolating wrongdoers with appropriate punishment, rather than penalising entire communities, as was the custom. Like Frere, and Outram before him (under whom Jacob had served, and who had influenced him greatly) Jacob believed in giving personal responsibility to his men and trusting them. He also worked hard at developing the local infrastructure, building a series of irrigation canals. Frere and Jacob immediately recognised an affinity – a consanguinity that was to be important to both of them.

Frere gave Jacob a free hand and protected him from bureaucratic interference. Jacob's tactics soon bore fruit, bringing peace and stability to a region that had previously known only violence and violation. Frere and Jacob proved an object lesson to other parts of the British Empire confronted by hostile tribes unused to colonial government. Frere recognised that the majority of his Indian subjects lived in fear; oppressed, enslaved, impoverished and ill-treated by local tyrants. He believed that by providing security and stability, by developing roads, sanitation and irrigation, he would encourage these so-called savages to become farmers and responsible citizens. He was on record as saying that he believed the world fell naturally into civilised societies on the one hand, savage and barbarous systems on the other. He believed the European presence would inevitably continue to undermine and replace any indigenous power, seeing this as an invariable fact rather than because of 'inordinate pride of race,' or a sense of destiny.

In 1855 Frere wrote:

"I have just returned from that wonderful place Jacobabad. Yesterday morning I went with Jacob nine miles into what four years ago was real desert… All is now…stubble and from the top of a surveying tower, as far as the eye could reach…we could see the fields extended, the cultivators and cattle not appearing to dream of the possibility of plunderers attacking them…"[35]

The peace that Jacob created on the border was lasting. This contrasted starkly with the Punjab to the north, which was centrally controlled. A Board of Control consisting of three Company officers had run the Punjab, which had been annexed in 1848, but soon power devolved to one man, John Lawrence. A Leveller, Lawrence was, like Frere, deeply religious, and certain in his approach to life. A man of fierce energy and a keen intellect, unlike Frere he believed in a firm rule based upon the Old Testament emotions of fatherhood, forgiveness and fear.[36] Although he was a strong protector of the poor, the paternalistic, stern administration he exercised was effective in leaving the indigenous tribes in no doubt as to who ruled and what the rules were. Punishment was unremitting to wrongdoers. Unfortunately this did not endear the British to the miscreants. Moreover, punitive retaliation to plunder took the form of burning crops and villages if reparation did not take place immediately. This merely encouraged the raiders to raid again in order to replace what they had lost. Although Lawrence and Frere shared a religious commitment, and professed to live their lives accordingly, there the similarities ended, and they did not see eye-to-eye on any question of rule and administration.

By 1854 Frere's wife was pregnant again. Karachi's climate was not conducive to bringing a new baby into the world, and she, together with their two daughters, returned to England. Her father was gravely ill, and he died in September, to be followed by his wife in January 1855. At least Mrs Arthur was alive to see her grandson, for in October 1854 Frere's first son, Bartle Compton Arthur, was born. There is in existence a charming letter that Frere wrote on October 29, 1854 to his daughter Kate. It brings vividly to life an account of his daily, now solitary, life:

> "I will tell you what I have been doing this morning. I was sleeping in the room where mamma and I used to sleep, and having no little girls to wake me, I told Peewo the peon to call me, and he came and said: 'Sahib, get up, it's six o'clock,' and I saw the sun was just going to rise behind the Clifton cliffs. So I got up and dressed, and went out, and it was a beautiful, clear, and very calm and cool morning....Everything in the distance was very clear, the hills towards Muggur Peer, and the town, and our house, and the new church, and the school, and the fishing village... and the reason that it was so clear was that a fresh North-East wind was blowing off the land and blew away all the smoke and fog and sea-mist; but as it blew off the shore on to the sea, the sea was very smooth; and there was a river steamer taking advantage of the smooth water to go by

sea to the mouth of the Indus, and so escape the creeks which we came through…Then I went to look at Mamma's favourite caper, which grows just at the edge of the cliff beyond the kitchen – there were some beautiful flowers on it, smelling very sweet…Then I went and walked round the cliff, and on the sheltered side I found a very pretty little hawk, and a large white-headed fishing eagle…In a sheltered nook there were three boats, fishing so close that I could see the fish they pulled up nearly as fast as they threw in their lines."[37]

Frere followed his wife back to England for a well-earned rest in the spring of 1856. Debilitated by the exhausting climate and overwork, he was suffering from bronchitis and malaria, which took some time to clear. Jacob was appointed Acting Commissioner in his stead. In December 1856 another daughter, Eliza, was born. Frere purchased Wressil Lodge, a large manor house on Wimbledon Park constructed from materials shipped from north-east England when the Duke of Northumberland's castle was demolished in the 1600's. He took the opportunity to spend time with his family, and his children were to remember those days as a time of great companionship and excitement. He was at his happiest with the young; his calm nature and easy charm enabled him to get along very well with his children. He was far from a stereotype of the stern, distant Victorian father.

He did not rest for long, however: soon he was lobbying the East India Company for help with his railway project. His frustration with authority was manifest in his letters to Jacob, in which he complained of differences between the Directors of the Company and the Court. The latter, comprising mainly of Whig politicians, were bent on making economies in India through salary reductions and reorganisation "with little reference to what people who have been twenty or thirty years in the country think safe or expedient."[38] His final letter to Jacob before leaving England again was even more pessimistic: "What I saw in England gave me little hope of any better governance for India."[39]

In March 1857, although not fully recovered, he returned alone to India, reaching Karachi on May 18. The parting from his family this time was very difficult for him. He was to write to his friend, G.T.Clark:

> "....if you ever had to pack your overland trunks, leaving your wife and little ones behind you, and feeling that however you might prosper, you could never see those same children again - that even if you returned in a very few years, they would be so altered that you would have to guess their names, and to discover, as in a stranger, tempers and dispositions with forming which you have had nothing to do. You know that the first uprooting from home is in youth, but the wrench then is a trifle to what it is when you are yourself the head of the home."[40]

What was awaiting him in Karachi was to ensure that it was some time before he was reunited with his family.

Chapter 4.

THE INDIAN MUTINY.

At the landing place in Karachi Frere was handed a private letter dated May 13 from the chief engineer of the Punjab Railways informing him of the mutiny of Indian troops at Meerut, near Delhi. All the British officers had been massacred along with women and children, and the so-called Indian Mutiny showed every likelihood of spreading. Frere immediately sent urgent messages to the Governor of Bombay, Lord Elphinstone, and to James Outram and John Jacob, who were engaged with their forces in military operations in Persia, urging them to return as soon as possible, and provide as many men as they could spare for the Sind. He also instructed the Acting Political Agent in the Kutch, east of Sind, to secure communications and take measures to maintain control. The rebellion had been foreseen by Outram, who had warned Lord Dalhousie that the Bengal Army was unreliable, and not well organised. He had also warned that there was unrest in the ranks over a number of grievances, and that a move by one regiment could quickly spread to the entire Indian army. Sepoys, or infantrymen, were poorly paid, and regularly agitated for a rise. Moreover, the annexation of territories where the Rajah died without natural heir, discussed above, had fostered deep resentment. The sepoys in the Bengal Army who rebelled were mainly from the province of Oudh, which was the latest territory to be annexed. In addition the intense activity of Christian missionaries led the men to be suspicious that their religious beliefs were being threatened and the caste system was to be broken down. This in turn led to the rumour that the paper wrapping new cartridges were waxed with pigs' fat. As the men broke the seal with their teeth, they were suspicious that there was a plot to transgress their religious taboos, which forbade the eating of pork. Sir John Lawrence attributed the mutiny solely to the cartridges, but subsequent historians have shown that there was considerable unrest before the cartridge issue emerged. Indeed, many of the rebels used the greased cartridges during the mutiny.

Frere recognised the dangers at once. Although the mutiny was, at the start, confined to the eastern and northern regions in which the Bengal Army operated, there was every possibility that it could spread throughout India. In particular the Punjab, in the extreme north-west, somewhat isolated from the main part of India, appeared vulnerable. Delhi had fallen to the rebels, thus preventing reinforcements from being sent to the Punjab through there. Sir John Lawrence was considering the evacuation of Peshawar, his headquarters in the region, in order to conserve his resources and save the Punjab. Frere believed strongly that the principal towns of Peshawar, Lahore and

Multan should be defended, even if it came to a siege. If the rebellion continued to spread, British rule in India could be swept away. To the west of the Punjab there were signs that the Afghanis were willing to support the rebels, and in turn would be supported by Persia and Russia. If Lawrence was to receive assistance the Indus would be a valuable (and now the only) conduit for providing help to the vital Punjab, but all available steamers were absent, supporting Outram in Persia.

Frere felt he must act at once, before matters spiralled out of control. He therefore proposed sending all available regiments upstream on the earliest available boat. The Officer Commanding the Sind regiments did not report to him, but to the Officer Commanding the Indian Army. Naturally he was resistant to taking such orders from a civilian, and apprehensive that by reducing his strength in the Sind he would be unable to resist an uprising there. This rebellion was outside anything he had encountered in his military career, and he was inclined to temporise. Frere had no time to argue procedures or consult Calcutta. By a mixture of tact, persuasion and assurance that he would take full responsibility for the decision, he managed to free 550 men of the First (European) Fusiliers and a loyal Baluchi battalion. This left Sind defended by a Bengal cavalry regiment whose reliability was questionable. One hundred and thirty-nine European troops and the Sind Horse protected the Bolan Pass against invasion by the Afghans or Persians. The Sind was highly vulnerable to an insurrection, and had the sepoys rebelled, putting British lives in danger, Frere would have been blamed for acting without higher authority. To his relief, within a few days he received a despatch from Lord John Elphinstone, Governor of Bombay and a nephew of the legendary Mountstuart Elphinstone, containing instructions that endorsed his actions. He had nevertheless taken huge risks.

The Sind crisis was to be pivotal to Frere's career. The frustration he had experienced with the bureaucracy of Bombay and its unwillingness to delegate responsibility or authority to local administrators was as nothing in peacetime compared to his experience now, in such a dangerous situation. Communications with Bombay remained lengthy and uncertain. At a time when the situation was changing every day, and urgent action was required, he felt it was imperative that he was free to take the decisions he felt necessary. Time and again he was balked by Bombay's insistence that they take the decisions. In many cases their actions were against his advice, or prevented him from moving forward. He thus attempted to ignore Bombay as much as he could, instigating action without authority whenever he considered it imperative. He took trouble to keep Lord Elphinstone fully informed of what he was doing and why, although by the time the Governor received his reports the deeds had been done. He was very fortunate that Elphinstone believed in him and was sympathetic with his position. He was therefore fully supported in his actions, and there can be little doubt that his swift decisions and perceptive reading of the dangers facing India contributed enormously to the containing of the rebellion. His swift action, taken before he was authorised to do so, meant that troops were deployed to the most crucial trouble spots in a prompt and timely manner. Moreover, he showed decisiveness, a sureness of touch and a calm control that enhanced his reputation.

Now the improvements at Karachi showed their value. The port was used as a major staging post for equipment in support of the British in the interior. Bombay bureaucracy again hampered progress: material for the assembly of four large steamers and four river flats (barges which conveyed troops and weapons towed behind steamers) sent out from England to Karachi the previous year had been sent on to Bombay on the insistence of the Bombay dockyard authority. There they lay, unused, until the builder, waiting in Karachi, prevailed, and they were sent on to Karachi without the workmen to assemble them. When Frere returned he found the material rusting on the beach. Frere complained bitterly to Lord Elphinstone of interference:

> "…(which) I have never seen exercised in any single instance save to the detriment of the public service. …any plan for improving our river Flotilla or Marine met with an amount of cold water at Bombay, quite sufficient to drown a landsman like myself. But I could stand it no longer when I saw what our countrymen did and are doing up country, heard their applications for help, and remembered that with a disposable force and excellent troops eager for employment, and a navigable river, and all the elements of a powerful steam Flotilla, we are sending tributes of two hundred men at a time in steamers that ought not to be allowed to run, to help men who

are marching twenty-five miles a day, for weeks together, in a Punjab May and June."[41]

Fortunately, Elphinstone fully appreciated Frere's strengths. Time and again the Governor supported him fully, overruling the bureaucratic decisions of Bombay civil servants in dispute with Frere. A classic instance of this involved the artillery. Most of the guns returning from Persia had immediately been sent on to other parts of India, leaving one troop of horse artillery in Karachi. Ninety volunteers from the 2nd European regiment were trained as artillerymen and formed into an effective battery. On August 15 the Commander-in-Chief at Bombay peremptorily ordered these artillerymen out of the Sind without reference to Frere, and Elphinstone was forced to intercede with a strong letter ordering that Frere should be allowed discretionary power to suspend orders for the withdrawal of troops from the Sind.

With the return of men from Persia came much-needed supplies. Forty-five tons of rifle bullets were available by July, and a huge camel train shifted supplies to Delhi, where the British were besieging the rebels. The returning Persian force was not allowed to stay in the Sind for long, however. On July 26 Frere received a request from Elphinstone for a wing of the 2nd European regiment to be sent to the Deccan. Despite his own shortages, Frere did not hesitate to comply, leaving him with a total of one hundred and thirty-five European infantrymen in the whole of the Sind. He reasoned that the improvements manifest in the Sind and the quiet, settled nature of the countryside would not lead to an uprising. The fact that the native regiments were, in the main, part of the Bombay Army, which unlike the Bengal force had largely remained loyal to their British officers, enhanced his feeling of security. The sight of so much material moving through Karachi probably had a salutary effect upon would-be mutineers in Sind, for all remained quiet until September.

Then news came of secret meetings being held in Hyderabad among the artillery. The Europeans moved swiftly to take possession of their guns and retreat into the fort. The 13th native infantry were also reported to be disaffected, and a hastily assembled task force was sent up river to secure the town. This alarm was followed by an attempted rising in Karachi. On September 14 1857 the sepoys of the 21st regiment stationed there rebelled. At two in the morning Frere was woken and warned of the disaffection, which at that stage was merely simmering in the barracks. He immediately drove to the camp, listening as he went to sounds from the native quarters, described as "like the humming of a hive of bees disturbed."[42] By the time he reached the parade ground the danger had been averted. The artillery regiment, with six six-pounders and two nine-pounders, augmented by four companies of Europeans, who fell in without the bugle being sounded, were assembled and a roll-call of sepoys carried out. Twenty-one men were found to be missing together with their arms. Order was restored without resistance, and the absentees subsequently tracked down outside Karachi and apprehended.

News then arrived that the native artillery in Shikarpur was mutinying, and as there was no European soldier within two hundred miles, this was serious. On September 24 at midnight artillery fire was heard in the town. The rebels had seized four guns and were firing them among the barracks and gun sheds. The police and 16th native regiment together with a loyal section of the artillery were quickly assembled and opened fire on the mutineers. As it was a particularly dark night there was considerable confusion. Firing continued for two hours before the troops and police rushed the gun-sheds and retook the guns. The mutineers were routed with three dead; it turned out that they only amounted to eleven in total. It was essential to the British that the ringleaders be brought to justice and Frere did not shrink from this duty. He persuaded the Commanding Officer that native officers, who dispensed justice as severely as the European court, and had the merit of communicating decisions, and explaining reasons to their fellow countrymen, should conduct courts-marshals.

The full story of the uprising has been told elsewhere: the atrocities committed, the retribution, the heroics and bravery of individuals. The Bombay Army, separate from that of Bengal, remained mainly loyal to its officers. Once the British had summoned adequate resources from abroad it was likely the mutiny would be quashed, and by the middle of 1858 they had regained control. Much soul-searching followed. Leading opinion-formers such as General Sir James Outram recognised very early in the campaign that harsh penal measures against the rebels would be counter-productive. He saw that the Company could not possibly rule India without the full co-operation of local leaders, but these people, the taluqdars (administrators who often owned their land) and zamindars (farmers who helped with tax collecting), had been among the willing participators of the mutiny.

He urged the new Governor-General, Lord Canning, to exercise clemency and understanding, and to restore property appropriated by the victorious British army. In this Outram succeeded.

Frere had been thinking along similar lines. He was anxious to include Indians in representative government, believing that unless this was done further uprisings would follow. The mutiny was a profound shock to all the assumptions underlying British rule in India. Reappraisal was necessary. As committed Christians, the men who ruled India could not accept that they were wrong. Many, including Sir John Lawrence, urged that Christian principles should be rigorously applied in order to bring enlightenment to the savages, and that unchristian principles should be eliminated from the Government of India. The implication of this thinking was that the paternalistic attitudes that prevailed before the mutiny should be reinforced. Frere thought differently. He wrote to Lord Stanley, Under-Secretary of State for India:

> "I feel convinced that the course proposed is not right – that as Christians we are not justified in using the temporal power of Government to enforce particular forms of religious belief, even when that belief is Christianity."

A devout Christian himself, he encouraged missionary work and approved of the progress that had been made in that area, but was nevertheless critical of the methods:

> "We rely on the temporal power of Government to influence the natives in matters of belief.

Disguise it as we may....I cannot see how we can, as Christians, defend in India a course which in England we should condemn as ineffectual for the promotion of true religion."[43]

A good example of his liberal attitude occurred when a chaplain posted an inscription on a wall in Hyderabad asserting that Mohammed was not a true prophet. Frere upheld the protest from Mohammedans and insisted it be removed immediately, because he could see it was taken as a deliberate insult. The chaplain, Mr Gell appealed to Bombay and stirred up controversy in the Bombay Press, but Frere held his ground and was supported by Government. In a letter to Lord Goderich dated January 5, 1859, he went further in setting out his beliefs:

"You can and you ought to assist the people to educate themselves....and you are bound as a Government to help them."

On religion he was forthright:

"With regard to missions, I hold that all that is required from Government is to leave them alone, and I look on any Government enterprise or support as in the last degree mischievous. Let the Government of this world keep the peace and do justice and mercy to the best of its power, and rule the people so that peace and plenty may prevail through the land, but let not Government presume to dictate to any of the meanest of its subjects what he shall believe, or, however indirectly, to bribe or coerce him into any form of belief."[44]

An important and sad loss for Frere was the death in December 1858 of General John Jacob. Jacob had been destined to play a leading role in the British reply to the mutiny and it was assumed that he would be given command of at least a major part of the Indian Army. His return from Persia had been delayed by the need to tie up the treaty while Outram brought his troops back post-haste. By the time he returned the command of the central army had been given to Sir Hugh Rose. Rose had distinguished himself in Syria and the Crimea before being appointed to command the Pune Division of the Bombay Army. Jacob went back quietly to Jacobabad. There he fell ill with violent fits of bleeding from the nose, and lack of energy. He complained of overwork, getting only three hours of sleep each night. He quickly deteriorated, and with medical resources rudimentary to say the least, he could not be saved. His successor, Major Green, wrote:

> "For fifteen years he had ruled these people; his name only was known, feared, and respected as no other has ever been, or ever will be; the enormous influence he exercised over these barbarians was even unknown to himself, nor could I have believed that any one man could, unseen, exert such influence."[45]

Frere's part in the Mutiny was recognised in England, where progress had been followed closely. Although comparatively unknown to the general public, his heroic decisions and action were brought to their attention by Lord Elphinstone. Frere received the thanks of Parliament and was awarded a knighthood (the KCB – Knight Commander of the Bath). The qualities Frere brought to his leadership were recognised by the Governor-General, who appointed him to the Viceroy's Council in Calcutta in October 1859. His promotion was no doubt aided by the ringing endorsement provided by Sir John Lawrence, Chief Commissioner in the Punjab, who wrote of him in May 1858:

> "From first to last, from the commencement of the Mutiny to the final triumph, that officer has rendered assistance to the Punjab administration, just as if he had been one of its own Commissioners. It was owing to his indefatigable exertions that the 1ˢᵗ Bombay Fusiliers arrived at Multan so soon as they did. He despatched the 1ˢᵗ and then the 2ⁿᵈ Belooch Battalion from Sind to succour the Punjab. The Chief Commissioner believes that probably there is no Civil Officer in India who, for eminent exertions, deserves better of the Government than Mr H.B.E.Frere."[46]

Frere took considerable risks during the mutiny, and succeeded. Acting without authority, he provided timely support to areas in greater need of help than the Sind. Yet, had the sepoys in the Sind rebelled earlier, and in greater numbers, it could have had disastrous consequences. He emerged with his reputation enhanced; it could easily have been otherwise.

Chapter 5.

CALCUTTA AND BOMBAY.

The sepoy uprising had a profound effect upon British policy towards India. Prior to the outbreak, the East India Company had come close to bankruptcy on more than one occasion, and there was unease in the British Parliament about the policies being applied. The cost of suppressing the mutiny had been huge. A liberal view was in vogue in England, and the annexation policy of Lord Dalhousie in particular came in for harsh criticism.

The mutiny changed attitudes in London radically. The Company could no longer be trusted to administer India safely, and the collapse of discipline in the Bengal Army demonstrated that major reform was necessary. The Government of India Act of 1858 established the sovereign authority of the Crown in India, and provided for a Secretary of State and a Council of India. A Viceroy representing the Crown replaced the Governor-General. The President of the Board of Control in London became Secretary of State for India, and the new Council of India combined the roles of the Board of Control and Court of Directors. The army was radically overhauled, providing for 80,000 European troops in India, double the existing number. These men would no longer be employed by the Company, but would be part of the Royal Army, enlisted for service anywhere in the world. Dalhousie's doctrine of lapse, the policy that dictated that in the event of a ruler having no natural heir his state would be annexed by the Company, was to be dropped. No support would be given to missionaries. Dalhousie was persuaded to retire. The new Viceroy, Lord Canning, knew Frere; uncle John Hookham had been a close friend to Canning's father, and Frere was to become a trusted adviser to the son just as his uncle had been to the father.

Frere's wife had joined him in Karachi. When it was known that he was to leave the Sind a public meeting was arranged to mark the occasion. More than five thousand people in Karachi signed a letter of gratitude to Frere. They represented every race and social class in the town. In his reply Frere could not resist the temptation to set out his strongly held feelings about the Company's bureaucracy:

> "…If I have been successful it has been by exposing to the utmost of my power the centralizing fashion which has of late years been so common, and which I have always considered to be one great cause of our late disasters….however earnestly and ably I might have laboured, the results would have been comparatively insignificant had I acted on any other principle than that of giving to every workman the freest scope and best aid I

could…it is this which, in almost every district, has enabled our officers, with very limited means, to crowd into a few years such a vast amount of improvement in roads, canals, railways, steamers, and other results and marks of civilization."[47]

In response the community of Karachi presented him with an address:

"…had your route lain through the province, instead of by sea, we are sure you would have found every step of your way crowded by a sorrowing populace. From the aristocracy of the land down to the humblest fisherman, every soul would have deserted their pleasure and their daily labour, and flocked round to give vent to the outpouring of their hearts."[48]

Frere and his wife sailed from Karachi on October 31 1859 on the steamer *Feroze*. Appropriately they travelled from Government House to the waterside by passenger train. The route was lined by massive crowds, reaching out with their hands for a last touch of the departing ruler. A farewell salute of fifteen guns from the fort boomed over the cheers of a huge crowd lining the harbourside. It was said that there was not a man in the length and breadth of Sind to whom Frere's face or voice was not familiar.

Their first port of call was Dwarka, a small fort two hundred miles to the south-east. It happened that they arrived there with fresh ammunition for the British garrison just as a sea assault from local malcontents was in progress, and they were able to watch the battle from the deck of the *Feroze*. It turned out to be a petty local outbreak that was easily contained, although several men were wounded and taken aboard the *Feroze*. Thereafter they stayed several weeks in Bombay, where Frere spoke at length with Lord Elphinstone and got to know the leading opinion-formers. Elphinstone had resisted Frere's appointment in Calcutta, arguing that he was too valuable to the Sind, but Canning had prevailed. Elphinstone gave in with a good grace, and remained supportive of Frere.

The welcome Frere received when he finally reached Calcutta was mixed. No Bombay man had ever served on the Supreme Council. Its members had previously come from the Bengal service, and the rivalry between the two Presidencies caused some initial tension. He was disapproved of by many of the diehard Europeans, who were already jealous of him for his elevation. At forty-five he had been promoted above many officers with greater seniority. Frere's tact, courtesy and willingness to enter into society quickly overcame these problems. His wife, as the daughter of a previous Bombay Governor, was well-versed in the diplomatic and social niceties of life in India, and their home became a centre at which the leaders of the English and Indian communities met on equal terms. Lady Frere visited the Indian ladies in turn, as she had been accustomed to doing in Bombay and the Sind. Her husband vigorously promoted female education, using his position to raise the social status of women.

Frere initiated public breakfasts to which anyone who wished to see him on any business could come. He was a courteous and attentive listener, and these breakfasts were popular. Overseas visitors or callers from other parts of India brought him valuable intelligence and information about affairs outside the rather insular Calcutta administration. Non-official Europeans, hitherto unable to make their grievances and needs known through any conduit other than the press, which was frequently strident and critical, found they were welcome at his table. He gained the trust and acceptance of many Indians, who saw in him an opportunity to have their voices heard at the highest level in the land. At Frere's instigation Legislative Councils were set up in Bombay, Madras and Calcutta in which both Indians and Europeans participated. They were not elected but nominated by the Government from non-officials. Three Indians became members of the Viceroy's Legislative Council, and four were appointed in Bombay. Frere argued against the restriction on ownership of firearms to Europeans and Eurasians only.

Frere immediately found common cause with the new Governor-General in opposing the policy of annexation of Indian states, and accepting the tradition of recognizing adoption. He believed that annexation had been an important grievance contributing to the Mutiny. The new Council in Calcutta provided an exciting opportunity for him to propagate his ideas. He found himself in sympathy with many of the reforms, but was opposed to the move from a Company army to the Royal Army, which looked like a knee-jerk reaction to the Mutiny.

He found he was joining an old friend on the Council in Calcutta. James Outram had distinguished himself during the uprising, featuring prominently in the relief of Lucknow. He was appointed to the Council as its military member in 1858 and, like Frere, saw this as an opportunity to promulgate a greater participation of Indians in positions of leadership and authority. Together they campaigned for a policy of reconciliation. Christianity would no longer be forced upon Muslims and Hindi. This stand attracted criticism in England where even the most liberal opinion still held that it was their duty to convert India to Christianity. John Lawrence was a strong supporter of this view. Frere remained a devout Christian to the end of his life, reading a portion of the Bible every day before breakfast. However he believed it was not his duty to convert India, as this would be a violation of the respect for the feelings and opinions of others, which he saw as the underlying conception of his faith.

Outram and Frere believed that the role of Indian officers in the army should be greatly expanded, and any acts of revenge against the population following the Mutiny stamped on. Government should be decentralised, authority being based upon the personal responsibility of individual officers. These officers should be selected on merit and not according to their position of seniority. Local rule by rajahs should be strengthened. Frere wrote:

> "How are we to restore the mutual confidence and good feeling between races now in so many provinces bitterly incensed against each other? It can hardly be done by rule…But much may be done by personal power and influence, if you trust good men."[49]

Elsewhere he was quoted as saying that if the only way Britain could hold India was through an army of occupation, one had to question what they were doing there.

In the aftermath of the Mutiny, Outram, for many years Resident in Lucknow, had urged that the taluqdars, important local dignitaries, should have their properties restored and should not be punished for their part in the mutiny if the British were to restore order in the long term. This proposal had been (reluctantly) accepted. In April 1861 a group of twelve taluqdars from the province of Oudh made a formal presentation of thanks to Canning for his interest and trust. Frere, visiting Lucknow with Canning in November of that year, noted:

> "Everyone spoke well of the results of the experiment made in entrusting the Talookdars with a share in the administration. I am convinced that it is the greatest and most urgently needed of all improvements on this side in India, and I cannot imagine how society and the administration have kept together so long without it."[50]

General Napier, who in 1861 succeeded Outram as the Military Member of the Supreme Council spoke warmly of Frere:

> "My first acquaintance with Sir Bartle Frere was when I was fitting out and embarking the Bengal troops for the campaign in China in 1860. [He must have forgotten their first meeting in

Karachi]. Sir James Outram was the President of the Council and Sir Bartle Frere a member. Sir James Outram, fresh from the exigencies of war, knew well how injurious would be the application of regulations adapted for peace measures to the wants of a military force under newly developed conditions, and in the application of his experience he was cordially supported by his colleague Sir Bartle Frere, who took an intense interest in, and a masterly view of, the wants of the troops, and the necessity of delivering them on the field of their work in the most perfect condition possible. Instead of having to fight for everything under the harrow of regulations never intended for such occasions, all official red-tape obstructions were brushed aside."[51]

Frere practised what he preached.

The Indian Army was completely reorganised. Frere saw this as an opportunity to advance his ideas, which were at some distance at variance with the customary way of doing things in India. It was plain that India could not be held with British troops alone. In a letter to Colonel Durand he set out his thoughts:

"…no army which it can be worth our while to maintain could hold India, unless we can revert to our old normal condition, when our subjects generally acquiesced passively in our rule, and when we were rarely reminded that it was necessary to use our Army, except against independent or semi-independent states. It seems to me utterly impossible that our present system of holding the country with European detachments scattered over it can be persevered in, without the destruction of all discipline and an aggravation of the feeling of general distrust, which makes Englishmen, as well as Natives, suppose that a detachment of Europeans is necessary at almost every Station.....we must continue to govern our own Indian Provinces hereafter, as we have generally done heretofore, through the respect and with the consent of the Natives, and to trust for the general maintenance of internal peace to our Police.....our attempts at centralization during the last twenty-five years have been the reverse of all this. They have been all by departments instead of by persons....Nowhere in India is it now possible to find any functionary of a grade higher than a village headman, who can say that he represents Government in all its departments; that he has himself undivided authority within the territorial bounds of his charge; and that he is responsible only to one superior representative of Government.....we find, as matter of fact, that our most successful Generals and expeditions have been either beyond the reach of post, or have succeeded only when imminent danger or exasperation, at repeated failures, led the nation to a tacit concession of dictatorial powers. We must, first of all then, get rid of what is incurably bad and dangerous. Race alone, to which we are now trusting, will be a most fallacious guide. Not only shall we dismiss many good and useful soldiers, and retain many bad and traitorous ones, but we shall perpetuate a most false and dangerous principle."[52]

Lord Canning retired in March 1862. Outram had gone back to England in 1860. Within a year of arriving in Calcutta, Frere had become the most senior member of the Council, and shouldered an increasing proportion of the reform work. The loss of his two closest allies put additional strains on him. His wife Catherine then fell ill, and was advised to return to England, leaving Frere feeling rather lonely and isolated. Canning's replacement was Lord Elgin. Although needed by Elgin as the most senior and knowledgeable member of the Viceroy's Council, Frere felt his time in Calcutta was coming to an end; that he had done as much there as he could.

Relief came from an unexpected quarter. Sir George Clerk was forced by ill health to resign his position of Governor of Bombay and Frere was appointed in his place, in spite of many senior members of the Bombay Presidency being ahead of him in rank and entitlement. His qualities had been recognised and appreciated by Canning, who on retirement from the Governor-Generalship recommended Frere for advancement. In many ways this was a source of great satisfaction to him. He was following in the footsteps of his respected father-in-law, which must have delighted his wife. Bombay had always been the state closest to his heart, the territory where his interests lay, and where he felt he could provide the most benefit of his leadership. Frere sailed down the coast from Calcutta to Madras on April 9, 1862. Catherine, who had already commenced the journey home to England, left her ship at Madras and joined him. From there they journeyed across country by the first train to cross India from coast to coast. From Beypore *H.M.S. Auckland* took them by sea to Bombay, which they reached on April 22. There they were welcomed warmly by many old friends. His arrival was however soured by the news that the ship transferring all his movable goods from Calcutta had foundered on a sandbank. Hardly anything was saved. Amongst the lost items were thirty-two cases of books and papers, collections of coins, antiquities, curiosities and hunting trophies, and all his letters and memoranda.[53]

Frere's work in Calcutta had been onerous and demanding. He had been looking forward to leave in England with his family, but now he was committed to at least five years more of heavy responsibility. His new post in Bombay, among many friends, gave him the opportunity and authority to apply his ideas and principles effectively. The Bombay Presidency covered a vast area, and Frere at once set out to visit as much as he could of the territory and familiarise himself with its officers and requirements. Canning had been the representative of the British Government's new liberal and progressive policy as applied to India after the mutiny, and Frere was now the senior defender of this policy. The Bombay Council consisted of three members besides the Governor – the Commander-in-Chief of the Bombay Presidency and two civil members responsible for financial and judicial matters respectively. Under an act of 1862 a Legislative Council for Bombay had been created, similar to Calcutta, with eight additional members to the presiding four. These eight members were to be nominated by the Governor, some being official, some non-official, and some Indians, thus significantly broadening representation. Frere saw that his first duty was to implement the changes decided by the Council.

Whilst many of the senior figures in the British Raj were prepared only to pay lip service to the changes, Frere took them very seriously. He was fortunate that many of his civil servants were former colleagues and old friends; like-minded officials who understood his thinking. He continued to give public breakfasts once or twice a week at which anyone could speak to him. Officials from outlying stations who sought his ear were invited to stay a week with him in Bombay. He saw it as a way of learning the needs of the local community, and in time enabling local legislation to prevail on matters of local interest. In this he was railing against the excessive centralisation of the bureaucracy that had grown up progressively: Calcutta had eroded the ability for local officials to take decisions on the spot. He went further. He believed that it was impractical for decisions affecting the lives of so many Indians to be taken in London, and he campaigned for many of these decisions to be localised. On November 15, 1866, he wrote:

> "Probably the most ardent centralizer in a French bureau would shrink from any proposal to manage the roads and bridges of the Ottoman Empire from Paris as a centre, though that would be a light task compared with what is now attempted in India."[54]

In November 1863 Lord Elgin, travelling over a mountain pass in the Himalyas, fell ill and died. His successor as Governor-General was Sir John Lawrence. A towering figure in India, Lawrence possessed very firm, conservative Christian opinions, and as Chief Commissioner of the Punjab had criticised Frere more than once, and shown his disapproval of the way Frere encouraged local participation. He had nevertheless publicly thanked Frere for his unhesitating support during the mutiny. Lawrence, at the end of his long career in India, had become set in his ways. Convinced of his own opinions and secure in his religious beliefs, he attempted to control everything from the centre. This policy had just about succeeded in the Punjab because he had informally bent the rules to meet local requirements, but it was not practical in overseeing the vast complexities of the country as a whole. Frere was dismayed. He wrote of Lawrence:

> "There is always in India some need for public servants acting without orders, on the assurance that, when their superiors hear their reasons, their acts will be approved and confirmed; and I hold that when you have extinguished that feeling of mutual confidence between superior and subordinate authorities and made public men as timid as they are in England, you will have removed one great safeguard of our Indian Empire. It does not take long so to bridle a body of public servants as to paralyse their power of acting without orders."[55]

Frere's worst expectations of Lawrence were soon realised. On September 8, 1864, he wrote to Sir Charles Wood, Secretary of State for India:

> "Sir John Lawrence has been good enough to allow me to communicate freely direct with him on all matters, and I have freely availed myself of his permission. But I can see that he regards me as the zealous but rather expensively inclined Commissioner of a district, with a number of deputies who, like the Commissioner, are a little inclined sometimes to run wild."[56]

Frere remained convinced that India could not be ruled effectively without the involvement of the local people. His experience had taught him that centralised control in such a vast country, with poor communications, left local authorities powerless to act in a timely way or adjust policies to local needs. In essence he was proposing that power be removed from the civil services in London and Calcutta and given to the Presidencies of Bombay, Calcutta and Madras. It was perhaps inevitable that his superiors would place every available obstacle in his path, and continue to hold the controlling reins very firmly. As in recent times, finance played a central part. If Frere were to succeed in encouraging Indian participation, developing the infrastructure and opening up trade, he would need funding from the centre. Not only were finances extremely tight after the Mutiny, and claims for reconstruction and renewal numerous, but the civil servants in Calcutta saw finance as a way of maintaining control over the Presidencies.

As a way of raising funds Frere encouraged the cultivation of cotton. The American Civil War, then in full spate, had meant that England's key supply of raw cotton had dried up, providing an opportunity for Indian cotton to supplant it. The funds required to develop the industry were promptly voted by the Bombay Council, but vetoed by Calcutta on the basis that it was not budgeted. Frere wrote on October 12, 1863 to Charles Trevelyan, finance member of the Supreme Council:

> "I cannot believe…that we should say: We will not make these roads for cotton or grain nor these works for irrigation, nor railway feeders, nor barracks….because a Budget rule, which we have made and remade half a dozen times and which we constantly violate, would be violated once more?"[57].

He was supported by Sir Charles Wood, Secretary for India in London, who wrote to Trevelyan that £3m must be devoted by Calcutta to the production and transportation of cotton, and that the Supreme Council could not "leave [themselves] open to the charge of dawdling and trifling with so vital a matter."[58] Frere got his way. Between 1861 and 1865 the annual value of cotton exported from the Bombay Presidency rose from £7 million to £31 million.

In April 1863 Frere arranged for the first census of the city of Bombay to be taken, and in August Calcutta gave assent to the necessary law. Frere felt that if he were to carry out much needed social improvements it was essential that he had a good idea of how many people lived in the teeming city. The census was scheduled for February 2, 1864, but a week before it was due the India Office in London instructed Frere to cancel it: they had not yet sanctioned it. Frere decided this was not a good enough reason, and that to suspend the work without explanation would cause alarm and misunderstanding. So he decided to proceed with the census without the act, on a voluntary basis. The result was a complete success.

Armed with the census, Frere turned his attention to health and cleanliness. Bombay with its high population and congested slums was among the most unhealthy of cities in India. More living space was desperately needed, and he started by clearing away obsolete fortifications, public buildings and factories, and utilising the cleared ground for new public buildings, recreation and homes. A trail-blazing piece of legislation, the Bombay Municipal Act, was passed in 1865, providing for the appointment of a Municipal Commission with executive power to manage finance and health. It was the first of its kind in India. It was not possible to build a new sewage system, due to the low-lying land on which the city was located, but waste collection was reorganised with a vast number of sweepers making inroads into the problem. By 1868 deaths in the city had fallen from 35.04 per thousand inhabitants to 19.20.[59]

As we have seen shipping was a subject dear to Frere's heart, and in order to improve marine commerce he initiated the reconstruction of Bombay's harbour in 1863, significantly expanding its shipping accommodation. Allied with this was the work he did in extending the railways north to Delhi and the Punjab as well as Karachi. This made the Punjab easily accessible from Karachi, and was the nearest route by eight hundred miles to the sea for twenty million people. He pointed out to Calcutta that not only would this network facilitate trade, but could have strategic military significance should the need arise to move troops, arms and/or supplies swiftly to other parts of the country. A new railway terminal was built in the Back Bay of Bombay on reclaimed land. As Calcutta would not finance the Reclamation Company, shares were sold to Indian entrepreneurs. Their value soared.

The combination of these new measures produced a boom in Bombay. Trade flourished, land prices soared and money in the form of gold and silver flooded in. The increased need for labour pushed wage rates up and drove up rents. Inflation rose steeply, and the cost of living doubled. Frere used the new-found wealth in the hands of Indian entrepreneurs and merchants to persuade them to finance the establishment of local schools and improve female education. His wife Catherine supported his efforts by inviting the wives and women relatives of the high Parsee caste to Government House. Frere was flying high, his imaginative schemes and his sympathetic Governorship producing encouraging progress and support locally. He was about to suffer a setback that was to sully his career record in the years to come.

The seeds of the problem he was to encounter had been sowed before he assumed the Governorship. The principal bank in his territory, the Bank of Bombay, had been founded in 1840 in order to foster trade. The entrepreneurial climate in Bombay was white-hot, but the Government of India in Calcutta became concerned that the bank was taking on unreasonable risks. In 1860, two years before Frere assumed the Governorship of

Bombay, Calcutta resolved to take on the responsibility itself. In compensation to the Bank it still permitted local advances to public companies on the security of their shares, although by an apparent oversight it was not necessary for these shares to be fully paid up. This left many of the shares without any substance as a security. A Bill to this effect was drafted and approved by the Secretary of State for India in London nineteen days before Frere took up office.

The Bill was a calamitous misjudgement. The American Civil War that was raging in the early 1860's had resulted in a dearth of American cotton, and the Indian cotton trade was flourishing. A feverish financial atmosphere developed, with individuals realising huge fortunes. As always in boom times, there occurred some overextended investment and bad business practices. When some of the investments made by the Bombay Bank turned bad it emerged that gross mismanagement had resulted in very heavy losses. The president of the Bank, an experienced banker appointed by Calcutta, had for many years neglected his duties and left all the control in the hands of the Bank secretary, who was under the influence of a wealthy local stockbroker, Premchund Roychund, one of the shareholders' representatives on the Board of the Bank. Roychund had favoured his friends, lending them large sums of money on inadequate security, so that a considerable proportion of the Bank's funds had been advanced on worthless pledges or overvalued shares. Speculators lost fortunes, and protested in the streets. Many of Frere's friends, who had participated in the boom and speculation, now turned on him, blaming him for their losses. When it was pointed out that he was not responsible for the misjudgements that had occurred prior to his appointment as Governor, they argued that he should have used his influence to stop the run. To make matters worse, the cotton industry, so successful in the early 1860's was suddenly confronted with renewed American competition when the Civil War there ended in 1865. More than half the capital of the bank was irretrievably lost. A run on the bank followed, and in order to stabilise it Frere applied to Calcutta for, and was granted, an advance of 150 lacs of Rupees (£1.5million). This stemmed the run, but not for long. A succession of bad debts and financial crises kept the bank in the news, with further panics, until it became evident in 1867 that the bank was close to complete failure. In January 1868, it was resolved to wind it up voluntarily.

Frere's hair turned grey as a result of the pressure under which he was placed. He was criticised in Calcutta and London for the "supineness and inaction" of the Bombay Government. A Commission of Inquiry was formed and evidence taken in London and India. Frere was examined as a witness, and in the report that followed the full extent of the misdeeds was disclosed for the first time. Frere defended the Bombay Government, which had assented to the disastrous change, although it had occurred before he became Governor. Nevertheless he was held to blame for giving only partial effect to instructions received from Calcutta and London, and failing to ensure that the bank was responsibly managed. He protested that the central control insisted upon left him unable to act on his own initiative, while the instructions he received lacked the benefit of local, detailed knowledge required. Needless to say, his attempts to redirect the blame to Calcutta were not well received, and his relationship with his masters became even more strained.

The Secretary of State, Sir Charles Wood, retired in February 1866. In winding up his tenure, he recommended the Star of India for Frere, and let it be known that he would like him to serve on the India Council, the Secretary of State's advisory body in London. Considering the criticism levelled at Frere this was a ringing endorsement from a very eminent senior statesman. Frere accepted with alacrity. His wife spent long periods in England, where the children attended school, and he had in recent years seen little of his family. In fact, he had not seen his son for ten years.

Frere felt that what good he could do in India had been achieved, and he needed to face new challenges. He was weary of the fights and disagreements with Calcutta, of an over-centralised organisation. It was time to move on.

Chapter 6.

LONDON AND ZANZIBAR.

F rere enjoyed his journey home. He made the most of his first opportunity for a holiday in ten years. With his wife and two eldest daughters he embarked in Bombay upon the steamer *Malta* on March 6, 1867. The Suez Canal was in construction, and he toured the work in the company of the architect, Ferdinand de Lesseps. At Malta he stayed in the old family house that had belonged to his uncle, Hookham Frere, now occupied by Lady Hamilton Chichester. Then he took a leisurely route back to England through Sicily, staying at Palermo for a while, Naples, Rome, Florence and Paris.

He rented a house in London in Princes Gardens, where his two youngest daughters, who had been living with their aunts, joined him. The family was once more united. He lived there for seven years, letting out Wressil Park, the family home in Wimbledon. The inclement weather that he encountered on his return, so different from India, soon affected his health. At the end of 1866 he had been badly injured when his horse shied at a passing camel and elephant, slipped into a ditch and fell over, crushing the muscles in one leg. He was on crutches for the remainder of his time in India, and felt the effects for the rest of his life. This injury, added to ten years of stress and toil, and the extremes of weather in India had left him weary and debilitated. He was forced to take a rest cure at Marienbad in Bohemia. Even during this two-month break he could not overcome the habits of a lifetime. He visited local elementary schools and was impressed with their excellence. He thought them in many ways superior to their equivalents in England.

Settled back in London, his work on the Indian Council, the Secretary of State's advisory body, was not onerous, and he enjoyed a rare period of calm, surrounded by his family. His wide range of interests and acquaintances brought many visitors to the house and he used these contacts to introduce to the Council anyone he felt might have knowledge or experience that could be useful.[60] The Council met once a week, supposedly in order to advise the Secretary of State on Indian affairs, but the Secretary of State largely ignored the Council, and communicated directly with the Viceroy. There were departmental committees on two or three other days when it was possible to raise important matters and express personal views.

Frere's presence was not entirely welcome. His views on India being governed by Indians were not popular with his masters, and the Secretary of State, Viscount Cranborne (later the Marquess of Salisbury) was a close ally of Sir John Lawrence and therefore not well-disposed to Frere. Salisbury was later to be one of Frere's bitterest enemies. Nevertheless Frere continued his campaign to delegate authority to the men on the spot, and his involvement certainly helped Napier, now Commander-in-Chief in Bombay, have a free hand in military decisions.

On the Council he also pursued the question of sanitary conditions, holding up the improvements he had brought about in Bombay as an example of what could be achieved. This brought him into contact with Florence Nightingale, who maintained a voluminous correspondence with him on the subject of soldiers' health, and the need to rid the towns and cantonments of contagious diseases. Through Frere's influence Sir Stafford Northcote, the Secretary of State for India who succeeded Cranborne in March 1867, met Florence Nightingale and set up a Sanitary Committee for India. Frere was proposed as Chairman. As always, the dead hand of bureaucracy in India made progress there painfully slow. Frere set out in a paper what needed to be done. Florence Nightingale wrote to him:

"It is a noble paper, an admirable paper – and what a present to make to a Government! You have included in it all the great principles – sanitary and administrative – which the country requires. And now you must work, work these points until they are embodied in local works in India. This will not be in our time, for it takes more than a few years to fill a continent with civilisation….God bless you for it! I think it is a great work."[61]

In November 1867, Frere was requested to assist Sir John Pakington, Secretary of State for War, in preparing a plan to reorganize the administrative departments of the British Army in India. He was recognised as one of the leading authorities on the subject. At Frere's suggestion a working party was formed consisting of himself, Major-General Balfour, a member of the Military Finance Commission in Calcutta, and General Sir Henry Storks. The result of their work was a Code of Regulations based largely upon the Military Finance Department in Calcutta, where Balfour had achieved major savings in expenditure. The cost of stores was reduced from £1,898,954 in 1867/8 to £1,086,116 in 1869/70.

When the Suez Canal was opened in 1869, Frere's experience in Africa, and his visit to the canal, were put to good purpose. He recognised immediately that the opening of the Canal would make the Middle and Far East much more accessible to the British. He urged the Prime Minister to take up shares in the Canal to provide a measure of control, but this suggestion was rejected by Gladstone (Disraeli was later to make such a move). Frere's awareness of the threat posed by the opening of the canal led him to propose a strengthening of the Indian Ocean fleet "now that the fleets of the Mediterranean may be within seven days' sail of Aden and twelve of Bombay."[62] He knew that the naval defence of India was weak, with scant training and poor organisation. He not only saw the augmentation of the fleet as a sound defensive measure but a possible opportunity to extend Britain's influence in the east. The government accepted his proposals in their entirety.

For the next five years Frere applied himself with diligence to his new office. His advice was sought by a wide variety of people requiring information about India. Lord Mayo, appointed Viceroy of India to succeed Sir John Lawrence, consulted Frere widely, and it can be seen that he applied much of the advice Frere gave him when he arrived in India. Frere lectured to a number of societies and wrote several articles on India, the east coast of Africa, (which had strong connections with India, as will be seen later), the Persian Gulf and Afghanistan. He was twice elected President of the Asiatic Society, and was a fellow of The Geographical Society, where he became President in 1873. He was talked of as a prospective Member of Parliament, but his position on the India Council precluded this.

By 1872 Frere, now 57, had served five years on the Council and felt his career was going nowhere. Then an opportunity arose which was to provide a new step forward. The move to abolish slavery was in full spate, with William Wilberforce and Zachary Macaulay campaigning widely, not only in Britain but also wherever they encountered it. The slave trade had been outlawed by the Slave Trade Act of 1807, but not enforced rigorously. The Slavery Abolition Act of 1833 outlawed slavery itself throughout most of the British Empire. The end of the American Civil War in 1865 gave the movement fresh impetus. The United States, hitherto ambivalent, provided unambiguous support to the abolition of slavery. However the slave trade on the high seas, mainly involving the transportation of slaves from African countries to the east, continued unabated until the Slave Trade Act of 1872. This empowered the

British Navy, after receiving appropriate authorisation from London, to detain ships suspected of slave trading. Unusually all the major powers were at peace at this time, and had the strength to impose their will on the world.

An occasion to exercise that will was not long in presenting itself. The island of Zanzibar, off the east coast of Africa, was a focal point for the slave traffic from Central and East Africa to Arabia, Persia and India. Hundreds of thousands of slaves passed through the great slave market on the island, controlled by Arab traders. This shocked David Livingstone when he observed the devastating effect on local populations, and he was quick to bring it to the notice of the British government. During Lord Palmerston's term as Prime Minister the Government had taken the lead in seeking to stop the slave trade, but he was no longer in office. In his evidence before the Slave-Trade Committee on July 17, 1871, Frere said:

> "It appears to me that the cardinal evil which you have to deal with is the oscillation of our own opinions in the matter…Our Government, representing public opinion, appears to me of late years to have been very half-hearted in the matter."[63]

Frere had become a friend of Livingstone following the explorer's visit to Bombay, when he had stayed with Frere. When Livingstone returned to Africa the two continued to write to each other. Frere was thus fully informed of Livingstone's views, and what he had witnessed. Accordingly he took a leading part in conjunction with the Anti-Slavery Society in pressing the government for action and speaking at public meetings.

The Arab slave-traders in East Africa transported their captives to the Middle and Far East in swift dhows that, with a south-west monsoon, could outrun any of the coastal steamers. An English squadron was deployed to intercept this traffic, but lacked sufficient timely information to check it in any significant way. Zanzibar's main trading partner was India, and through that trade Britain was able to exercise considerable influence on Zanzibar. On August 31, 1868, Frere wrote to Gifford Palgrave, whom he had met in India and was a consul in the Foreign Office:

> "I am sure you would find little difficulty in making a settlement of the slave-trade questions concerned with Zanzibar. The only real difficulty is to get the Government and influential classes in England to make up their minds as to what they want....both the Indian and English Governments think that, by shutting their eyes and doing nothing, they can avoid the diplomatic entanglements and the outlay of money which they so much dread..."[64]

Commencing in 1822 several treaties had been agreed with the Sultan of Zanzibar either outlawing the slave trade or limiting it severely. All had been ignored by the slave masters, who stood to lose a fortune if the trade ceased, and had sufficient influence with the Sultan to ensure the treaties were not upheld. Due to the ineffectiveness of the attempts by the Royal Navy, with ten ships at their disposal, to police the entire East African coast, stronger measures were required to intercept the slave boats. A Parliamentary Select Committee, convened in July 1871, recommended that a major effort should be made to persuade the Sultan to ban the trade completely. An important public meeting at the Mansion House in London, convened by the Anti-Slavery Society, led in August 1872 to the Government, under pressure from the public, announcing its intention to take action. Frere, by dint of his public stance on slavery, was chosen to head a temporary mission with wide discretionary powers to persuade the Sultan to cease the trade. He was well placed to do so: Livingstone's report, referred to above, had prompted correspondence, common cause and a growing friendship between the explorer and Frere. As a friend of Livingstone Frere had been kept in close touch with the situation. He had taken a leading part, speaking at public meetings and working with the Anti-Slavery Society to press the Government to act. Moreover his contacts in India would be useful, as much of the slavery finance was provided by Indian companies in Bombay.

Frere prepared the ground carefully. First he visited Paris in an attempt to persuade the French to withdraw their co-operation with the traders, who frequently flew French flags, so that British ships could intercept and search slave ships without offending the French. This attempt fell on stony ground, so he moved on to visit the pope and King Victor Emmanuel in Rome. The king was well briefed about the mission, and was sympathetic. He presented Frere with a newly forged gold medal to give to Livingstone. The pope showed great interest in Frere's mission, and gave it his blessing, expressing regret that he had nothing more substantial to give.

From Italy the party sailed to Alexandria, then took the train to Cairo, where they stayed a week. The ruler of Egypt, the Khedive, was an intelligent man with a good grasp of the slavery problem. Egypt was the destination of many of the slaves coming from East Africa, and the Khedive knew the Sultan of Zanzibar well. He gave Frere advice on what he could expect in Zanzibar, and claimed for Egypt the position of "leader of civilization" in Africa.[65] He wished, with Britain's help, to suppress the slave trade, and pointed out that he and his predecessor had done much to check it. Throughout this journey his son, now 19 years old, accompanied Frere.

Frere arrived in Zanzibar on January 12, 1873. In the harbour were Rear-Admiral Cumming's flagship, *Glasgow,* and the British cruisers *Briton* and *Daphne,* and the American *Yantic.* On the afternoon of January 13 Frere led a party of forty-eight men ashore, including the off-duty officers of the three men-of-war, in full uniform for a formal reception by the Sultan. Frere presented the Royal letter and papers offering a treaty. In exchange for the public slave-markets being closed and all transport of slaves by sea ceasing, the British government would discharge the subsidy owed by Zanzibar to Muscat. This had fallen seriously in arrears after the failure of the crops the previous year. These proposals met strong resistance from the Sultan's Council, who made it clear that if he agreed they would look elsewhere for a Sultan.

For a month the Sultan hesitated and deferred his answer. The slave trade was too profitable to be given up easily. Frere's first meeting with the Sultan had not gone well. Doctor John Kirk, the local acting British Consul, who had formed a friendship with the Sultan before he succeeded his brother, and was well trusted by him, represented Frere at subsequent meetings. Long and frequent interviews had little effect, as the Sultan's advisers, the Mlawas, who has a vested interest in keeping the slave trade going, were always present.

Whilst these negotiations were proceeding, Frere used the time to visit the countryside. He also went to see the slave-market, which appalled him:

> "The slave-market is a hideous sight – a dirty, uneven space surrounded with filthy huts. The common slaves – generally children seated in lines or batches – were miserably thin and ill; hardly any had more than a few rags to cover them."[66]

He returned on February 8 to be told that the Sultan courteously but flatly refused to sign the treaty. Frere was not surprised, but he remained confident of ultimate success based upon the power and authority at his command. He suggested to Kirk that the American, German and French Consuls should be enlisted to apply pressure on the Sultan. The U.S. Secretary of State, Hamilton Fish, promised to lend enthusiastic support and the Captain of the *Yantic* wrote to the Sultan urging him to sign the treaty. However the American Consul, W.G. Webb, undermined this effort by letting the Sultan know he would support him if he would just limit the slave trade, not end it. With German support for the British and Fish insisting that the Americans also agree, it looked as though pressure would tell on the Sultan, and he would sign the treaty. However the French consul, de Vienne, who returned from Paris on February 9, suggested to the Sultan that he should apply for French protectorate status, and this encouraged the Sultan to maintain his resistance.

Frere sailed away south on the *Enchantress*, accompanied by the man-of-war *Briton*, promising to return in a month in case the Sultan changed his mind. His plan was to visit all the places on the coast of East Africa where the slave trade was practised so that he could be fully informed on the subject. He also wanted to make it clear to the slave masters that this was an official visit with the full might of England behind it. "I do not think I could have thoroughly understood the whole question without seeing what I have thus seen," he wrote to his wife, "and I hope it will enable Government to do what is needed effectually to put down the Slave-trade. It has been very hard work in every way, from heat as well as sheer physical labour."[67] On his return to Zanzibar on February 27, 1873, Frere filed a report with Lord Granville on his conclusions:

> "It is hardly an exaggeration to say that all trade passes through Indian hands. African, Arab, and European all use an Indian agent or Banian to manage the details of buying and selling; and without the intervention of an Indian, either as capitalist or petty trader, very little business is done…Two inferences must be drawn from these facts – first, that everything connected with African trade is at least as much an Indian as an English question…India, therefore, must share

with England the responsibility for what they do, and the obligation to protect them in their lawful callings. Secondly, England, through India, has an immense practical hold on East Africa. The Sultan and his Arabs can do nothing for good or evil without the Indian capitalist. The present difficulty is how to use this hold for the purpose of putting down the slave-trade, which has grown with the growth of the Indian interests on this coast. The question would be simple if we had to deal with the Sultan alone; but he knows we have joined France in guaranteeing his independence by the treaty of 1866; and the influence of France is actively exerted to prevent his concurring in our views regarding the slave-trade."[68]

Frere's tour caused him to think expansively. He recognised the potential of the East African coast, with its natural resources and good labour supply. An imperialist by instinct, he needed little encouragement to think of extending the British Empire. Britain effectively controlled East Africa: why not link it with British possessions further south? His thoughts received impetus from a member of his staff, Frederic Elton. Elton had served in India, and shared Frere's views on colonies. His duties included securing mining concessions, suppressing the slave trade and recruiting labour, with particular reference to South Africa. His knowledge of Africa was invaluable to Frere. The development of their working relationship was to have important consequences later, when Frere was in South Africa. Frere's memorandum on his negotiations with the Sultan makes reference to his thinking at the time;

> "There is a tempting opening for an empire in East Africa at the disposal of any great naval power; but common honesty forbids us to undertake a great philanthropic enterprise of this kind, and to find in it the coarse material reward of extended dominion."

Britain had "succeeded without seeking it and almost without knowing it, to a dominant position and immense commercial interests in East Africa."[69]

An air of uncertainty prevailed in Zanzibar. As long as the slave-trade question remained unresolved, trade of all kind would be at a standstill. The Sultan appeared relaxed: with France's backing and popular support from the Arabs on his stand he could not see how the English could oppose him. Frere remained patient but determined. He was resolved to get his way. He would prefer this to be by conciliation, but any agreement he achieved needed to be genuine and permanent. He was uncertain whether the English government would countenance strong-arm tactics, but in a way he did not care. As we have seen, Frere was strongly resistant to the overweaning hand of central government on local operations. Now he used the wide discretion he had been given to devastating effect. He issued a final warning to the Sultan and sailed for Muscat. From Mombasa he sent a further letter informing the Sultan that no transport of slaves by sea would any longer be permitted. The British squadron, increased to

14 ships, would henceforth blockade the port of Zanzibar and inspect all shipping using it to enforce this ban. In informing the Foreign Minister, Lord Granville, of what he had done, he suggested that the British Government should lay an embargo on the Sultan's custom houses and employ the custom house officials, who were almost all Indians or British subjects, to stop the slave trade. This far exceeded his authority, and was probably illegal.

The initial reaction in London was one of horror. The Law Officers of the Crown advised that these imposed terms infringed the independence of Zanzibar, guaranteed by Britain and France since 1862, and would therefore amount to an act of war. Further consideration by Granville, however, led to the conclusion that the threatened blockade would probably be effective, and he instructed Kirk to issue the ultimatum to the Sultan. Admiral Cumming was ordered to return to Zanzibar at once with all available ships.

When Frere reached London on June 12, 1873, he faced a major storm. The Prime Minister, Gladstone, was aghast, and the Cabinet in uproar. His actions were condemned as an unauthorised act of war. His supporters pointed out that there was a precedent for Frere's action: a slave trade incident in Brazil had been resolved by a similar measure. Fortunately for Frere, within two days news was received that the blockade had convinced the Sultan to abolish slavery. The anti-slavery movement championed Frere and Gladstone moved quickly to endorse him. Within a year the number of slaves exported by sea had fallen from between 16,000 and 23,000 to 1400, of which 217 were apprehended. The Queen appointed him to the Privy Council, and during a long interview with him showed a close interest in, and intimate knowledge of, his expedition. She sent for a map and made him describe for her the entire action. He remarked afterwards: "The Queen knew more about it than all her Ministers."[70] The Corporation of London gave him the freedom of the city and the universities of both Cambridge and Oxford bestowed honorary degrees on him. When the Liberals were defeated in a general election in February 1874 and Benjamin Disraeli became Prime Minister, Frere was offered the choice of a baronetcy or Knight Grand Cross of the Bath (GCB). He chose the former, but Queen Victoria bestowed the latter on him as well.

This episode was to leave a lasting impression, for Gladstone and Frere from that point on came to loathe each other. Gladstone had been embarrassed by Frere's action. The Prime Minister had first condemned it and then been forced to endorse it by the anti-slavery movement. Frere regarded Gladstone with contempt: he considered him a shifty politician who had avoided responsibility for his part in the errors made during the Crimean War. Disraeli shared his contempt.

News came in January 1874 that Livingstone had died. In 1867 Livingstone had written to Frere requesting his help. His wife Mary, left alone in England for most of their married life, had become an alcoholic and died of malaria attempting to follow him to Africa. Their four remaining children were left destitute in England. His son Tom, at the University of Glasgow was unable to progress further with his studies due to lack of finance. Livingstone, still in a remote part of Africa, could not help, and wanted Frere to see whether the government could provide assistance, as he had never previously asked for anything himself. Frere sent a letter to Gladstone, then Prime Minister, dated December 25, 1869: "I have been rather at a loss to know how I could be of any use to these poor orphan-like children of a man whom I reverence as a real hero, a true apostle…But it seems to me that the nation owes something to the father….it may be long ere the nation can repay him, if it ever can repay him at all, save through his children."[71] Considerable correspondence followed, until in 1871 he obtained a grant for the Livingstone children from the Queen's Bounty.

Enjoying a period of great popularity after his Zanzibar coup, and having his cause strongly advanced to Queen Victoria by his staunch ally, Florence Nightingale, Frere looked to reactivate his dream of an expanding British Empire, with its authority extending in a crescent from East Africa up the coast of Africa and across to the south coast of India. He also believed it would be possible to control the Persian Gulf, his argument being that this would provide a stout defence against any plans by Russia to make a move towards India or use its ally, Persia, to expand in the Middle East. Russia remained the main potential enemy and, as in 1840, the fear was that any threat to India would come through Afghanistan or along the Gulf coast.

Frere was being talked of as the next Viceroy of India, and doubtless there is nothing he would have liked more than this appointment. Perhaps his aired views were circulated with an eye towards this appointment, but it was not to be. His unilateral action in Zanzibar, successful though it had been, had frightened the British Government. The last thing they wanted at the present was an independently minded Viceroy who was sympathetic to local aspirations. Instead Lord Lytton was appointed, and Frere was cast back into the India Council. His disappointment at the setback was assuaged by the news that he had been appointed to escort the Prince of Wales on a proposed tour of India in 1875, as a forerunner to the Queen being declared Empress of India on January 1, 1877. Lord Napier wrote: "The event of the Prince's coming is a great one for our prestige in India. It is a want that has been unfulfilled since the time of the best Moguls."[72]

Frere had long believed that the people of India, who would be impressed by the sight of a visible chief, should see royalty in the flesh. It was his view that the eastern mind seeks a visible chief on whom to bestow its allegiance. He saw the formality and splendour of ceremonies and processions in India as an important manifestation of authority. In this respect Frere was an unreconstructed imperialist.

Frere was now sixty, and some thought he might be thinking of living a quieter life. This new mission was one he felt was too good to miss. He threw himself into the preparations with great zeal. He attended to every detail of the trip, buying tropical gear, obtaining £100,000 from Parliament for official gifts, and arranging security. The Prince landed at Bombay in November 1875 to a most impressive reception. Durbars, balls, picnics and other festivities followed in quick succession. From Bombay the Prince visited Ceylon (Sri Lanka) and travelled on to Madras and Calcutta. Then via Benares. Khanpur and Lucknow he arrived at Delhi before returning to Bombay. The tour was considered a great success, marked with ceremonial parades and lavish banquets at every stop. More importantly, accompanying the future king enabled Frere to gain access to the opinion-formers in India and officials at the highest level. He pressed upon them his concerns over the threat posed by Russia and the need to strengthen defences. In 1873 the Russians had captured Merv, and appeared to be looking towards Afghanistan. Even the Secretary of State, Lord Salisbury (alias Lord Cranborne) was sufficiently alarmed to pay attention to what Frere had to say. He asked Frere to report on frontier affairs and relations with the Amir.

When Frere begged leave of the Prince to visit the Punjab nobody objected. He wished to see the grave of his brother, Richard, who had died in Rawalpindi thirty-three years previously. From Rawalpindi he went on to the main city in the Punjab, Peshawar. A walled city, it was situated close to the mouth of the Khyber Pass, and therefore of key strategic importance in protecting India from the west. There he found that the defence of the Khyber Pass had been neglected, offering invaders an easy access to India. There was confusion in the command, and an inability of local commanders to act as they saw fit. The dead hand of bureaucracy lay across them. He was appalled. The diligence with which the frontier had been guarded in the 1840's had been dissipated. He wrote to Lord Salisbury setting out his views in a very forthright manner. He urged that power should be devolved onto the Punjab authorities so that they could assume responsibility and have the freedom to act on what they observed.

His enquiries also revealed that the Emir of Afghanistan, Sher Ali, was hostile towards England and unlikely to be co-operative. General George Pollock, the hero of the relief of Kabul in 1842, was uncertain what the Calcutta government's attitude was towards Afghanistan, and in accordance with his instructions had not kept in touch with developments over the border. Calcutta had not kept him informed on British policy, and standing orders to frontier officers were to adopt a non-interference policy. Frere advocated a new approach to Afghanistan. He wanted an envoy sent to Kabul to ensure that the Emir did not agree to an alliance with the Russians. A clear understanding should be reached with the Emir as to the aims of both parties. If the Emir refused to co-operate, then "we must look for alliances and influences elsewhere than in Kabul; …in Kelat, at Kandahar, Herat, and in Persia."[73] He protested against the "constant inculcation of a non-interference and know-nothing policy, the standing orders to frontier officers, the spirit of the orders being to turn their backs and shut their eyes and ears to all beyond the frontier."[74] He also proposed that the British reoccupy Quetta to safeguard the Bolan Pass, the most likely route an invading force would take to enter India. Sir John Lawrence, now in retirement, took exception to this meddling, and retorted tartly, reminding everyone of the Afghan disaster that had started in similar circumstances. Frere refused to be cowed. He believed the age of small, independent states was over; that they would all be subsumed by the great powers, and that Britain had better be aware of this and prepared to compete. Although he could make no headway with the hierarchy in Calcutta, on the way home Frere met Lord Lytton journeying out to take up his position as Viceroy, and told him of his concerns, giving him copies of the letters he had written to Lord Salisbury. Lytton totally agreed with Frere's views on Afghanistan, and acted to rectify the weaknesses soon after his arrival.

Frere returned to London on April 21, 1876, in triumph. The tour had been a great success, and the royal family held him in high esteem. Warm acknowledgement was made of his part in the success of the tour. He was regarded as an authority on the Indian Empire, and was consulted as such by politicians and opinion-formers. His name was again touted as a future Viceroy. He continued to develop his thoughts on the Empire, and how it could or would develop. He reiterated his belief that the world was being carved up by the major powers. Russia was in an expansionist mode, a newly united Germany threatened to dominate continental Europe, and the United States of America, after the Civil War, were showing signs of becoming what they were called, united, with all the potential might that was at their disposal. Unless Britain competed on the world stage, the Empire would be in danger on several fronts. His imperial views sat oddly with his belief that power should be devolved and local authorities be given responsibility for decision-making and administration. But Frere remained within the conventional Victorian mindset, that the British way was best, and more importantly right.

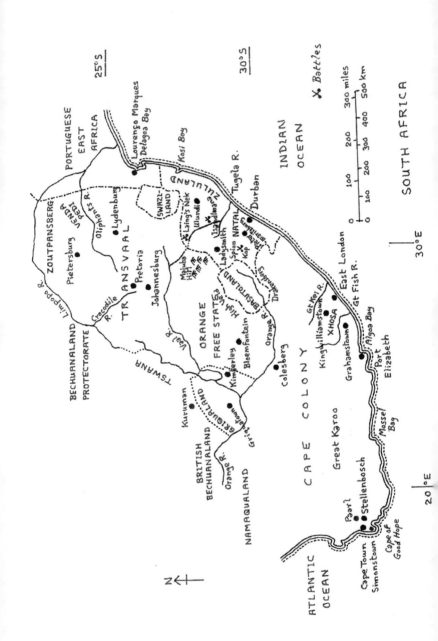

SOUTH AFRICA

Chapter 7.

SOUTH AFRICA.

It was natural that Frere's thoughts should turn to Britain's position in Africa. He felt that with the opening of the Suez Canal the Indian Ocean had become much more accessible to several nations, and unless Britain secured its influence in Africa, most notably in the east and south, not only would others eclipse the British presence there but they would present a new challenge to India. Russia's ambitions posed an immediate problem. The Turkish Ottoman Empire was in terminal decline, and its demise threatened control of the Bosphorus. If Russia's Black Sea fleet could not be contained, Britain's Mediterranean dominance would be threatened. A Russian blockade of the Suez Canal would leave Britain dependent once again on the long sea voyage round the Cape to reach India, which would in turn become more difficult to defend. Moreover, Russia would gain access to the Indian Ocean, with all that implied for India and Africa.

There was another reason for Britain to take more interest in Africa. South Africa represented an attractive prize: not only did it promise vast resources but it was strategically situated to control the sea lanes to the east. In 1652 the Dutch had established a refuelling and provisioning post for its ships at the Cape of Good Hope. They had limited ambitions for their new colony, and between then and 1800 expansion only occurred as farmers moved away from Cape Town in search of fresh pastures. When in 1795 the Dutch monarchy was overthrown and Holland became something of a satellite to France under Napoleon, Britain sent a squadron of four warships to secure the Cape. On July 9 they sailed into Simon's Bay and landed soldiers. By September 15 they had gained control of the small Dutch settlement in Cape Town.

The colony had been close to bankruptcy for years. Diamonds and gold were yet to be discovered in South Africa. The Dutch had encouraged agriculture, and many of the Boers, as they were called (Dutch for farmers) were granted land outside of Cape Town. This led to expansion in search of rich pastures, and by 1800 many Boers had settled on land away to the east and north of Cape Town. Unfortunately, being self-sufficient and independently minded, they contributed very little to the colony's coffers. Wheat was exported to Batavia, but very little else left the Cape. The wine produced at that time was very poor. The only interest Britain had in Cape Town at that time was as a naval base, to serve as a refuelling stop on the way to the Far East. English replaced Dutch as the official language, and English administration and court systems were introduced.

In 1820 the British sponsored 4,000 immigrants from Britain to settle in Algoa Bay. £50,000, a considerable sum in those days, was assigned to the venture, but the purpose was not altruistic. Chronic unemployment in Britain following the end of the Napoleonic Wars had led to violent demonstrations and mass meetings. Resettlement would help alleviate the situation. Many of these immigrants were tradesmen: cobblers, carpenters, millers and shoemakers. The British saw them as a buffer between the Boers, expanding east, and the resident indigenous tribes. In addition, the immigrants would be required to act as part-time soldiers on the eastern frontier, where local tribes were showing some aggression. The immigrants were not told of this expectation.

In 1824, with British help further up the eastern coast, traders set up a trading post at Port Natal. In 1835 this was renamed Durban after the Governor of the Cape, Sir Benjamin D'Urban. Both British colonies struggled to survive. The Cape was afflicted by a fall in wool prices, as Britain's woollen textiles faced increasing competition in Europe and woollen substitutes from Asia. Recurring plagues of locusts and drought made successful farming difficult. Development of transport systems was halted for lack of funds. The small white population in Natal lived in constant fear of African raids, or invasion from the neighbouring warlike Zulus with their huge army. Many politicians in England regarded the colonies as a liability not worthy of further investment.

In 1828 the Cape authorities passed an ordinance making "Hottentots and other free people of colour" equal before the law, and removing legal restrictions on their movements.[75] More importantly, the Slavery

Abolition Act of 1833 which outlawed slavery throughout most of the British Empire was enforced in the Cape in December 1834, setting 38,000 African slaves free and depriving the 25,000 Dutch, German and French Huguenot settlers of their labour pool. Many of the Dutch settlers found the idea that Africans would have equality with white Christians repugnant. They depended upon the indigenous population for a source of cheap labour. Determined to live by their own rules and not within the British colony, they could not accept the new regime. This led to the Great Trek. Groups of families moved north by ox wagon across the Orange River in 1836, and then north of the Vaal River, seeking to set up trading links with the Portuguese at Delagoa Bay. Many turned east across the Drakensberg Mountains, spreading into the fertile hills of Natal. By 1840 some 6,000 of them had left the colony in the Cape. One of the leaders, Piet Retief, listed the grievances they suffered, including "severe losses" arising from the emancipation of slaves, although he was careful to disclaim all practices of slavery. He said he hoped the British government would allow them to govern themselves without interference in the future.[76] The British had no such intentions. They were intent on maintaining a stake in the hinterland. In 1836 the Cape government passed the Punishment Act, which laid down that the trekkers, who came to be known as the Boers (Dutch for 'farmers') would be held accountable for any crimes they committed south of twenty-five degrees latitude. As this covered territory up to a point north of what was to become Pretoria, it was an attempt to maintain jurisdiction over most of South Africa, including Natal.

As they moved north the trekkers clashed repeatedly with African tribes. Hardy men at the outset, these trekkers developed into formidable warriors. Heavily armed with muskets and knives, they did not hesitate to take the fight to the resident tribes. When threatened they drew their wagons into a tight circle (a laager) and fired from between the wheels. The Africans, although numerically superior, were armed mainly with assegais (six foot long wooden spears with iron tips which could be thrown). They could not match the firepower of the trekkers, who were able to move further afield and settle on fertile land vacated by their adversaries.

The cost to the British of enforcing law and order at some distance was onerous. They soon tired of the exercise, and in 1852, at the convention of Sand River, Britain recognised the independence of the Zuid-Afrikaansche Republiek (ZAR) in territory north of the Vaal River, to become known as the Transvaal. In 1854 a similar treaty was signed in Bloemfontein recognising the independence of the Orange Free State, taking its name from the Orange River. The inhabitants of these fledgling republics were spread thinly and widely across a large expanse of countryside. These families were remote from administrative centres. The governments of the republics were constantly short of funds. They had difficulty keeping discipline within the dispersed communities or raising taxes from the subsistence farmers. Their problems were compounded by the fact that they were surrounded and outnumbered by indigenous Africans who could threaten to overrun them at any time.

The futures of the two Boer republics were to be transformed by the discovery of diamonds and, much later, gold in alluvial deposits. The first diamond was found by accident close to the Orange River by a farmer's son in 1866. It was used in a children's game of 'five-stones' before a neighbour recognised it as a diamond. Isolated stones were discovered in the years that followed before in 1871 the richest diamond seam in the world was discovered beneath a farm which was to be transformed into the town of Kimberley. Fortune hunters from all over the world were attracted to South Africa. Both the Orange Free State and Transvaal claimed the land on which they were found, which was known as Griqualand West. The Griquas, a mixed race of Europeans, Khoi, San and Tswana tribes inhabited this semi-independent area adjacent to the Orange Free State, but also bordering on the Transvaal. Naturally the Griquas contested the claims, making a case for independence. A court of arbitration, presided over by Robert Keate, Lieutenant-Governor of Natal, found in favour of the Griquas. However the inhabitants recognised that Griqualand was unlikely to remain independent, given their new-found mineral wealth, and chose to become a protectorate of the Cape Colony. In 1871 it became a separate Crown Colony, but was formally annexed to the Cape in 1880.

The prospect of instant wealth also attracted large numbers of Africans from all parts of South Africa to the diamond mines. Guns were in plentiful supply, and the white miners used them to pay the Africans for their labour. By the end of 1876 it was estimated that 200,000 Africans possessed guns, representing a major threat to the stability of the country. It encouraged the more hawkish elements among the Africans to think they might possibly rid their land of Europeans.

In 1874 a new Tory government led by Benjamin Disraeli came back to power in Britain and adopted new foreign policies. The formation of the German Empire in 1871 after Prussia defeated Denmark and France, and the expansionist policies of Russia, had changed the balance of power in Europe. Britain under the previous Prime Minister, Gladstone, had adopted a passive stance. Disraeli, an unashamed imperialist, aimed to re-establish Britain's pre-eminence, particularly in industry and commerce. Frere shared the Prime Minister's ambitions to expand the Empire. The Industrial Revolution had given it the lead – a lead that was being eroded as other powers emerged. Disraeli aimed to extend the presence and influence of Britain overseas, and he appointed as his Colonial Secretary a like-minded expansionist, Henry Herbert, fourth Earl of Carnarvon. In 1866 Carnarvon had successfully introduced a bill to confederate Canada into a union of separate states within a single political entity, and he and Disraeli proposed to establish a similar structure for South Africa.

At a time when the major European powers were eager to acquire territory overseas, Carnarvon was mainly concerned about defence. He saw the Cape with its naval base at Simon's Bay as a crucial link in the imperial network, and vital to a secure route to India. It was also important as a trade link to Ceylon, China, Singapore and Australasia, even after the Suez Canal had been opened in 1869. It was a concern that Frere shared. Carnarvon believed that South Africa, with a coastline of over one thousand miles and no settled regime in the interior, was extremely vulnerable to interference by other powers, most notably Germany and Russia. He was anxious to develop the imperial defence system so that the colonies were not only secure, but also loyal. South Africa needed to become a fortress against foreign intervention. This became particularly important once the mineral wealth lying below South African soil was revealed. The revenue from the mines could be used to improve defence systems. The coaling station at Cape Town was defenceless, undermanned and not well run. Communications between South Africa and England were laborious: no direct telegraph existed, and the military presence in the Cape was minimal. Although it was unlikely that a major expedition mounted from Europe could succeed in reaching the Cape before the Royal Navy intercepted it, rebellion by local inhabitants allied to a small raiding force would wreak havoc on the colony.

Carnarvon was concerned that the Transvaal would succeed in attracting foreign powers to provide aid and would therefore remain outside Britain's sphere of influence. Although gold had first been discovered in the Transvaal in 1871, the early strikes were of alluvial deposits. These did not yield large amounts, and few men grew rich by them. They contributed very little to the Transvaal's coffers. (It was only once the main Witwatersrand reef was discovered in the 1880's that the full promise of the goldfields was realised). However in 1876 a senior engineer had noted that the Transvaal had greater and more varied resources than those of any other South African territory. Carnarvon wrote in late 1876: "The Transvaal must be ours."[77]

The new ZAR in the Transvaal was a very weak structure. The republic was dependent upon the British-controlled ports of Durban and Cape Town. The Boers' dream was to construct a railroad from Pretoria to the sea at Delagoa Bay, in Mozambique, north of Natal and Zululand a possession of Portugal. Their plan was to make the Republic truly independent from the British and gain access to world markets. In order to foil the ZAR's plans Britain claimed possession of Delagoa Bay, under protest from Portugal. International arbitration conducted by Marshal MacMahon of France decided in favour of the Portuguese claim. The President of the ZAR, Thomas Burgers, sought financial assistance from Europe. Germany showed some interest but was not prepared to confront British interests in South Africa directly. With scant revenue being raised from inhabitants, development of the local economy could only be achieved through loans, which Burgers raised in Holland at ruinous rates. The ZAR treasury ran up debts of £250,000, a huge sum in those days. The Boers were reluctant to pay taxes, though they were in favour of taxing the resident Africans heavily. Revenue was urgently needed to develop the infrastructure and establish orderly markets.

The Boers who established farms required a supply of local labour. In this they were in competition with the diamond mines further south, and sugar farmers in Natal. As early as 1872 Carnarvon's predecessor, Lord Kimberley, had considered confederation in order to control the supply of labour. The prospect of steady work and reasonable wages attracted Africans from the territories to the north of South Africa. An independent Transvaal interfered with the movement of migrant labour. There was already evidence that the Boers intercepted migrants moving south and forced then onto the farms.

By 1876 the Transvaal was bankrupt. The tendency of Boer farmers to settle in the fertile lands adjacent to the Transvaal provoked indigenous tribes, and repeated clashes took place. Carnarvon, alarmed by the expansionist tendencies of the Transvaal Boers, and encouraged by the urban English settlers to intervene, considered his next move. To simply dissolve the republic would be seen by the outside world as wrong. Any take-over would either have to be by consent of the majority of settlers or because of a complete change in the structure of the South African territories.

A secure South Africa was imperative, and in Carnarvon's mind this did not involve just the Cape and Natal, but the two Boer republics and the troublesome African territories within the bounds of South Africa. It was almost inevitable therefore that Frere should be asked by Carnarvon to go to South Africa. On October 13, 1876 he entered into correspondence with Frere on the subject. These letters are quoted at some length because they set out clearly what was intended. In the light of the controversy that later occurred, this intent is significant.

> "I venture in what I consider a very important and critical matter, to ask whether you can give the Government the benefit of those valuable services that have so often and so signally been proved on other occasions? You are probably aware of the general position of affairs at the Cape. We have been on the edge of a great native war; and, though I trust that the danger is passing, if not past, the position is one of extreme delicacy from its political as well as its native complications,

and a strong hand is required. But the war between the Transvaal Republic and the natives have had this further effect: it rapidly ripened all South African policy….It brings us near to the object and end for which I have now for two years been steadily labouring – the union of the South African Colonies and States. I am indeed now considering the details of a Bill for their confederation…(you are) the statesman who seems to me most capable of carrying my scheme of confederation into effect, and whose long administrative experience and personal character give me the best chance of success…I will only add that if, after having done this great work, you feel yourself able to stay on for two or three years to bring the new machine into working order, as the first Governor-General of the South African Dominion, I shall hail the decision both on personal and on public grounds."[78]

Frere replied:

"I should not have cared for the ordinary current duties of Governor of the Cape of Good Hope, but a special duty I should look upon in a different light. And there are few things which I should personally like better than to be associated in any way with such a great policy as yours in South Africa, entering as I do into the imperial importance of your masterly scheme, and being deeply interested personally from old Indian and African associations in such work."[79]

Frere's predecessor, Sir George Grey, had strongly advocated confederation fifteen years earlier, arguing that the European settlements existed under separate governments surrounded and vastly outnumbered by local natives. In Natal, for instance, there were between 17,000 and 18,000 settlers and 300,000 Africans; in the Transvaal the ratio was 35,000 to 350,000. Only confederation would provide the necessary protection. When he tried to merge the republics with the British colonies he was censured for disobedience and in 1861 recalled. Carnarvon, on taking office, reinstated Grey and restarted the move towards confederation. In September 1876, before Frere was appointed, Carnarvon had arranged a conference in London to consider bringing together the two British colonies with the two independent republics under one, united constitution. This conference was boycotted by the Cape and Transvaal governments, but attended by representatives from Natal, the Orange Free State and Griqualand West.

Nominally Frere was to be appointed Governor in the Cape at a salary of £7,000 per annum, rising to £10,000 after confederation, twice the salary of the then Governor. In addition to his Governorship he was also to be High Commissioner of Native Affairs, giving him involvement in the other British territories of Natal, Griqualand West, Basutoland and Pondoland. Frere negotiated an additional special allowance of £2,000 per annum for two years, arguing successfully that in the transitional period the "unavoidable calls upon the salary of the Governor would be greatly increased beyond their ordinary amount."[80] His initial brief was to secure South Africa's defences and to draw together what had become a disparate group of settlements into some form of confederation. Lord Salisbury, who had served with him on the Indian Council, and with whom he had frequently clashed, opposed the appointment. He described Frere as "quarrelsome and mutinous." He remarked of Frere that when they served together "Impatience of control is a common defect in men of [Frere's] able and fearless character and his impetuosity of disposition."[81] This criticism was to come back to haunt Frere and his superiors. Certainly Frere was on record as believing that the responsibility of officials to their superiors "should always be retrospective in the shape of praise or blame for what is done."[82] His record in Bombay and Zanzibar showed his tendency to act without authority when he judged the situation to require it.

Before Frere could reach South Africa, however, events in the Transvaal presented Carnarvon with a pressing problem, and an opportunity. Discovery of alluvial gold deposits in the Lydenberg area north-east of what is now Pretoria in 1873 prompted a gold rush, and brought the Transvaal settlers into conflict with the local Pedi tribe and their chief, Sekhukhune. Individual attempts by the Boers to take the law into their own hands and settle on farming land occupied by African tribes could not be resisted by the weak Transvaal government. The Pedi, the most powerful tribe inhabiting the Transvaal, strongly opposed the expansionist plans of the Boers. Their capital at Tsate in the Leolu Mountains was heavily fortified, and Pedi migrant labourers had been able to acquire modern firearms with their earnings in the diamond fields. The President of the Transvaal, Burgers, rashly decided in 1876 that the Pedi needed to be brought under control, and mounted an expeditionary force of 2,000 Boers, 600 Transvaal auxiliaries (who were indigenous Africans) and 2,400 Swazi warriors. Dissension between the Swazis and Boers occurred early in the campaign, leading to the Swazis deserting. Faced with the daunting task of storming Sekhukhune's stronghold the Boers quickly lost their appetite for confrontation and streamed home to their farms.

News of the withdrawal gave Carnarvon an excuse to press ahead with confederation. On September 22, 1876, believing that conflict between the Boers and the Pedi threatened the peace of all South Africa, he wrote to Sir Henry Barkly, then Governor of the Cape Colony:

> "There can be no doubt that the safety and prosperity of the Republic would be best assured by its union with the British Colonies…should the people of the Transvaal Republic consider it advisable…to invite Her Majesty's Government to undertake the government of that territory…I am of opinion that the request could not properly or prudently be declined."[83]

Germany was showing signs of establishing a position in Southern Africa. It had a trading post in South-West Africa (now Namibia) and in East Africa. President Burgers saw an opportunity to seek financial help from Germany. He had on more than one occasion petitioned the Chancellor, Bismarck, to intervene and take the Transvaal under his wing. Although Bismarck had declined, and maintained friendly relations with Disraeli, the threat remained present. Carnarvon urgently sought permission from Disraeli to go ahead with confederation without taking it to the Cabinet. Disraeli agreed. "I concur…must leave the matter to you."[84] The Transvaal could not be allowed to pursue its own development outside the grand scheme if confederation was to succeed.

Who could Carnarvon find to bring the Transvaal within the British fold? The answer lay in a seemingly innocuous administrator. Sir Theophilus Shepstone, born in England in 1817, grew up in a missionary family in the Cape Colony. Fluent in African languages, in 1846 he was posted to Natal as Diplomatic Agent and was then appointed head of Native Affairs in Natal. He was regarded as the foremost authority on the Zulus, a large and warlike tribe who occupied the country north of Natal, and an expert on African affairs. He supported Carnarvon's confederation intentions and was enthusiastic about extending British paramountcy to the highveld. Carnarvon saw in Shepstone someone who would be of great assistance in pressing forward with confederation. The Colonial Secretary had first met Shepstone in September 1874 in London. Shepstone was making the case for a separate black kingdom between the Transvaal and Zululand to facilitate migration routes, open up Central Africa to trade from South Africa, and deny the Boers access to the sea.[85]

In September 1876, when Carnarvon wrote the above letter to Barkly, Shepstone was back in England to receive a knighthood and to attend the confederation conference. He returned to South Africa with a brief to confer with Burgers on the question of confederation, and to inquire into the "origin, nature and circumstances" of the war with the Pedi. Carnarvon also told Shepstone that should he deem it expedient and if "sufficient number" of its residents were willing, he was to take over the Transvaal and become its first British Governor under the British flag. Carnarvon clearly envisaged this as a progressive move towards confederation.

In fact, the Colonial Secretary's ambitions were far wider. On December 12, 1876 he wrote:

> "I should not like anyone to come too near us either on the South towards the Transvaal, which must be ours; or on the North too near Egypt and the country which belongs to Egypt. In fact when I speak of geographical limits I am not expressing my real opinion. We cannot admit rivals in the East or even the central parts of Africa: and I do not see why….the Zambesi should be considered to be without the range of our colonisation."[86]

The competition for possessions in Africa between colonial powers was well under way, and the Colonial Secretary felt that British ambitions should not be usurped.

Shepstone adopted an extremely cautious approach. When he arrived back in Natal he paused for ten weeks, consulting and listening to local opinion. He was particularly concerned about the effect of any move he made in the Transvaal on the unpredictable Zulus, who constantly clashed with the Transvaal Boers over grazing land. He knew that Cetshwayo, the Zulu king, was in communication with Sekhukhune, chief of the Pedi tribe, and a concerted attack by the two tribes was not out of the question. Finally on December 27 Shepstone set out for Pretoria, accompanied by 24 members of the Natal Mounted Police and 8 civilians. It took him 4 weeks to reach the Transvaal capital. Along the way he stopped to consult with everyone he met. Those he saw recognised that the British would provide additional defence against an attack by the Pedi. To his surprise (and to some extent disappointment) Shepstone found that the Pedi did not pose an imminent threat. They were being successfully contained, and the situation was calm.

The Republic's finances were still in a parlous state. The fiercely independent Boers refused to pay the taxes levied upon them by the Republican government, and there was no money to service the considerable public debt. The republic's ability to borrow money had been exhausted, bringing to a halt all mining and trade. Shepstone claimed he had received a petition in support of annexation from 2,500 residents suffering from the economic collapse and inability to mine or trade. What he had not done was talk to a single Boer farming on the high veld, the vast open plains. They would have told him how much they valued their independence, and that all they wanted was the president, Burgers, to be replaced.

The Boers soon realised that Shepstone's agenda was not the same as theirs, and the Volksraad (People's Council) passed a motion rejecting annexation. Shepstone responded by pointing out that not only did Sekhukhune pose a real threat, but that the Zulu king Cetshwayo was known to be antagonistic towards the Transvaal and had said he was keen to "wash his spears" in the blood of white people. Shepstone offered Burgers a compromise: he would stay his hand if the Volksraad would carry out necessary reforms. Finances, education and security all urgently needed improving. The state was bankrupt; taxes were not being collected, education was rudimentary, there were few magistrates or judges to uphold the law and the farmers, an independent-minded group at the best of times, would not conform to the Transvaal governments requirements.

Burgers could not control his Council and the offer was rejected out of hand. Ignoring Boer opposition, Shepstone proceeded to proclaim the annexation of the Transvaal on April 12, 1877 There were virtually no protests. The settlers were conscious that British troops were close at hand across the border backed up by the full resources of the British Empire. Most of the English-speaking residents welcomed annexation, and some of the Boers living close to the borders saw the value of strong defensive support against the Africans. However most of the rural Boers were still adamantly opposed to the move, and this faction's leader, Paul Kruger, immediately set out for London and Europe to protest and seek reversal of the annexation. The Boers threatened armed resistance, but Burgers warned them that any violence would jeopardise Kruger's mission.

Frere took up his position as Governor of the Cape and High Commissioner for Native Affairs in 1877. He landed at Cape Town on March 31, accompanied by his wife and three daughters, Lily, Mary and Georgina. His son, Bartle, was not with them, but with his regiment in Gibraltar. The official residence was in a small fort close to the beach. The house itself, within the walls, was a pleasant two-storey mansion built in the Dutch style.

Unfortunately this house had not been designed for family living, and was therefore unsuitable for his wife and daughters, so they moved into Government House in the middle of Cape Town. It was rather run-down and in dingy surroundings, but conveniently situated. He was unaware of developments in the Transvaal, for he had been on the high seas for several weeks

Frere's first impressions of Cape Town were not favourable:

> "In some things the place reminds me of a less tropical Ceylon. The climate, the flowers, and the magnificent Table Mountain are all that has been described, but it would be difficult to imagine anything more sleepy and slipshod than everything about the place, or more dirty and unwholesome than the town."[87]

Frere saw his first priority was to secure Cape Town from foreign attack. He was convinced that Britain would soon be at war with Russia, and that this could conceivably spread into conflict involving all the major nations of Europe. The Cape of Good Hope could become a key location in such circumstances, particularly if Russia chose to threaten Britain's possessions in the east. The fort was inadequate as a defence against a sophisticated attack from the sea, and the batteries that were in place had been established before the building of a breakwater and port, and were thus of little defensive value, being too far from the sea. The main military garrison was sited at Simonstown, on the other side of Table Mountain, a day's march away. Moreover, there was no man-of-war permanently available to resist a sea attack. In Frere's opinion Cape Town was wide open to invasion by a foreign force with even modest armaments. He wrote to London:

> "…Table Bay is still open to any vessel with a single rifled gun, and a Privateer might levy a contribution from our Banks before a man-of-war could come to help……The Russians know this well, and when their Squadron was here two or three years ago, the officers used to tell their partners at balls that they did not intend to wait to be taken by the English Channel or Mediterranean fleets, but to pay visits to the Cape and Indian ports where they would levy contributions."[88]

When Russia declared war on Turkey on April 24, 1877, the threat to the Cape became tangible and immediate.

Frere discovered another serious problem that was to be an important element later in his governorship: lack of good communications. There was no direct telegraphic link with London, the nearest being in Cape Verde, nine days away by ship. The fastest telegram on record took sixteen days from Cape Town to London. The post took up to six weeks. Internally, the telegraph had only reached Kimberley from Cape Town. Other South African towns felt isolated. Frere remarked that "the inefficiency of our postal arrangements is one great source of our weakness in S. Africa. We should certainly not hold India many years with such defective postal arrangements."[89] (By

1855 India had 5,050 miles of cable laid, linking the major cities there, and an Indo-England cable through Turkey was opened not long after this).

Such was the naval power that Britain possessed that European waters were dominated by the British fleet. However, so far south, that power was not evident. Lacking defences, the Cape was wide open to exploitation by foreign powers. Frere, pending a requested grant from the British Government, authorised work on a temporary battery to defend the naval stores at Simonstown, and agreed plans for four new batteries to defend Cape Town, including a floating gun platform. He assessed that the minimum requirement was 12 large naval guns, although he was unlikely to be given the funds for them. It should be remembered that prior to the discovery of diamonds and gold in significant quantity in South Africa the British Government regarded the colony as something of a nuisance and a drain on resources, and was loath to sanction expensive developments, so the necessary funds would have to be wrung out of London. This was bound to take time – time which Frere felt he did not have.

Even more pressing issues were about to beset the new governor. Carnarvon's proposals for a confederation had been sent to the South Africans for ratification through their legislature. No sooner had Frere arrived in Cape Town than the Prime Minister of the Cape Colony, James Molteno, afraid that the Cape would have to pay for the expensive wars against African tribes in the Transvaal and Natal, voiced his opposition. Then Sir Henry Bulwer, Lieutenant-Governor of Natal, intimated that he was against confederation and had not submitted the draft Confederation Bill to his Legislative Council, even though he had been aware of the proposals since December 1876. He was concerned that the Cape would dominate such a confederation. Finally, in May 1877, President Brand of the Orange Free State rejected the confederation proposals, distrustful of any British proposals on principle, and furious with the decision to annex the Transvaal.

To what extent Frere was aware of Carnarvon's instructions to annex the Transvaal has long been debated. He must have recognised that some form of inclusion involving the two Boer republics was necessary if confederation was to be achieved, but as his reaction to the news that Shepstone had subsequently annexed the Transvaal was to show, he clearly did not know that Shepstone had been authorised to take over the Transvaal if he deemed it necessary.

News that Shepstone had annexed the Transvaal reached Frere on April 16, 1877, shortly after his arrival in Cape Town. Shepstone was convinced that he had adequate support in the Transvaal for the move. In a letter to Frere dated April 11, 1877, he insisted:

"There will be a protest against my act of annexation ….but they will at the same time call upon the people to submit quietly, pending the issue; you need not be disquieted by such action, because it is taken merely to save appearances and the members of the Government from the violence of a faction that seems for years to have held Pretoria in terror when any act of the Government displeased it. You will better understand this when I tell you privately that the President [Burgers] has from the first fully acquiesced in the necessity for the change, and that most of the members of the Government have expressed themselves anxious for it – but none of them have had the courage openly to express their opinions, so I have had to act apparently against them."[90]

He went on:

"You will see when the Proclamation reaches you, that I have taken the high ground. Nothing but annexation will or can save the State, and nothing else can save South Africa from the direst consequences. All the thinking and intelligent people know this, and will be thankful to be delivered from the thraldom of petty factions by which they are perpetually kept in a state of excitement and unrest because the Government and everything connected with it is a thorough sham."[91]

Shepstone had not consulted Frere before announcing the annexation. This therefore came as a surprise to him. It also surprised the British Government, which had authorised Shepstone to act when the time was ripe, but had not expected it to happen so fast. Frere's first reaction was: "Good heavens! What will they say in England?"[92] He was forced to defend an act that he had not been involved in and of which he knew nothing. Whilst he was the titular head of the British presence in South Africa, the Colonial Secretary had authorised Shepstone to rule the Transvaal. He had little alternative but to support Shepstone. Staying true to his tenet of devolved responsibility and trusting the judgement of the man on the spot, he wrote to Carnarvon

"It seems to me that, as matters now stand, criticism as to what Shepstone is doing is as misplaced as suggestions how to hold his paddle would be to a man shooting a rapid. Our best course is cordially to support him in all reasonable ways as long as he appears to be doing his best to carry out our views and instructions."[93]

How much time Shepstone would have to assume control of the Transvaal and introduce the essential reforms was a moot point. Cetshwayo, the Zulu king, with a powerful army, hitherto looking upon the British as an ally, was now confronting them in the Transvaal. The Boers had made unsubstantiated claims on Zulu territory, and Shepstone inherited the dispute. The concern was that the Zulus would take advantage of the unsettled situation in the Transvaal to take back the land they claimed had been taken from them by the Boers. Local observers supported this feeling. A Royal Engineer in Pretoria, Colonel Durnford, writes:

"Cetshwayo…would undoubtedly have swept the Transvaal, at least up to the Vaal River, if not to Pretoria itself, had the country not been taken over by the English."[94]

Sir Arthur Cunnynghame, commanding the British force in the Transvaal on July supported this opinion:

> "I am convinced that had the country not been annexed it would have been ravaged by the native tribes. Forty square miles of country had been overrun by natives and every house burned, just before annexation. Every day convinces me that unless the country had been annexed it would have been a prey to plunder and rapine from the natives on its eastern border, joined by Secocoeni [Sekhukhune], Mapock, and other tribes in the Transvaal. Feeling the influence of the British Government, they are now tranquil."[95]

Frere was concerned that Kruger, campaigning in Europe on behalf of the Transvaal Boers, may persuade Germany to weigh in on his side. Writing in late April after consideration, he once more defended Shepstone's action to Carnarvon:

> "I have already seen enough to be sure it will require great care to prevent the whole Dutch section of the population feeling deeply on the subject. None of them seem to realize, as I had expected, that it was quite impossible for the Transvaal to go on any longer as it has been doing for the last two years, and that if they were cordially to adopt what you had offered, they might obtain more security for reasonable self-government than they or their forefathers ever hoped for."[96]

Frere's notes at the time show the importance he placed on producing a new constitution for the Transvaal as soon as possible. Although the Boers objected to the proclamation, annexation was received by the urban dwellers with some relief. There were no public protests, credit was restored, trading recommenced and property prices started to rise. Hitherto there had been no English soldiers in the territory, and when the 13th Light Infantry marched into Pretoria in May the whole population turned out to meet them and cheer. Frere wrote to Carnarvon on May 21:

> "There can be little doubt that the annexation of the Transvaal has materially altered the position of all parties…with regard to confederation. It has immensely strengthened the position of all who desire confederation, by making it more of an absolute certainty and necessity than it was before." [97]

He remained concerned about the followers of Burgers, the President, whose dream of a great anti-English South Africa was now in tatters.

Frere hit his first obstacle to confederation on his own doorstep, in Cape Town. The British Government was in the process of passing a Bill through Parliament enabling confederation of the South African colonies at such time as they saw fit, so there was no secret about the British intention. The Cape government, obsessed with its own issues such as the supply of cheap labour and the movement away of the Boers, showed no interest in the process whatsoever. Nor did it wish to assume responsibility for anything outside its own borders. As the senior colony it envisaged that a heavy burden would fall on its shoulders under confederation – a weight it did not wish to bear. It professed ignorance of the Transvaal annexation and took no steps to engage in the process. The Prime Minister, John Molteno, refused to say whether he was for or against confederation.

Frere needed to test the opinion of settlers in other regions of South Africa. He lacked knowledge of the country, and was disinclined to trust the advice he was receiving from individuals with a vested interest in their positions. The only alternative was to find out in person, and he set out on a fact-finding tour of South Africa. He also aimed, by dint of diplomacy and his personality, to persuade local leaders of the merits of confederation.

Chapter 8.

THE EASTERN CAPE.

It was Frere's intention to visit all the provinces in order to gauge reactions to the proposed confederation. Leaving Cape Town in August 1877, he first went to the eastern Cape. In the first half of the nineteenth century the Cape Colony had sought to extend its borders east and north, seeking more farmland. As explained previously, in 1820 the British had established a settlement in the eastern Cape with the aim of securing a base at the port called Algoa Bay, which was to become Port Elizabeth. The settlers found existence very hard. There were already some white farmers living in the area: Boers who had trekked away from the Cape and had settled on farms there. Harsh conditions and disease took their toll, but the greatest threat came from hostile African tribes who saw the arrival of settlers as a challenge to their territory. Raids on settlers' farms were frequent, and close communication between the tribes to the east of Port Elizabeth, and the Zulus some distance to the north of the territory, led the settlers to fear a general uprising which would sweep them away. Constant requests to the government in the Cape for help with the frontier defence and more stringent laws against cattle rustling were ignored.

The Xhosa people, whose various tribes inhabited the eastern Cape, were a proud race, unlikely to yield their land easily. Pressure on farming land increased dramatically in the 1840's when Britain's own wool crop could not keep pace with the demands of the textile mills booming on the back of the Industrial Revolution, and sheep were introduced to South Africa. Between 1839 and 1861 wool exports from South Africa increased by more than 500% to 24 million kilograms. This led to more and more territory being annexed to the Cape Colony at the expense of the Xhosa. Where possible, agreements were negotiated with local chiefs and the peace was preserved, but there remained many flashpoints. In order to establish tenure, Residents were appointed by the British in the territories where colonists settled. These officials represented the colonial power and offered protection to settlers. In theory the tribal chiefs were in command of the territory, but in reality it was the British who ruled, supported by superior weapons and professional soldiers. The tense situation was not helped by missionaries, who moved into the eastern Cape with a fervent desire to convert the indigenous population to Christianity. The strong convictions of the missionaries antagonised the local tribes and caused them to fear for their independence and preservation of their customs.

Frere's first port of call was Port Elizabeth. He noted that the harbour was defenceless, "at the mercy of any little steamer that can carry a rifled gun."[98] The settlement's isolation and lack of defences meant that the colonists were strongly in favour of confederation. Most of the settlers were of British origin, and unlike the Boers they welcomed the umbrella offered by the Crown. Frere travelled on to Grahamstown, the next significant town after Port Elizabeth, where many of the original British settlers had made their homes. There he heard of the frontier problems. To the north of the Kei River (known as the Transkei) lived two semi-independent tribes, the Gcalekas on the coast and the Fingoes inland. Internecine fighting between the individual tribes over border disputes had recently broken out, which had not been curbed by the large body of well-armed British police. Frere crossed the border into the Transkei, meeting Colonel Eustace, Resident with the Gcalekas, at Butterworth. He let it be known that he was prepared to listen to any grievances that Kreli, the chief of the Gcalekas, might have. Kreli found excuses for avoiding him. When Frere travelled on to Kingwilliamstown, the nearest town in the eastern Cape to the river Kei and therefore close to the border with Transkei, he found it full of farmers and their wives and families, who had been driven off their land. A mixture of Africans and Europeans heavily populated the area to the north. The land was overgrazed, and a recent drought had brought the economy to the edge of collapse. Both the Gcalekas and the Fingoes had turned on the settlers, who had occupied land which the tribes believed was theirs, and the homesteads in the rural districts could not be defended. Frere was forced to live in the barracks with the 24th Regiment, as no other suitable accommodation was available. There he was to remain for seven months.

The fighting became widespread and the entire territory was thrown into a state of uproar. The situation was not helped by the rather ill-defined nature of the relationship between the settlers and the tribes. The Fingoes, praised by the Cape Government for their industry and forward-looking, lived in territory where they had been resettled after a period of slavery to the Gcalekas, and were therefore nominally British subjects. The Gcalekas in the Transkei were semi-independent, being in part answerable to the Cape Government through a Resident. The Fingoes had responded well to active magistrates intent on helping them, and had managed their affairs successfully, while the Gcalekas, fiercely independent, concentrated on cattle farming. When, at the bidding of a prophet, the Gcalekas killed most of their oxen, they found themselves impoverished and disadvantaged. The young men, seeing their neighbours the Fingoes prospering, believed they could drive them out – and the English, if necessary.

The area was administered by two members of the Cape Government, John Merriman, Commissioner of Crown Lands, and Charles Brownlee, Secretary for Native Affairs. The organisation of the armed forces in the territory was inadequate. The police, the civil order and the army, the last of which was British, acted independently, and all three reported back to higher authorities in Cape Town. Thus the local authorities had no say in their conduct, and could not direct them to act. The battles which took place between the Gcalekas and Fingoes were observed by these forces, but none of them could intervene without approval from Cape Town, four or five days' communication away. "Unless I had seen it myself I could not have believed in such a state of things," wrote Frere "murders and cattle raids were of almost daily occurrence, and were hardly suspended whilst I was on the spot, and all this not from any one person's fault, but simply from 'drifting.'"[99]

Frere had seen this before: it echoed the bureaucratic central control he had railed against in India. In the face of stubborn resistance and complaints he established a daily emergency council meeting under the British Commander-in-Chief, Sir Arthur Cunynghame, with instructions to act as it saw fit to control the rebellious tribes. It achieved immediate success. By the end of October the colonial forces had pushed the Gcalekas northwards across the Bashee and Umtata rivers. The tribe lost 700 men, 20 chiefs and 13,000 head of cattle. The officer commanding the colonial forces considered the uprising to be over, and abandoned pursuit. Soon the Gcalekas returned to attack a colonial contingent and join up with another tribe, the Gaikas. The Gaika tribe lived among settlers in the north of the province, south of the Kei River, and were considered to be British subjects. Frere was appalled at the way the police treated the Africans:

> "…I find a very serious difference of opinion between myself and Mr Merriman [Commissioner of Crown Lands and Public Works], as to the mode in which the question is to be treated. He is for carrying matters with a very high hand, in a manner which must bring about a collision with the Gaikas…I cannot see the legality, necessity or justice of such violent remedies."[100]

Frere's experience in India had taught him the value of working with the local population rather than against them.

> "How shall we attach them to us and gain their confidence? I say, by ruling them justly and strictly, but mercifully not by letting loose volunteers and burghers to carry fire and sword through the country."[101]

Merriman and Brownlee objected to attempts to override colonial command. They were responsible to the Prime Minister of the Cape Colony, John Molteno, who was adamantly against handing over control of colonial forces to a British General. By January 1878, having been detained for six months by the unrest and unable to reconcile the local needs with the distant hand of Cape control, Frere abandoned any concern for the Cape government's feelings. The problem needed to be resolved fast; he was wasting precious time on less important issues than that of annexation and confederation. He determined to take active and personal control.

Molteno tried to persuade Frere to return to Cape Town. When that failed he joined Frere in Kingwilliamstown. Between January 10 and February 1 a series of meetings took place between the two, without any agreement. Molteno saw their differences in terms of colonists versus the British Government, represented by Frere and the British army. He instructed the colonial officers to act on their own responsibility, without reference to Frere or the military commander. This was unacceptable to Frere, and Molteno indicated that this was a resigning matter. Frere agreed, but Molteno then retracted. Frere replied that he had no alternative but to dismiss the Prime Minister and his ministers, as their actions were illegal.

This was a bold move. Ostensibly Molteno and his ministers, having been democratically elected, had the support of the Legislative Assembly. Given colonial sensitivities, Frere was bound to face criticism, but he could see no alternative: the Crown could not be dictated to. It bore responsibility for all subjects, including the indigenous tribes. In Molteno's place Frere invited Gordon Sprigg to form a Ministry. Born of a Puritan family in Essex, Sprigg was a member of the Legislative Assembly in Cape Town. His home was a farm within a few miles of Kingwilliamstown, which meant that he was thoroughly familiar with the problems of the eastern Cape. Sprigg had gained the respect of Frere, with whom he felt he could work. He had a reputation as an ambitious politician who favoured an aggressive approach to troublesome African territories, and believed that all Africans should be disarmed. When he left his farm his wife remained living there, and shortly thereafter had to be rescued when the farm was attacked and the cattle carried off.

On February 7 a skirmish took place which was to have considerable influence on the thinking of the British army. A combined force of Gaikas and Gcalekas attacked a small detachment of British troops in the Transkei. These troops were from the 24th Regiment, seasoned soldiers who had seen action in many a battle in North America, Europe and India, and were to feature prominently later in the war against the Zulus. They were led by Captain Upcher, who turned out to be an able leader, and well prepared. Although significantly outnumbered, the British opened up with artillery into the massed ranks of advancing warriors.

Frere takes up the story:

"They [the attackers] held on after several shells had burst among their advanced masses, but they could not live under the fire of the Martini-Henry [the new rapid -fire repeater rifle]. The 24th are old, steady shots, and every bullet told, and when they broke, Carrington's Horse followed them up and made the success more decided that in any former action. It has been in many respects a very instructive action; not only as regards the vastly increased power in our improved weapons and organization, but as showing the Kaffir persistence in the new tactics of attacking us in the open in masses. At present this is their fatal error."[102]

Frere's next step was to take all the armed forces under his personal control, thus ensuring that the colonists could not act independently. These he delegated to Cunynghame's successor, his new Commander-in-Chief, General Frederic Thesiger (later Lord Chelmsford), who arrived in Kingwilliamstown on March 4, 1878. Born in 1827, Thesiger was the eldest son of the first Baron Chelmsford, a former Tory Lord Chancellor. Using his father's money he had purchased a Lieutenant-Colonelcy at the age of thirty and served in the Crimea and India, where he saw active duty in the last stages of the Mutiny. He was seen as a safe pair of hands, if light on active duty, although he had distinguished himself under Napier in Abyssinia. When he arrived in South Africa he was aged fifty, a tall, fit man and an excellent horseman. He was well liked by his troops, being interested in their welfare, and remained calm under fire. However he was versed in outmoded tactics unsuited to Africa, and could easily be swayed by contrary advice, leading to vacillation. Lacking command experience, he was to make some fundamental errors.

He started well. Leaving political considerations to Frere, he concentrated on pulling together the disparate forces operating in the eastern Cape, and repairing some of the breaches which had resulted from the dispute between Cunynghame and Merriman over control of the armed forces. He created well-defined military districts with responsibility clearly delineated. Although Thesiger commanded only two thousand British Regulars, and few colonists (most volunteers having returned to their farms), the united command quickly produced results. The British professionals took the offensive in late April. Sandilli, chief of the Gaikas was killed and Kreli, chief of the Gcalekas, became a fugitive. By June 29 much of the fighting had ceased, and an amnesty was proclaimed to all that would lay down their arms, although the Transkei remained unsettled for some time to come.

In retrospect the success that Thesiger enjoyed in the eastern Cape was to have disastrous consequences. He had been able to overcome the local tribes with some ease, adopting professional military discipline and possessing superior firepower. He had swept his enemy away in a number of skirmishes, leading him to believe that the Africans could offer no serious resistance. As a consequence, he had learnt little about tactics should he face a more sophisticated foe. This ignorance was to come back to haunt him when he faced the Zulus.

A cousin of Sandilli, Umhala, who had received "a good Christian education" and who acted as a court interpreter, was tried after the war on suspicion of sedition. His diary was found to contain some inflammatory remarks, but no concrete evidence of sedition, and he was acquitted. When the Resident Magistrate in Kingwilliamstown refused to reinstate him, the Bishop of Grahamstown asked Frere to intercede on Umhala's behalf. Frere's reply is an interesting indication of how he viewed the Africans:

> "Umhala's case seems to me to illustrate one serious but little-noticed defect in much of our teaching in this country where natives are concerned. I allude to any direct teaching of the duty of obedience to the law. Among ourselves such teaching would usually be quite superfluous. The duty is indirectly taught in our families and among our schoolfellows, better than it could be taught in any formal lesson, and is thus more perfectly learnt and realized among the most law-abiding nation in Christendom. But the Kaffir has no such advantages, and the consequence is that controversies and arguments…have for them a significance quite different from what they have for us….the Kaffir who has learnt the whole duty of Christian man, with the exception of that law of civil obedience to constituted authority… may naturally translate much of the argument

into assegais and red ochre, and be dangerously perverted from obedience to laws which really hold society together."[103]

Frere again raised the theme of local representation by writing to the Colonial Secretary. He observed:

"There is nothing like a native branch of the Civil Service, such as is so useful in India. There is a great want of clerks and interpreters in the English offices…Chiefs have been allowed greater power, both within and without the Colony, but it is by right of birth as chiefs, not as Government servants. I cannot find a single instance of an educated native being employed to do any Government work…such as magisterial or revenue duty…When anything of the kind is proposed, it strikes even the best friends of the natives, as unpractical, if not an impossibility… None of the objections I have heard stated appear to me of any force. It can hardly be said that educated natives, carefully selected and trained, are unfit for the duties or responsibilities of deciding the ordinary police or magisterial duties of a Kaffir kraal…I think a beginning might be made by organizing a service, which, without being excessively native, should give opportunities for the employment of natives in the public service and for advancing them when found worthy."[104]

Frere was able to return to Cape Town, where Sprigg was making a good impression. The new Prime Minister's proposals for reform of defence measures, involving the police, burghers, volunteers and yeomanry, created a local uproar, but the success of Thesiger in suppressing the rebellion, carried the House. Sprigg presented a financial statement – "the first full and plain and honest account the House had had for some years."[105] He proposed increased custom duties, a new house tax and an excise duty, all of which were approved. To Frere's immense satisfaction, Sprigg also promised strong support for confederation. The two men were to work in harmony for the remainder of Frere's stay at the Cape. At last Frere had an ally who would maintain a stable and supportive regime in the Cape while he tackled the more intractable problems facing him. He could rely upon Sprigg to support confederation, and as the strongest of the local governments in South Africa, give him a base to fall back on.

In South Africa tranquillity and peace did not last long at that time. When the protectorate, Griqualnd West, was absorbed fully by the Cape Colony in February 1878, the Griquas rebelled over the denial of ownership rights to the land and claims on the diamond fields. Unrest spread to most areas of the Cape Colony and affected adjoining territories, prompting Frere to interpret the uprisings as "a general and simultaneous rising of Kaffirdom against white civilization" blocking the way to confederation. This led him to the view that as long as African chiefdoms were allowed to exist, peaceful confederation would be under challenge.

He wrote:

"I [have formed the] conviction that Shepstone and others of experience in the country were right as to the existence of a wish among the great chiefs to make this war a general and simultaneous rising of Kaffirdom against white civilization….there [is] a widespread feeling among them…that the time has come for them all to join to resist the flood of new ideas and ways which threatened to sweep away the idle, sensuous elysium of Kaffirdom, such as Gaika and Chaka and Dingaan fought for and enjoyed; that they too had got guns and could shoot as well or better than the white man, and had, besides, numbers and valour on their side…..If Shepstone is able to give Sekhukhune a decided check, it will tell on the Zulus and keep them quiet for a time; but you must not expect peace on that border till the chiefs have satisfied themselves who is master….unless they are very unlike their cousins here, they are more easily governed than most Indian nations, but they must be *governed*, not neglected and left to follow their own devices. They are very teachable, and can be made to take all the cost and much of the labour of their own government, but the impulse and the standards of right and wrong must be European." [106]

The rebellious tribes in the Cape needed to be subjugated, and troops were sent to quell the uprisings. The sense that Frere had acquired of turbulent people forever on the brink of rebellion was reinforced, and was to lead him into considerable difficulty.

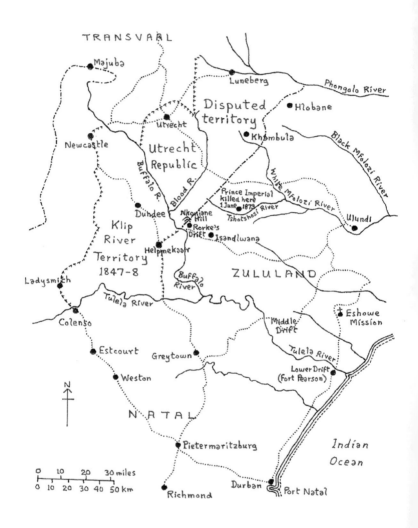

NATAL, TRANSVAAL and ZULULAND

Chapter 9.

THE ZULUS.

Although the eastern Cape was now pacified, conflict still broke out spasmodically in other parts of South Africa. As we have seen, the Transvaal Boers, ever in search of fresh pastures, clashed with the tribes living within the borders of their territory. This threat they could cope with. What was of greater concern was the challenge presented by the Zulus in the neighbouring territory, lead by King Cetshwayo. The Zulus were a proud, warlike people, with an army of more than thirty thousand warriors. Frere recognised that whilst they remained independent and potentially in conflict with the settlers in Natal and the Transvaal, his plans for confederation would be in jeopardy. To ignore them would be to live with a constant threat on the borders of his new, unified South Africa. He would have to come to terms with the Zulus.

Zululand was a hilly, fertile country north of Natal, adjacent to the Transvaal and bordered in the north by Mozambique. It had been inhabited by a number of small tribes until Shaka ascended the throne of the (small) Zulu tribe in 1816. By a combination of strict discipline and superior military tactics he subjugated other local tribes and built a powerful base in Zululand. He absorbed some of the surrounding tribes into the Zulu system, others he annihilated. It has been estimated that he killed around one million people in the process.

The Zulus clashed with the trekkers soon after they arrived in Natal from the Transvaal and Orange Free State, over the Drakensberg Mountains. The Boers were seeking suitable land on which to settle, and initially the two sides attempted to resolve disputes peacefully. Soon, however, distrust on both sides led to bloody conflict. The Boer leaders were treacherously murdered when they attended a meeting at the kraal of Zulu king, Dingane, who had succeeded his brother Shaka. A decisive moment came in 1838. A major battle took place at what came to be called Blood River, which the Zulus knew as the Ncome River. The Boers, entrenched in fortifications on the Natal side of the river, used concentrated firepower from modern, repeating rifles on the massed charge of the Zulu army to kill three thousand men without any fatalities themselves. Not a single Zulu got within ten yards of the laager. The defeat made Dingane's position uncertain. His brother, Mpande, fearing for his life, fled to Natal but returned with a large force of emigre Zulus and a Boer commando. They defeated the main Zulu army in January 1840, causing Dingane to flee to the north, where he was assassinated. Mpande was proclaimed king by the Boers.

Mpande was in no position to oppose the Boers, who promptly claimed all the land between the Tugela

River in the south and the Black Umfolozi River to the north, deep in Zululand, where they marked their new boundary with two large stones. They also seized thirty-one thousand cattle from the Zulus and retired south of the Tugela River. There, bounded in the north by the Drakensberg Mountains and in the south by the sea, they established the Republic of Natalia. A flood of refugees from Zululand followed, mainly from lesser tribes who had been conquered by the Zulus. This influx provided the new settlers with a pool of labour, much needed for their new farms. The Boers had no intention of settling on the land they had taken from the Zulus. They could not defend such a large expanse of territory, and although they registered claims to farms there, they used the land mainly for grazing and hunting game. In fact the Zulus continued to govern there and expelled Boers guilty of misdemeanours such as cattle rustling.[107]

The British authorities in Cape Town were unhappy. Natalia was yet another independent Boer republic. Its major port, Durban, provided an excellent harbour for trade and defence, and raised again the spectre of an invading foreign power gaining a foothold in South Africa. To prevent this the British raised the Union Jack in Durban in 1842. The Boers resisted strongly, besieging the fort in the heart of Durban, but a heroic horseback ride of 600 miles to Grahamstown by Dick King to raise the alarm led to a strong British force arriving on the frigate *Southampton* on June 25 to relieve the garrison. The Boers, outgunned, retired to their capital, Pietermaritzburg, and finally agreed to yield to British sovereignty. Natalia was annexed to the Crown in 1844, and renamed Natal. In 1845 it became a district of the

Cape Colony. A Lieutenant-General took up residence in Pietermaritzburg in December 1845. Natal was declared a British Crown Colony on July 15, 1862.

Between 1840 and 1843 some Boers had moved east of the Tugela River into a triangular tract of land bounded by the Buffalo and Tugela Rivers, and to the north by the Transvaal. In 1843, in return for a hundred cattle, Mpande put his mark on a rather loose title deed ceding the Boers grazing land between the Buffalo and Blood Rivers. Although this land was part of the territory seized by the Boers after their Blood River victory, it was technically part of Zululand. It had never been farmed. By 1854 there were nearly two hundred Boer families resident in this wedge of land. Mpande did not challenge them, although the original agreement had given them grazing rights only. In September 1854 Mpande agreed to the farms remaining. The Boers immediately proclaimed this wedge of land the Republic of Utrecht. In 1859 this small republic was subsumed within the Transvaal.

The curbing of Zulu power led to a thirty-two year period of peace, during which time Mpande was clever enough to remain on good terms with the Natal settlers and their British masters. When his reign came to an end, however, the situation changed. There was no clear process of succession: Zulu chiefs had many wives and therefore many sons, who vied for the crown. Mpande fathered twenty-three sons. Often a man of the Zulu hierarchy first married when he was young, and therefore his first wife was a junior wife. Succession was often reserved for the eldest son of his Great Wife, chosen relatively late in life. Mpande never took an official Great Wife, leaving succession uncertain.

Mpande favoured Mbuyazi, the eldest son of his second wife. However the eldest and most aggressive of his sons was Cetshwayo, born in 1832 to Mpande's first wife. He was cast rather in the mould of Shaka and Dingane than his father. He set about ruthlessly eliminating rival brothers. He forced two of his brothers, fourteen year-old Mthonga, and Mgidlana, fearing for their lives, to seek sanctuary in Utrecht. The Boers offered to hand them back and recognize Cetshwayo's claim to the throne in return for his cession of land east of the Blood River, further into Zululand than they had strayed previously, to a point further down the Buffalo River near Rorke's Drift – good pastures which they coveted. Although this was part of the Zulu kingdom, Cetshwayo agreed. The Treaty of Waaihoek was signed in March 1861, and the princes were handed over on the condition that their lives were spared. Three months later Cetshwayo, encouraged by the British, who opposed Boer expansion, unilaterally rescinded the agreement, leaving the rights to land east of the Blood River in dispute. The Boers ignored this move and continued to settle there.

Cetshwayo, distrustful of the Boers, now turned to Natal to support his claim to the throne. Theophilus Shepstone, at that time in charge of "Native Affairs" in Natal, saw his chance to consolidate relations between the colony and the Zulus. Like Frere, he believed that confederation would only be possible with the inclusion of Zululand in some way. He could foresee a time when the British would want to take over Zululand, and he preferred to see it allied to Natal rather than the Boers. He also had plans to secure a corridor for migrant labour from the north to pass south into Natal between the

Transvaal and Zululand. Burgeoning sugar farming on the coast and farms inland had a rapidly expanding need of labour which the Zulus would not fill. The territories to the north of South Africa could meet the labour need, provided they could reach Natal without being diverted by the Transvaal Boers or obstructed by the Zulus. The corridor he required was through the territory disputed by the Boers and the Zulus.

It was important to Shepstone that the recognition of Cetshwayo's claim to the throne should be conditional upon promises of better governance. Victorian morality and sensibility caused the British to be appalled at the apparent savagery of the Zulus, their careless disregard for the sanctity of life, and the harsh autocracy of the king, as Frere was to show in his letters later. They were determined to "civilize" the Zulus, and in particular to instruct them in the Christian ethics which underlay colonisation. Attempts to persuade the Zulus to adhere to the British code were to be at the heart of the conflict which followed later, and which were to cause so many of Frere's problems.

Mpande died in October 1872. Cetshwayo, forty-five years old, was now the heir apparent, although he was not popular with all the Zulus. A number of brothers and half-brothers could realistically lay claim to the throne. In such an unsettled situation, Cetshwayo turned again to Shepstone and requested that, as "father" to the Zulus, he formally perform the coronation. The procession of Shepstone into Zululand with a well-armed escort in late July 1873 caused some consternation among the Zulu commanders, who believed that the British long-term objective was to possess Zululand. Many of Cetshwayo's most senior men did not see the need for colonial endorsement, and resented the implication that the Zulu king was being patronised. Shepstone moved cautiously, reaching Eshowe on August 12. There he was kept waiting by Cetshwayo for sixteen days. The Zulu generals insisted on holding their own coronation ceremony before he arrived, so that when Shepstone was finally admitted to the royal kraal and placed a rather pathetic, tawdry, paper crown on Cetshwayo's head the act had lost its impact, and was regarded as a non-event by the Zulus. Nevertheless Shepstone reminded Cetshwayo of the conditions he had imposed when confirming his right to be heir apparent. This was to be important later.

Shepstone's plans for Zululand received support in 1875 from the new Lieutenant-Governor of Natal, Major-General Sir Garnet Wolseley. A darling of the Victorian public, Wolseley boasted a distinguished service career in Burma, the Crimea, India and West Africa. He had served under Outram in India and was with him at the relief of the besieged garrison in Lucknow during the Indian Mutiny. His success had led him to become rather self-regarding and keen to seek publicity. He was known to hold the opinion that only soldiers were capable of resolving complex problems, and that he was pre-eminent among them. He made sure that his connections with aristocracy were maintained. His overweening self-confidence tempted Gilbert and Sullivan into lampooning him as "the very model of a modern Major-General." Frere was to clash with him later.

Wolseley had been persuaded to take on the post in Natal before Frere took up his position in South Africa as Governor-General. He could see that the problems accumulating there needed urgent attention from a clear-thinking military man. Carnarvon, uneasy that the tribal chiefs in Natal were too independent and insubordinate, gave him the task of reforming Shepstone's Native Policy. The colonists lived in constant fear of an uprising, and Wolseley quickly came to the conclusion that the only solution was to annex Zululand. This would enable the Natal authorities to introduce a uniform "native policy for the region, and facilitate confederation." Shepstone believed it would take only a thousand British soldiers to win over Zululand, and Wolseley, new to the territory, accepted his judgement. Carnarvon was not enthusiastic: it had never been imperial policy to expand British possessions in South Africa beyond strategic considerations of defence, and he preferred to be patient and wait for confederation to take place. True confederation would provide for a degree of local rule and administration, thus avoiding some of the burden that annexation would bring with it.

Wolseley was aware of the potential problems arising over the territory occupied by the Boers in Zululand, and had no sympathy for the Boer cause. In his journal he wrote:

> "I have only to give the King [Cetshwayo] the slightest hint & he would pitch into the Tvl there & then. I wish I could do so without compromising the Govt at home; when his messengers arrive I will see what can be done. It is a glorious opportunity for England for we ought to try & force the Tvl into our arms.[108]

Wolseley was recalled to take up the post of High Commissioner in Cyprus in 1876, before Frere arrived in South Africa, and was replaced by an able administrator, Sir Henry Bulwer.

The annexation of the Transvaal in 1877 added a new dimension to the Zulu problem. Cetshwayo had maintained friendly relations with the British, and Shepstone in particular, whom he referred to as my "father Somtseu." (Somtsewu = father of whiteness). Cetshwayo saw the British as potential allies in his opposition to the Boers, but now the annexation aligned Britain with the Boers. The Lieutenant-Governor of Natal, Sir Henry Bulwer assessed the position of Cetshwayo as:

"Probably he has no wish to try conclusions with the English unnecessarily, but his temper of mind is such that he is quite prepared to fight, not merely to defend himself and his authority as an independent King, but to fight on the slightest provocation, regardless of all consequences."[109]

Frere was to heed this opinion when he weighed up the situation in 1878.

Word came that Cetshwayo was seeking an alliance with the Zulus' traditional enemies, the Swazi, so that they could attack the Transvaal from two sides. This aggression was mainly sparked by further expansionist moves by the Boers, this time into territory north of the Phongolo River, considered by the Swazis as theirs. Shepstone immediately sent a messenger to Cetshwayo explaining that the Transvaal was now under the sovereignty of the

Queen, and he was to stand down his army. Cetshwayo's answer was some time in coming:

> "I thank my father Somtseu for his message. I am glad that he has sent it because the Dutch have tired me out and I intended soon to fight with them once, only once and to drive them over the Vaal….It was to fight the Dutch I called them [the impis] together. Now I will send them back to their homes."[110]

It is difficult to know how sincere Cetshwayo's reaction was. He found himself facing not just a rather weak collection of Natal settlers intent on maintaining the peace, and independent Boer farmers unable to form a cohesive resistance to the massive Zulu army, but two colonies, Natal and Transvaal, united under the British flag. Cetshwayo was an intelligent man, and sufficiently knowledgeable about the world to be aware that the British had substantial military resources at their command. It is difficult to believe that he would have willingly engaged the British in a full-scale war, knowing that the likely outcome was defeat and the destruction of his kingdom. The question was: did he have full control of his army?

This is not how the situation appeared to Frere. Although Cetshwayo paid lip service to his undertakings, he had also revived the ruthless military regime initiated by Shaka. Frere was aware that the Zulus could field an army of more than 30,000 warriors. Shaka had refined its military system to be extremely flexible. There was no standing army: the king called up his warriors from their farms when he required them. The system was based upon an "ibutho", a gathering of young men (some as young as 14 years old) who built their own collection of homes and lived together. They initially herded cattle or worked in the fields while honing their military skills. They would remain together until called upon to fight, (which they would do in units called amabuthos) and would return to their homes once the fighting was over. Young men remained single until they had killed in battle ("washing of the spears," as it was called) when they would be allowed to take a wife. This system meant that the young warriors of Zululand were very keen to wash their spears, and the army remained in a high state of readiness and willingness. The need to kill in battle enticed them to embrace a very aggressive stance: they looked for conflict. In Shaka's days this provided a decided edge over rival tribes.

During the late, rather lax years of Mpande's rule, traditional customs had not been well observed. Many young men had taken young girls as their lovers. In September 1876 a number of girls who had taken men of corresponding age rather than marry veterans who had washed their spears were slaughtered in cold blood and their bodies put on display. This was too much for the Natal authorities to ignore, and the Lieutenant-Governor, Sir Henry Bulwer, remonstrated with Cetshwayo. The king's answer was belligerent: he defended his action as being in keeping with Zulu law, and ended:

"Go back and tell the white men this, and let them hear it well. The Governor of Natal and

I are equal; he is Governor of Natal and I am Governor here."[111]

Alarmed, Bulwer noted:

"It is evident…that he has not only been preparing for war, but that he has been sounding the way with a view to a combination of the native races against the white men."[112]

Shepstone, attempting to come to grips with the problems in the Transvaal, was also becoming concerned about the Zulus' stance. Cetshwayo encouraged the import of guns, and by 1875 there were estimated to be 10,000 guns per annum entering Zululand either from Natal or Delagoa Bay. (The guns were rather antiquated, and as there was no attempt to train the Zulu army in their use, they proved to be ineffectual in battle). An enigmatic white man, John Dunn, who had spent much of his life in Zululand and had several Zulu wives, facilitated this trade. He was close to Cetshwayo and acted as agent for him. Dunn, born in 1833 to an English settler, had grown up in the company of Zulu nursemaids and their children in Durban. Consequently he spoke fluent Zulu. Possessing a rudimentary education, and uncomfortable in colonial society, he moved to Zululand at the age of eighteen. There he drifted aimlessly for a year. Living off game, he was enlisted as an assistant border agent for his knowledge of the Zulus. With him went the fifteen year-old daughter of his father's European assistant, a mixed-race woman from the Cape. Once settled in Zululand, with coloured children, his future was sealed. His unique knowledge of the British colony and his life in Zululand, supported by fluent capability in its language, made him a valuable aide to the king. This was particularly important when written matter was involved, as few of the Zulu hierarchy could read.

The question of rights to the land east of Blood River, part of Zululand, reappeared. The Boers claimed they had purchased the land from the Zulus; the Zulus argued that they had merely leased the land for a definite period for grazing, and that they now wanted it back. In 1875 the Boers had proclaimed a new boundary line that took in a large area south of the Phongolo River. This was land that had belonged to the Zulus since the reign of Shaka, although it was part of the territory seized by the Boers in 1840. To make matters worse, they commenced taxing the Zulus living there, and when they refused to pay took their cattle in lieu.

Shepstone met Zulu envoys, headed by Mnayamana, now Cetshwayo's Chief Minister, on October 18, 1877 in Utrecht, to negotiate a settlement. To say the boundary lines lacked precision would be an understatement. The Transvaal had published seven maps between 1870 and 1877 showing seven different lines varying by as much as seventy miles. There were three areas involved: the Utrecht district, ceded to the Boers by Mpande and now part of the Transvaal; land north of the Phongolo River, occupied by the Swazi and not an integral part of Zululand, which had been settled on by the Boers; and the area east of the Blood River ceded to the Boers by Cetshwayo in exchange for the return of the young princes. Shepstone insisted that the Zulus should give up the Utrecht district, situated between the Buffalo and

Blood River, and accept the Boers' boundary claim to the other two areas. The Zulu delegation quickly realised that the man who was saying this was no longer their "father" but an advocate for the Boers. One of them stood up and accused him of betraying the son of his old friend Mpande. Shepstone lost his temper, turned away and muttered to one of his team that he would march a force across the Tugela to show them who was in charge.

In a further attempt to diffuse the argument, Shepstone sent a message to Cetshwayo on December 8, 1877, suggesting that the British Government appoint an independent arbitrator. Shrewdly Cetshwayo accepted the principle of arbitration, but suggested a preliminary investigation by commissioners in Natal. Bulwer, relieved that war had been averted, appointed a Commission to consider the Zulu claims to what was to be known as the Disputed Territory. It was to consider only Boer claims between the Buffalo and Blood Rivers (the Utrecht district), and the land east of the Blood River. Land north of the Phongolo River was not to be considered; Cetshwayo understood that claims to this territory were to be referred to the Britsh authorities separately. The Utrecht district contained a number of Boer farms, whilst the land within Zululand, east of the Blood River, was used mainly for grazing. Although some Boers had established farms there, they had been forced to leave by the Zulus.

Michael Gallwey, Natal's first Attorney-General and an Irishman of some integrity and independence chaired the Commission. Other members included Shepstone's younger brother, John Wesley Shepstone, acting as Native Secretary in Natal, and a soldier, Colonel William Anthony

Durnford. The Zulus were unhappy that John Shepstone was part of the Commission, but while burdened by the disadvantage of being Theophilus' brother, he had expert knowledge of the Zulus. The Commission met for the first time on March 12, 1878 at Rorke's Drift.

The Zulus, not confident that the Boundary Commission would be unbiased and would consider their case on its merits chose for the moment to ignore the negotiations. They made a number of raids into the disputed territory, forcing families to flee. At the same time, and probably in connivance with the Zulus, the Swazi attacked farms in the Luneberg area, north of the Phongolo River.

From this moment on Shepstone appears to have taken a strikingly different attitude towards the Zulus. He had initially liked and trusted them, but had always considered the advantages of Zululand coming under colonial rule. Now he gave full voice to his opinions. On January 5, 1878, he wrote to Carnarvon that African society

> "must be looked upon as an engine constructed and used to generate power, the accumulation of which is now kept pent-up in this machine…those forces have continued to accumulate and are daily accumulating without safety valve or outlet…Had Cetywayo's thirty thousand warriors been in time changed to labourers working for wages, Zululand would have been a prosperous peaceful country instead of what it now is, a source of perpetual danger to itself and its neighbours."[113]

To add to Frere's problems, in February 1878 the Colonial Secretary, Lord Carnarvon, resigned. In 1877 Russia had declared war on Turkey in support of the Balkan countries, which were trying to break free from the tottering Ottoman Empire. Russia saw this as an opportunity to consolidate its alliance with these countries, and to recover some of the losses suffered during the Crimean War. Most notably, it was anxious to remove Turkey's dominance of the Black Sea. Although Turkey was well equipped with modern weapons supplied by its western allies, and possessed a large army, it was vulnerable to attack. Its leaders adopted a passive, defensive stance, not believing Russia would invade. However Russia succeeded in crossing the Danube and making progress towards the strategic capital city of Constantinople (now Istanbul). Britain was very concerned about the potential consequences of Russia occupying Constantinople and controlling the entrance to the Black Sea. The Prime Minister, Benjamin Disraeli, foresaw the possibility of war looming. He requested from Parliament a £6 million vote of credit and approval to send warships to the Dardanelles in order to keep the entrance open. Carnarvon, the least anti-Russian of the Cabinet, objected to any aggressive act, believing that the last thing Britain wanted at this stage was another war with Russia. Unable to agree with his colleagues, Carnarvon felt that he had no alternative but to resign.

This was a major blow to Frere: Carnarvon was not only his greatest supporter, but also the architect of confederation. It was difficult enough for him to carry the day against local opposition; without his champion the future direction of South Africa was very uncertain.

An inexperienced politician, Sir Michael Hicks Beach, replaced Lord Carnarvon. A former Irish Secretary, Hicks Beach had made a name for himself in the House of Commons with straight-talking speeches. He had not previously been exposed to African affairs, so came to office knowing little of what was happening in South Africa. He had not been privy to the confederation plan. He was a staunch anti-Russianist, and with the crisis in Europe pre-eminent in the Government's priorities, it was natural that he would pay less attention to Frere's needs and proposals than Carnarvon had. The implication was that South Africa was being consigned to a less important position in colonial affairs, and the Colonial Secretary would not be in sympathy with the expansionist dreams of Carnarvon and Frere. Moreover, Frere would no longer receive automatic support for the decisions he took.

Frere's first inclination was to resign. He wrote to Carnarvon:

> "If you have really left the Colonial Office, it adds another, and the strongest of all reasons for my wishing to follow you, and to rest after forty-four years of continuous service with very little holiday."[114]

A life of public service, and his strong feelings of loyalty and imperial convictions, well recorded in his correspondence, caused him to stay in post. However the resignation of the ardent champion of confederation was to lead to radical changes in British attitudes towards South Africa. Frere's first briefing to the new Colonial Secretary, Michael Hicks Beach not only raised the level of alarm signals but also is instructive in terms of what was to follow. Concerned about the possibility of European intervention in South Africa, particularly following the annexation of the Transvaal, Frere argued that there were a number of anchorages around the coast which were undefended, and would easily provide an invading power with landing stages. It was possible that a general European war might result in Holland being absorbed by Germany, which would give the Germans the excuse to interfere in the Transvaal and Orange Free State, where a number of Boers with Dutch heritage had settled. Britain's ability to defend its position in South Africa would depend to some extent upon having a settled internal situation, and this was far from certain. Frere had seen at first hand how quickly disturbances could escalate, and how difficult it was to suppress the local population. He foresaw the possibility of war with the Zulus....

"....or with other independent tribes in contact with us, or our allied neighbours, along all our frontiers in the Cape Colony and Natal, as well as the Transvaal Territory."[115]

He stressed that "unless something could be done to ensure the just and humane treatment of our native neighbours the risk could not be disregarded."[116]

Hicks Beach's first letter to Frere gave rise to great concern:

"The negotiations, through Bulwer, with Cetshwayo should be pushed on, and the dwellers of the disputed territory be protected from aggression meanwhile; but our power should not make us relax our best efforts to obtain a peaceful solution."[117]

The Boundary Commission's hearings continued for five weeks, and when the Boers' evidence came under scrutiny it was apparent that they could not legitimately claim the territory. Frere had listened to the settlers' arguments, and believed that the Commission would support the Boer claim. Thus when it reported to Frere in July 1878 in favour of the Zulu claim, he was at a loss to know how to handle it. The report read:

> "The evidence shows that this so-called 'disputed territory' has never been occupied by the Boers, but had always been inhabited by the border clans, who have never moved their homes, and that the only use ever made of the land by the Boers has been for grazing purposes, which in itself proves nothing."[118]

It found the documentary evidence supporting the cession of land defective, and that in any case the Zulu chief had acted without the consent of his people, represented by the Council of Chiefs. It added that the Transvaal government of Boers had never exercised any jurisdiction over the disputed territory in terms of levying rent or taxes, and had never imposed government on the inhabitants. Although the land to the west of the Blood River was not central to their deliberations, the Commission declared that, as it had already been subsumed into the Transvaal, it was to be awarded to the Transvaal as it exercised sovereignty over it with the tacit acceptance of the Zulus.

This was not what Frere had expected. Nor did he find the situation very comfortable. He had been delegated sweeping powers by the Colonial Secretary, including the right to resort to military force in order to settle any internal disputes. He was also empowered to deal with local issues, even if they did not come within British jurisdiction. The way in which the land was to be assigned was left to Frere to decide, but it was obvious that whatever his decision was neither side would be satisfied. The Boers would lose their settlements south of the Phongolo River. The Commission had not considered the land north of the river, where many Boers had settled and had not been harassed by the Zulus, although the Swazi had opposed them. Cetshwayo was prepared to concede this territory, but his closest advisers opposed the concession.

The dilemma facing Frere was serious. If he upheld the Commission's findings, the concession to the Zulus would significantly hamper his plans for confederation. By acknowledging independent Zulu rights, how could he then incorporate Zululand into a confederated South Africa? Yet by originally agreeing to the Commission he could hardly go against its unequivocal findings. He had to find a way of pressing forward with confederation without compromising the Commission.

Frere did not respond to the Commission's recommendations immediately. The findings were irrefutable, yet he was inclined to support the Boers' cause. We have seen evidence of his deep Christian convictions, and his beliefs coloured the way he saw the world. He wrote:

> "The Boers had force of their own, and every right of conquest; but they had also what they seriously believed to be a higher title, in the old commands they found in parts of their Bible to exterminate the Gentiles, and take their land in possession. We may freely admit that they misinterpret the text, and were utterly mistaken in its application. But they had at least a sincere belief in the Divine authority for what they did, and therefore a far higher title than the Zulus could claim for all they acquired."[119]

Frere saw his choice as stark. Either he sided with the Boers and disregarded the Commission's findings, in which case the Zulus would be justified in taking the disputed territory as of right, provoking a war, or he upheld the findings. It was his opinion that in the latter case the Boers would rebel, and the Zulus would seize the opportunity to invade Natal.

From the time that Frere accepted the request from Carnarvon to proceed with confederation, he was clear-sighted enough to recognise that confederation would not be feasible without exercising some control over the Zulus. The more he got to know of the situation, the more convinced he became that this would have to be through some form of annexation. Now the Commission's findings had given him another problem. His first move was to send his trusted general, Thesiger, to Natal to assess the colony's military resources. He also asked him to solicit the views of both sides in the land dispute before he finally decided on the settlement. But he was pessimistic about the Zulu response:

> "My mistrust is not because they are semi-savages; but because they are a military nation, and Cetshwayo's whole object is to keep up their military character. They generally believe themselves to be invincible – under similar circumstances I would not trust to any people… to abstain from aggression. I do not believe anything will induce them so to abstain, unless they are thoroughly convinced of our superior power; and I do not see any chance of their being so convinced till they have tried their strength against us and learned by sad experience. This will in no way make me slacken in my efforts to preserve peace by careful abstinence from all cause of offence. But, on the other hand, I would neglect no precaution in preparing for the worst."[120]

Colonial Secretary Hicks Beach had been kept fully informed of the Zulu border dispute, and he advised Frere that "When you do arbitrate, your arbitration must be upheld, at whatever cost."[121] It was clear that the impending dangers in South Africa alarmed the new Colonial Secretary, for his letters to Frere took on a much more aggressive note. He laid down a course of action based on two principles: the grant of self-governing institutions to the Boers and the settlement of the Zulu land question. These were now urgent prerogatives, with the how and when left to Frere's discretion, but Hicks Beach recognised that there was the distinct possibility of armed resistance by the Boers and/or war with the Zulus. He made a point of saying to Frere that the likelihood of war with Russia was not to interfere with the resolution of these measures, and that "I take it for granted that if [Chelmsford] and you consider more troops are required, you will ask for them"[122] He instructed that Zulu raids upon persons and properties in the disputed territory were to be stopped. Then he added: "I leave you, as you see, very wide discretion!"[123] In the light of this Frere was entitled to feel that he had the Colonial Secretary's support for a proactive stance towards the Zulus.

In July 1878 a serious incident caused more tension between the two nations. Two wives of a Zulu chief, Sihayo, living near Rorke's Drift had started affairs with younger men. When they were discovered, the women and their lovers escaped to Natal. Mehlokazulu, the son of Sihayo, crossed the Tugela with a raiding party of 30 mounted men with guns and a large force on foot, found his father's young wife and dragged her back to Zululand and executed her.

A few days later he returned to find the other woman, his mother, and had her shot. It was not unusual for the Zulus to deal with transgressions of this sort by executing the miscreants. Cross-border incursions of this nature were not uncommon; normally the Natal authorities returned the errant refugee without demur. This time Bulwer remonstrated with Cetshwayo, whom he believed was ignorant of the raids, and requested that the raiding party be turned over to him. Cetshwayo showed no signs of surrendering the men responsible for the death of the two women, saying that the women and their lovers deserved to die. They had not been killed on Natal soil, and no Natalians had been touched. Mnayamana, Hamu and Zibhebhu, his senior generals, could see the trouble this recalcitrant stand would bring, and argued that the country should not be destroyed on account of "minor people. Let them be caught and handed over."[124] Cetshwayo did agree that the transgressors should be punished, and sent Bulwer £50. Bulwer rejected the money, and turned the affair over to Frere, who was to re-open the demand when he came to negotiate with Cetshwayo.

It is probable that this incident coloured Frere's attitude towards the Zulus, whom he regarded as uncivilised savages. Referring to the Sind, where he had so successfully developed the local infrastructure and left a legacy of improvements to trade and society, he was to write later what amounted to his philosophy of empire:

> "…no notice was taken of tribal ties or local custom as excuses for offences against British law….The excuse of 'custom' in such case was ignored or treated as an aggravation of the offence, inasmuch as it was proof of premeditation…. the tribes were made to understand that the prosecution of a feud was not permitted by our Government; no allowance was made for the excuse that the murder or robbery would have been venal or permissible under the Native Government."[125]

Pressure was mounting on all sides. The Boers, already unhappy with the annexation of the Transvaal, were likely to react adversely to Frere's decision, whatever it was. The Zulus felt threatened by both the British and Boers, and Cetshwayo was under some pressure from his Council to reclaim land from the Boers. Thesiger had reported back that the colony's military resources were in a deplorable condition, leaving the settlers unable to defend the border with Zululand that stretched for more than 100 miles. On August 24, 1878, he submitted a memo to Bulwer entitled "Invasion of Zululand; or, Defence of the Natal and Transvaal Colony from Invasion by the Zulus."[126] He recommended that the only hope of preserving Natal was to invade Zululand, press the Zulu army back towards the centre of the country where the king resided and destroy it before it could spread out and attack Natal from several points. He proposed placing five separate columns at various points along the Zulu border, but reckoned that even with troops from the Cape his force would not be adequate. Reinforcements were urgently required. The five-column proposal was significant: it was appropriate in preparing to attack the Zulus, but woefully deficient if it was designed to defend the long Natal border.

The sense of matters coming to a head was accentuated by the treatment of missionaries. Several different faiths had been active in Zululand for some time, without any success. The Zulus treated them with disdain, and were often irritated by their tendency to meddle in affairs of state. The Anglican bishop of Natal, John Colenso, had provided sanctuary for one of Mpande's sons, Mkungu, before Cetshwayo was crowned. Cetshwayo had threatened to expel all missionaries in 1869 but had been advised by Dunn that this would lead to his country being annexed by Natal. Robert Robertson, an Anglican minister who had harboured ambitions of becoming close to Cetshwayo, was disillusioned. He set out to bring down the king by writing to the Natal Mercury newspaper and addressing anyone who would listen:

> "…try and fancy yourself in the King's kraal in the heart of the Umfolozi Bush with thousands of wild Zulus around you who, whatever else they might have learned from the white man have learned the name of the Evil one and call themselves 'the boys of Satan.' You have heard of course of the new line of action which the King and his advisors have lately adopted towards the missionaries. Three Christians have been killed and it was intended to kill others."[127]

Robertson wrote to Frere, who told him to address his complaints to Bulwer. On November 16 Robertson advised Bulwer that Cetshwayo was "ready for war."[128] He also suggested that provided no taxation was imposed upon them, most of the Zulu people would accept British rule readily.

The Boers in the Transvaal led by Paul Kruger and Piet Joubert were alarmed by the possibility that they would end up losing territory to the Zulus. It seemed to them that their interests were being subordinated. The preparations for a possible Zulu war, now evident in Natal, caused them considerable unease. Would British soldiers be used to subdue their own aspirations as well as the Zulus? A second Boer delegation to London petitioning for restoration of the Transvaal Republic presented a long petition to Hicks Beach, who told Frere: "It is the old story, against annexation….[they] are quite intractable on the subject." There was no possibility of Britain "giving up the country: but stating my readiness to consider, and if possible to remedy, any complaints they may bring before me."[129] They were turned away empty-handed, and Hicks Beach warned Frere that there could be trouble when they returned to South Africa. He advised Frere to strengthen to the utmost the British forces in the Transvaal.[130]

Thesiger was alarmed that Bulwer did not seem to be taking the threat from the Zulus seriously. Bulwer advised Thesiger that he did not believe the Zulus were intent on war, and warned the general not to assume that they would disintegrate as a nation if attacked. He was reluctant to tackle the responsibility for implementing any decision the Commission might make over the boundary dispute, and was resisting the movement of any additional troops into Natal in case the Zulus misunderstood it.

Pressure was mounting on Frere from all sides, and a sense of events reaching a climax prevailed.

Chapter 10.

ULTIMATUM.

Up to this point Frere had been dealing with issues in Natal and Zululand from Cape Town. Now both Bulwer and Thesiger urged him to come to Natal. Although Bulwer had established the Boundary Commission, he did not want the responsibility of announcing its findings himself. Thesiger, at odds with the Natal government over defence needed Frere's support to impose his views. It was time for Frere to see for himself. He sailed for Natal from Cape Town on the Royal Mail Ship *Courland,* arriving in Durban on September 23, 1878. He immediately travelled on to Pietermaritzburg, capital of Natal, to meet the Crown's top representative in Natal, Lieutenant-Governor Bulwer. His first reaction was that Natal as a Crown Colony had become somewhat isolated and reactionary to change. The capital, Pietermaritzburg, was a sleepy little country town, isolated from the bustling commerce of Durban and the far-flung farmers' needs. The Natal legislature harboured strong prejudices against the Boers, and the colonists resented any interference from the Cape. Historically the government of the Cape Colony had exercised considerable influence, and the nascent Crown Colony of Natal was concerned that decisions taken by the administration in South Africa tended to consider the Cape's opinions and needs in preference to other territories. In contrast to the patent animosity between the Boers and the Zulus, Frere found evidence that the English in Natal had maintained peaceful relations with the Zulus, supporting them against the Boers. Aware of the menace posed by a large, warlike people on their border, the settlers of Natal had chosen the option of appeasement rather than confrontation.

The first issue confronting Frere was the findings of the Boundary Commission. Bulwer pressed Frere to take full responsibility for implementing the recommendations of the Commission. Frere considered the Commission's decision one-sided and unfair.[131] He ascertained that in the territory east of the Blood River there were seventy-five farms occupied by Boers, with homesteads, and a further twenty farms now unoccupied. To return this territory to the Zulus would result in the homesteads being swept away. He was concerned that to accede to the findings of the Commission completely would further alienate the Boers against the British Government, and lead to hostilities between the Boers and Zulus. He wanted the Zulus to compensate the Boers for the land they were forced to give up. Bulwer believed that would reverse the award. Frere finally agreed the Commission's findings should stand, but in an attempt to mollify the Boer's feelings and give them something from the Commission, he secretly inserted modifications. These stipulated that the Boers should either be compensated for property given up, or if they chose to remain and become Zulu subjects their rights would be protected. He argued that sovereignty over the land, decided in favour of the Zulus, should not affect the individual rights of resident farmers. He added that a British Resident would be charged with this duty. Privately, he recognised that the only long-term solution was for the British to annex the territory.

Thesiger had succeeded to the title of Lord Chelmsford when his father died. As officer commanding the British forces in Natal he believed that no decision would satisfy the Zulus. He was anxious to prepare his army for a war by securing the frontiers of Natal and protecting himself from an attack in the rear (by the Pondos in the south). Shepstone, who now saw his responsibility as defending the Boers in the Transvaal against Zulu aggression, advised Frere that there could be no permanent peace until the Zulu nation was broken up.

Cetshwayo's attitude was becoming more aggressive at this time. Frere's first letter to Hicks Beach from Pietermaritzburg was gloomy:

> "I regret that I find the position of affairs in this Colony far more critical even than I expected…..Zulu regiments are reported as moving about on unusual and special errands, several of them organizing royal hunts on a great scale in parts of the country where little game is to be expected, and where the obvious object is to guard the border against attack…a recognized mode of provoking or declaring war."[132]

Having taken stock of what he found, Frere wrote further to Hicks Beach from Government House, Pietermaritzburg:

"…..the people here are slumbering on a volcano, and I much fear you will not be able to send out the reinforcements we have asked for, in time to prevent an explosion…..The Zulus are now quite out of hand, and the maintenance of peace depends on their forbearance……the peace of South Africa for many years to come seems to me to depend on your taking steps to put a final end to Zulu pretensions to dictate to H.M.Government what they may or may not do to protect H.M.Colonies in South Africa, and that unless you settle with the Zulus you will find it difficult, if not impossible, to govern the Transvaal without a considerable standing force of H.M. troops."[133]

Frere, lacking a deep knowledge or experience of the South African scene, fell back on his Indian experience: "Sir Henry [Bulwer]…never had much to do with military affairs, and many things which are burnt into one after a few years dealing with Natives in India have to be explained to him."[134]

Frere found that Natal was, in his estimation, twenty years behind the Cape defences. He knew from the experience of the settlers that it was the practice of the Africans to launch attacks suddenly and without warning, depending on the unpreparedness of the Europeans for their success. These views were not merely hypothetical:

in 1834 ten thousand Zulus had swept across the border, murdering, burning and pillaging homesteads. Then in 1838 the Zulu king Dingane had attacked Boer encampments on the Blaauwkrantz River, killing 600 men, women and children. Nevertheless, the Natal authorities showed a marked reluctance to co-operate with Lord Chelmsford in military preparations. Frere made his position clear in a letter on October 28, 1878:

> "I can only repeat my own conviction that the continued preservation of peace depends no longer on what the servants of the British Government here may do or abstain from doing, but simply on the caprice of an ignorant and bloodthirsty despot, with an organized force of at least 10,000 armed men at his absolute command."[135]

Frere had been alarmed by unusually large and well-armed groups of Zulus hunting near the mouth of the Tugela and close to Rorke's Drift on the banks of the Buffalo River. To make matters worse, on October 7, it was reported that armed Zulus had seized a British surveyor and his companion on Natal territory. The surveyor, Smith, was surveying the road from Greytown (north of Pietermaritzburg and quite close to the Tugela River) to Fort Buckingham, taking with him a trader called Deighton. Part of their brief was to report on "what would be necessary to be done to make the drift passable by wagons etc."[136] Close to the river they encountered a small party of Zulus who wanted to know what they were doing. When the men started to inspect the drift, and walked out to a small island in the middle of the river, the Zulus took this to be an invasion of their territory. They detained the men for an hour in an attempt to get them to explain their movements, before releasing them on the instructions of a passing headman. The presence of numbers of Zulus close to the border, and the aggressive action against Smith, led Frere to fear a move against Natal by the Zulus. Bishop Colenso, however, believed that Smith and his companion were reconnoitring a suitable crossing point in preparation for a British invasion of Zululand.

The Commission had only considered territory south of the Phongolo River. Now news came that German settlers at Luneberg, north of the Phongolo River but not within the disputed territory, had been ordered by Cetshwayo to leave their farms. Frere proposed to stand firm and defend the farmers, but the Natal Government showed no sign of supporting him, preferring to refrain from provoking the Zulus in any way. The alliance between Cetshwayo and the Swazis was becoming manifest: in September the Swazis, with the connivance of Cetshwayo, mounted raids into the country around Luneberg, which the Zulus had not hitherto claimed.

Frere held strong opinions on citizens' rights. His strong Christian principles, his liberal tendencies and imperial conscience all led to the conviction that, irrespective of race or colour, all citizens were entitled to the same protection of person or property. He immediately wrote to Colonel Wood, commanding a British force at Utrecht, requesting that he intervene. Without waiting for Chelmsford's orders, Wood sent two companies of the 90th regiment to protect the farmers at

Luneberg. The raids were a disturbing sign that the Zulus were not prepared to be passive over the question of land rights. Luneberg was close to the disputed territory, but not actually in it.

Frere, concerned at the build-up of the Zulu army and what he saw as the ever-present threat of an invasion of Natal by Cetshwayo, was all for leaving the Zulus in no doubt what the options facing them were: either they accepted the Commission's findings without alteration or they would be faced with war. Frere alerted Hicks Beach to this in a letter dated October 7:

> "It will be to me a most agreeable and unexpected surprise, if we succeed in avoiding a collision and obtain anything better than an armed peace. I have seen no cause to alter or modify the opinions I expressed…as to either the critical position of affairs, or the insufficiency of local preparations to meet it."[137]

The Natal authorities viewed this approach with horror, still believing war could be averted. They argued that their "native policy" – living in peace with the Zulu nation, not interfering with their customs and offering employment in Natal - had worked for thirty years. Meanwhile every letter Frere despatched to Hicks Beach reminded the Colonial Secretary of his urgent requests for military reinforcements.

Finally Hicks Beach posted his response to the Commission's findings:

"As to the Zulu boundary question, …I think that the boundary line indicated by them must almost necessarily be accepted by us, though I fear it will be most unpopular in the Transvaal; and may encourage Cetshwayo to war, from the natural belief of a savage that we only yield from weakness……Of course Cetshwayo must be kept in order, and compelled to give up Zulus who violate….Natal or Transvaal territory. And if we could get the disputed territory from him by purchase, that might be the best way out of the difficulty."[138]

Hicks Beach's cautious approach was clarified in his next communication to Frere by telegram dated October 12:

"It may be possible to send out some special service officers, but I feel some doubts whether more troops can be spared. As the hostilities in the Cape Colony are now at an end, would not the police and volunteers be sufficient for the Cape, and might not all the Imperial troops be sent to Natal and Transvaal, with the exception of a small garrison for Cape Town?"[139]

Frere felt under pressure. His advisers all agreed that the Zulus could attack Natal at any moment. The boundary dispute was a touchstone, and if he could not negotiate an amicable settlement it might provide the spark to bloody conflict. Hicks Beach's refusal to provide reinforcements confirmed Frere's worst fears: that the

British cabinet either did not recognise the seriousness of the situation or was not prepared to back him. He replied on November 5:

"Special service officers useful and acceptable, but troops asked for urgently needed to prevent war of races. Cape Colony and Diamond Fields have done their duty nobly, and are relying almost entirely on Colonial forces recently raised, and only half organised…..State here as described by Sir Garnet Wolseley three years ago. On the other side of fordable river Zulu army, forty to sixty thousand strong, well-armed, unconquered, insolent; burning to clear out white men. Wolseley's estimate of force required to bring them quickly and surely to reason not too large. Diplomacy and patience have absolute limits…..if victory is to be ensured on terms which will bear examination hereafter a sufficient force of H.M. disciplined troops under H.M. officers should be employed." [140]

To add to his problems, Frere could see that affairs in the Transvaal were going to have a significant influence on his stance towards the Zulus. He felt that since annexation the territory had gone from bad to worse. Shepstone, though an expert on African matters, turned out to be an "execrably bad manager."[141] There was "no visible government" or any form of representation. Sekhukhune and the Pedi had not been curbed, and the Transvaal was bankrupt. Hicks Beach was agitating for Shepstone to be removed from office, but Frere still supported him. He wrote that in view of Shepstone's long and excellent service "he ought not to be removed except by promotion."[142] Frere argued that if the Transvaal economy could be developed it would remove some of the Boer grievances and make annexation more palatable. Shepstone's status was anomalous, as he had been put in place in the Transvaal by the Colonial Secretary without reference to Frere, so Frere requested that Shepstone be instructed by Hicks Beach to consult him (Frere) before considering any changes to the Transvaal constitution.

Apart from the Zulu army massing on the border, Frere had concerns over the Zulus already living in Natal, who might well link up with the Zulu army should it choose to invade Natal. The white population of Natal stood at less than 20,000. The Tugela River, into which both the Buffalo and Blood Rivers flowed, and which then wound its way over 200 miles to the Indian Ocean, separated Natal from Zululand. From March to October, when the South African summer started, the river was easily fordable, and therefore presented a very long border across which the Zulus could enter. This meant that Natal was vulnerable to invasion at any time in the following four months. Later he was to argue in defence of his decision to invade Zululand:

> "the great object seemed to me to be to avert Zulu inroads from Natal, and if Cetywayo decided for war to make his country the theatre of it….The temper of our own natives was then unknown, and if the Zulus once began making raids into Natal a far larger force than we possessed would be required to protect our own

border, and at the same time to carry the war into the enemy's country....it was only by acting on the offensive and taking up positions in Zululand that we could hope to preserve our own Colony from the horrors of Zulu invasion."[143]

News came that Wood's protection of the Luneberg farmers had provoked Cetshwayo to put his army on a war footing. Frere advised Hicks Beach that Natal could not afford to postpone any necessary measures of military defence, but the Colonial Secretary was adamant:

"Her Majesty's Government are not prepared to comply with a request for a reinforcement of troops. All the information that has hitherto reached them...appears to them to justify a confident hope that by the exercise of prudence and by meeting the Zulus in a spirit of forbearance and reasonable compromise, it will be possible to avert the very serious evil of a war with Cetshwayo."[144]

Frere was unwilling to forbear and compromise, it appears, arguing that the brief he had been given on his appointment as Governor-General was in part "to promote the good order, civilization, and moral and religious instruction of tribes, and, with that in view, to place them under some settled form of government."[145] Due to the vulnerability of the colony to a Zulu invasion – and Frere was convinced that the number of available troops was woefully inadequate – he believed the only way of neutralising the Zulu threat was to pin them down in Zululand by advancing into their territory.

Cetshwayo had for some time been alarmed by the military preparations he saw taking place across the border, and complained to Bulwer:

> "I hear of troops arriving in Natal, that they are coming to attack the Zulus, and to seize me; in what have I done wrong that I should be seized like an 'Umtakata' [wrongdoer], the English are my fathers, I do not wish to quarrel with them, but to live as I always have done, at peace with them."[146]

On December 11, 1878, Zulu envoys arrived at the Natal frontier near the mouth of the Tugela to hear the results of the Commission. Three British officials met them there with two documents. The first was the Boundary Award, which was read, translated and delivered to the envoys to take back to Cetshwayo. The second contained a list of "requirements" which Cetshwayo would need to agree to if the Award was to be implemented. The intent, so Frere wrote, was for a final settlement with the Zulus. He placed huge importance on this list. Writing to Sir Robert Herbert in the Colonial Office in London he noted that "…everything in South Africa hangs on this question – Transvaal contentment and Transvaal finance, and all chance of Confederation depend on its being settled, to say nothing of the peace on this border."[147] In fact these requirements amounted to an ultimatum. In return for the Boers giving back land in the disputed territory a British Resident would be stationed in

Zululand, functioning in much the same way as Residents did in India. All Zulu men would be allowed to marry as they came to maturity, and while the obligation for them to serve in war would not be interfered with the regiments were not to be called up without the consent of the British Government. In addition, within twenty days the two sons of Sihayo would be handed over to the Natal authorities as previously demanded. Missionaries who had settled in the country were to be left unmolested. Frere reasoned that this settlement would be acceptable to the Boers, who would see the Zulu threat removed. He hoped it would be agreed by Cetshwayo on the grounds that he did not wish to fight the British, would prefer them on his side (thus shoring up his reign) and could justify it on the basis of the land regained. However he had grave doubts about Cetshwayo's ability to restrain his army.

Whether Frere ever believed that Cetshwayo would accept the ultimatum is open to question. Given the resistance of the Zulu generals, and the humiliation implicit in agreeing terms which denied fundamental tenets of Zulu culture and rule, Frere must have known this was highly unlikely. This belief was reinforced by reports from missionary refugees and agents that Cetshwayo had no intention of complying with the ultimatum and that he was saying "there is now nothing for it but war."[148] Given Frere's overriding objective of confederation, it probably did not matter much to him which way Cetshwayo decided. If he accepted the ultimatum, the British, through a Resident in Zululand, would exercise enough power to include the territory in a confederated South Africa. Alternatively, as he was supremely confident that the Zulus would be swiftly defeated in a war, should it come to that his aims would be achieved.

Frere wrote to Shepstone on December 4 stating his belief that war was inevitable. He maintained that there was little room remaining for "pacific negotiations" and that Cetshwayo would not stop his young men proving their strength.[149] Accustomed to negotiating with senior commanders, if not the king himself, the British saw the Zulu practice of attempting to parley by initially sending lowly messengers as evidence that Cetshwayo was not serious, and merely temporising.

Frere could argue that he had legal grounds for declaring war on Cetshwayo. When the Zulu king was crowned in 1873, one of the conditions of the Coronation Laws was the right to depose him if he did not govern according to British notions of justice and fairness.[150] He could claim that Cetshwayo's failure to meet the ultimatum would constitute a breach of these laws, although whether the Zulu king was aware of this nuance is debatable. Frere's Christian sensitivity would have left him in no doubt as to the savagery of Zulu customs. There is no evidence that Hicks Beach himself was anything other than fully in agreement with Frere's strategy at this stage. He consistently deferred to Frere, saying he was the best person to judge the situation. As late as October 1878 he was still agreeing with "all that was said and done" by Frere.[151]

The question remains: knowing the ultimatum would probably be rejected and war would ensue, why did Frere press forward, and not play a waiting game? Apart from his concern that the young Zulu warriors were spoiling for a fight, and may not be contained by their leaders, and the vulnerable Natal defences along an extended frontier, there was the experience of Frere and Chelmsford in the eastern Cape. Once the military had been properly marshalled and discipline applied to their confrontations with local tribes, superior firepower and training had easily defeated the Africans. Their success there led them both to believe that the Zulu army in open battle would be no match for the British. They expected the war to be over in a few weeks.

With hindsight, it was never likely that Cetshwayo would accept such an ultimatum. The notion to him of disbanding his unconquered army – his major asset – was inconceivable. Historians have long argued that Frere knew this, and used the ultimatum to escalate the war he felt was both necessary and inevitable. Chelmsford had advised him that, based on his experience in the Cape it would take a mere two months to conquer Zululand. Frere calculated that communications with London were such that two months was all he needed. He would be able to counter any objections with a fait accompli. Hicks Beach only received the text of the ultimatum on Christmas Eve, and recognised at once its implications. On Christmas Day he sent a telegram reinforcing what he had already stated very firmly to Frere: there was to be no war with the Zulus. Frere replied on January 15 rejecting his logic, and on January 25 sent a detailed report backing his arguments. By then the notorious battle of Isandlwana had been fought and lost.

Chapter 11.

WAR.

Before Frere sent the text of the ultimatum to Hicks Beach (on November 16, 1878), he was made aware that the British Government did not agree with him that war with the Zulus was inevitable. Clearly Hicks Beach did not fully realise how far matters had gone. On November 10 Frere received a communication from Hicks Beach informing him that the Prime Minister and Lord Salisbury did not share Frere's concern that South Africa would be defenceless against a Russian attack. However, having resisted Frere's request for reinforcements, urging him to avoid war at virtually any cost, Hicks Beach and the Cabinet appear finally to have been persuaded that support was necessary. On November 28 he cabled Frere informing him that two infantry battalions would be sent. It was re-emphasised that the Cabinet was "most anxious not to have a Zulu war on our hands just now."[152] Frere received the news on December 16. Before that he had written to the Colonial Secretary on December 10 arguing that the Zulus represented a clear and immediate threat. On December 23 he wrote again to Hicks Beach:

> "My own impression is that it is quite impossible for Cetshwayo to submit without calling in our aid to coerce the Frankenstein he has created in his regular regiments. Even if he was sincere and convinced of our superior power – neither of which I believe – he would find a large residuum of his soldiers who are fully convinced of their own superiority to us and will not give in without a trial of strength…I hope the preparations already made will secure our own borders from any inroad in force, and if the time allowed passes without complete acceptance of our terms, I hope that Lord Chelmsford's plan for moving in three converging columns on the Royal kraal, will go far to paralyse opposition and to secure success with as little sacrifice of life as possible."[153]

Frere went on to thank Hicks Beach for agreeing to send reinforcements, but ignored the instruction that they were to be used for defence only:

> "I can assure you that I have asked for no more than were absolutely necessary to secure speedy peace with the least possible bloodshed, here and in the Transvaal. The die for peace or war had been cast long before I or Bulwer or even Sir Garnet Wolseley came here. You will find clear proof of this in every one of Wolseley's

important despatches, and every month since has aggravated the crisis."[154]

Whether Cetshwayo was in a position to control his eager young soldiers is a crucial consideration. Frere clearly believed he could not; that the desire to "wash their spears" would lead the amabutho (members of the ibuthos) to disregard any caution their king might show. The Zulu nation was still a collection of disparate factions, and it is arguable whether Cetshwayo's will would have prevailed. Shepstone, to whom Frere still listened for advice, believed that the majority of Zulus were opposed to war with the British, but advised Frere that should war be declared on them they would resist strongly.

Cetshwayo consulted his assembled Council over the terms of the ultimatum. One of the most contentious clauses involved the sons of Sihayo. By crossing into Natal and killing the women who had eloped, they offended colonial sensibilities. Most of the Council was in favour of handing over the sons of Sihayo, but Sihayo was one of Cetshwayo's favourites, and the king was adamant that this would not happen. Public opinion in Zululand supported him. In the course of this debate it emerged that John Dunn, the white man close to Cetshwayo, had played down hostile intent by the British, leading the king to believe they would not attack. To surrender the sons of Sihayo was one of the least onerous demands of the ultimatum. To disband their army, to yield to a British Resident was tantamount to unconditional surrender of Zulu independence. A proud nation could not accept this without a struggle.

Hamu and Mnyamana opposed the king at the Council, and when Hamu returned home he immediately sent out feelers to Chelmsford, offering to defect to the British if they invaded Zululand. Heartened by signs of disagreement among the Zulu hierarchy, Frere sent messages that any chief who collaborated with the British would be relocated in Natal during the conflict and afterwards reinstated with a degree of independence, owing allegiance to the Queen.[155] Hedging his bets, Hamu also opened negotiations with the Swazi on his northern border. He was finally to defect in early February, too late to influence the course of the war. He headed for Wood's encampment at Kambula, but was pursued by Cetshwayo's men, and sought refuge in Swaziland.

There were grounds for hope that some of the other Zulu leaders would defect. As we have seen, the Zulu nation was a loose confederation of local chiefs, each with their own following and own territory. Many of them feared the outcome of the argument with the British, and bore no specific loyalty to Cetshwayo. However, the experience of the tribes in the eastern Cape, and the conditions under which the Africans in Natal lived and worked, showed them what to expect under British rule. Their independence would be forfeited, and they would become nothing more than serfs. Thus they had very little to lose by supporting Cetshwayo in his resistance.

On January 1, 1879, the twenty days provided for the return of Sihayo's sons expired. Recognising that this non-compliance signalled a refusal by the Zulus to accept the ultimatum in its entirety, on January 4 Frere placed the enforcement of terms in the hands of Lord Chelmsford. Reinforcements arrived on January 9. When the full thirty days time limit of the ultimatum expired on the 10th, British troops moved to enter Zululand. They could have reasonably expected the campaign to be short, sharp and victorious. The Zulu army, which under Shaka had used tactics not seen before on the battlefield, had not been modernised. Tactics remained largely the same, movement predictable, weapons outdated. Although possessing rifles, the Zulus had not been taught to use them skilfully, and were poor shots. The British army with modern repeating rifles should have been more than a match for them in a pitched battle. Chelmsford had taken the trouble to issue all his commanders with tactical instructions arising from the experience of facing African attacks. He based these instructions on what he had seen in the eastern Cape. What he did not realise was that whereas the Xhosas were prone to remain passive until attacked, the Zulus preferred to take the fight to the enemy. This was a crucial difference in tactics that was to hurt Chelmsford.

There remained the arrogance of invincibility among the British. Had the campaign been immediately successful, the disobedience of Frere, and the questions over his motives and decisions, would have been swept away in a tide of relief and euphoria. Once he had been able to "draw the Monster's teeth and claws" as he put it, Zululand would be accommodated in the confederation like an Indian "subject ally."[156] There can be no doubt that Chelmsford had prepared assiduously for the war. His force had been augmented with British infantry from elsewhere in South Africa. He had at his disposal 17,929 men. Of these 5476 were British regulars, 1193 irregular colonial horse, 9350 black auxiliaries and the remainder non-combatants. The border agent Fynney presented an expert assessment of the Zulu army. He estimated the number of their fighting men at 40,000, although recent assessments put this number at nearer 29,000 active men in the field, still the largest gathering ever fielded. He explained the battle system which had succeeded so well for previous Zulu kings: highly mobile regiments covering prodigious distances on foot to surprise their enemies; strict discipline, precise, rehearsed manoeuvres that relied upon the right and left flanks – the 'horns' – gradually encircling their foe as the centre held firm. Officers had clear responsibilities and were obeyed. Chelmsford had the report printed and distributed to every officer. Struck by the success of the new Martini-Henry breech-loading rifle with a range of up to 1,000 yards, accurate and powerful, Chelmsford was confident of winning any set battle against the Zulus, virtually whatever the odds.

Chelmsford's strategy was a sound one. He had refined his original plan to deploy five columns by reducing them to three: in the north, centre and near the coast to press the enemy back towards the centre of Zululand and converge on the Zulu king's headquarters at Ulundi. Column One with 4,700 men under Colonel Charles Pearson would cross the Tugela at the Lower Drift and make for Eshowe, fifteen miles to the north. Another column of 2,250 men under Colonel Evelyn Wood would march south-east from Utrecht while the main force of 4,700 lead by Chelmsford himself would cross the Buffalo River at Rorke's Drift, a small Scandinavian mission station.

The main force crossed into Zululand at dawn on January 11, 1879. Thick fog and drizzle made the river crossing onerous. The water in the drift covered the men's shoulders, and the current was swift. The British soldiers, used to these conditions, locked arms and rushed the stream, getting across without loss. Several of the Natal African auxiliaries were not as adept, and were swept away. In the lead was the 24th Regiment, known as the South Wales Borderers. This regiment had a proud history. Formed in 1689 as Sir Edward Dering's Regiment of Foot, it became the 24th Regiment of Foot in 1751, having been considered the 24th in the infantry order of precedence since 1747. Initially formed in Warwickshire, it moved its base to Brecon in Wales in 1873, and recruited mainly from the surrounding counties. This resulted in its name of the South Wales Borderers, originating from 1881. The regiment saw battle in many parts of the world, most notably during the Peninsula War, Canada during the American War of Independence, and India. During the Indian Mutiny Frere had sent it to the Punjab from the Sind. There it preserved a precarious and important peace. Chelmsford was familiar with the regiment's abilities, for it had distinguished itself in the eastern Cape under his command.

The force made very slow progress over rocky, broken terrain. Chelmsford was a cautious general. He insisted on clearing the territory of Zulus as he advanced, thus ensuring he would not be surprised from the rear. His ox-led transport was cumbersome and slow; the engineers had to precede the main column in order to make the rudimentary tracks passable. To drag the guns and carry supplies and ammunition required more than 2,000 oxen, 67 mules, 220 wagons and 82 carts.[157] The first engagement occurred on January 12 at Sokexe, close to Rorke's Drift. By coincidence this happened to be Sihayo's home, although he had already gone to Ulundi to be with the king. His son, Mkumbikazulu, one of the sons cited in retrieval and murder of the women who had fled to Natal, defended stoutly, but was outnumbered by the British troops who captured the cattle and burnt Sokexe. Mkumbikazulu was killed.

It took seven days of preparation work, with engineers laying a road for the wagons, to make it possible for the column to cover the ten miles between crossing into Zululand at Rorke's Drift and Isandlwana, the first staging post with good water and wood for a camping site. They reached the landmark conical hill on January 20. From there, with the hill behind him, Chelmsford could survey a wide, open valley with clear views extending over four miles to the east and two miles to the north. Here he felt safe: his experience in the eastern Cape had led him to believe that his enemy would only fight when attacked. Although experience of skirmishes in South Africa had emphasized the advantage of entrenchments, none were attempted here as the line would extend to over a mile and the ground was too stony to dig. The alternative defence was to draw the wagons into a laager, but a number of these were required to transport supplies on a regular basis. Chelmsford, aware that he still had eighty miles to cover before he reached Ulundi, the Zulu capital, was reluctant to become bogged down by elaborate precautions which would slow his progress. As long as his scouts gave him adequate warning of impending attack he was confident he could prevail.

Unknown to Carnarvon, the Zulus were concealed on the floor of the Ngwebeni valley some seven miles away.

At the same time as the British crossed the Buffalo into Zululand the Zulu army had assembled at Ulundi, and "seemed to stretch from there right to the sea" so large did it appear. Cetshwayo, who was aware of the three enemy columns, had decided to concentrate on the main force, which Chelmsford was accompanying. On the afternoon of January 17 between 20,000 and 25,000 Zulu warriors moved out of Ulundi down the Mahlabatini Plain across the White Umfolozi River. In four days they covered fifty miles, arriving close to Isandlwana on the 21st.

On January 22 Chelmsford committed a fatal error. Attracted by fires in the hills off to the south-east, he led roughly half his force out of camp, believing he would confront the Zulu army in the hills. The remainder, some 1,770 men, feeling secure in their commanding position, still did not prepare adequate defences. They believed an attack on their position was extremely unlikely. Chelmsford was soon out of the broad valley and into a range of rugged hills traversed by dongas (shallow ditches). Once there he found that the wide vistas of the open plain gave way to restricted views ahead of him. He encountered very few Zulus, and certainly no Zulu army, but could not be sure they were not close by.

Meanwhile a British patrol riding out from the base camp at Isandlwana to the end of the valley came across some Zulu herders and gave chase. The herders ran over the crest of a slope and disappeared. One of the pursuers, close behind, suddenly pulled up his horse in alarm. It has long been held that he was on the brink of a precipice looking into a deep, wide ravine. This was the Ngwebeni Valley, where twenty thousand Zulu warriors sat in silence. It is said that although they had not planned to attack that day, the fired-up younger warriors spontaneously spilled out of the valley. Yet recent research has shown that it would have been impossible for the patrol, which left the camp at 11 a.m., to have returned when they did, at noon, with the report of their discovery if they had gone as far as the Ngwebeni Valley. Experiments have shown that even at full gallop the round journey would have taken an hour and a half, and as the patrol did not leave the camp at a gallop, it was more likely they would have taken upwards of two hours. It appears more likely that the army had formed up outside the valley but below the crest of the iThusi hill facing Isandlwana, on the Nqutu plateau, in preparation for an attack.

The effect on the waiting Zulus of the sight of the British soldier was electric. Impulsively they surged forward without orders from their commanders. The British horseman wheeled, shouting the alarm and the patrol raced back to the camp. Within minutes the Zulus had reached the crest of the hill and looked down onto the plain. To the British the sight of such a host appearing over the rim of the hill, spread out as far as the eye could see, was awe-inspiring. For a distance of two miles the horde filled the horizon, making their trademark humming noise which sounded like a million angry bees. Forming their traditional horn formation, they spilled into the valley and fanned out over the plain to converge upon the camp. It was the first serious battle these warriors had been in for a long time and all their energy and courage was invested in it.

Chelmsford had found little evidence of the Zulu army in the hills to the south. His detachment was soon strung out through the countryside, with the artillery making particularly slow progress over rugged terrain. Small clusters of Zulus were engaged, and either killed or captured, leading Chelmsford to believe that they were forerunners to the main army. One prisoner confirmed that the main body of the Zulu army was due from Ulundi that day. At this point the unmistakable sound of cannon fire came from the two guns left in the camp. Chelmsford and his staff rode to the top of a hill and looked back. They could see the bright flashes of a few shells exploding against the escarpment at the end of the valley facing Isandlwana. At that point a message arrived from the officer commanding the Isandlwana camp: "… the Zulus are advancing in force from left front of the camp."[158] This puzzled Chelmsford. The camp was just visible from the hills where he was, and looked normal, with small figures moving about among the tents. Soon the cannonade died down, and Chelmsford assumed that if there had been an attack it had been beaten off. He assumed it must have been by an advance party and not the main army. Although the force left in camp had been significantly diminished by his departure, he was confident of their ability to resist successfully any Zulu attack, and thus did not consider returning.

The officer commanding the artillery, Colonel Harness, was some way behind Chelmsford at this time. His four guns were negotiating a series of dongas running across the plain. Harness had also heard the firing, and looking back saw a European officer approaching at full gallop. The message he brought was: "For God's sake come back with all your men; the camp is surrounded and must be taken unless helped."[159] Harness immediately turned his guns around and started for Isandlwana.

Major Gosset, a member of Chelmsford's staff, was present at the time, and Harness asked him to take the message to Chelmsford. Gosset had observed the camp from the hill, when all appeared to be normal, and knew that Chelmsford considered the defending force to be more than adequate. He tried to dissuade Harness from turning around, but when Harness insisted he rode off to see Chelmsford. It seems that Gosset never gave the message to Chelmsford directly, and that whatever he did say to Chelmsford's staff, he did not repeat the warning verbatim, which would have rung the alarm bells. What Chelmsford did hear simply seemed to be another report of what he had observed himself. By the time he realised the scale of the battle, it was too late for him to intervene.

The details of the battle are well known. The defenders fought well, causing the Zulus to falter more than once in the face of ferocious firepower, but without fortifications they were cruelly exposed on the open veld. Numbers told in the end, and the camp was inundated. A volunteer later related: "We shot hundreds but it seemed to make no impression, they still came on."[160] The end came when the impis to the right of the main body of Zulus, the "right horn," adopting their traditional tactic of moving forward in an attempt to outflank the enemy, made its way around the back of the Isandlwana hill and engaged the redcoats from the rear, effectively cutting off any means of retreat. Of the 800 white soldiers, British and colonial, 779 were killed, whilst of 907 Africans fighting with them 471 perished, the remainder escaping because they were less conspicuous than the redcoats. It was estimated that between 2,600 and 3,000 Zulus died in the battle.[161]

Faced by overwhelming numbers, attacked from front and rear, there remained only one escape route. A narrow track ran back from Isandlwana to the Buffalo River. This track remained open, as the Zulus had chosen to attack the camp rather than cover the track. Those few who did escape fell back over the Buffalo River into Natal to the mission post of Rorke's Drift, where there was a hospital and a garrison. The awful news they brought caused great alarm. Tasting victory, it was inevitable that the Zulus would follow the survivors back to Rorke's Drift. The garrison was in no position to resist the might of the Zulu army, and was handicapped by a number of incapacitated men in the hospital. A withdrawal was considered, but it was soon pointed out that the Zulus would quickly catch up with wagons encumbered by the sick and injured. Better that they stood and fought.

Thus occurred one of the legendary defences in British military history. For twelve hours 131 men and 8 officers held out at the small mission post against some 4,000 Zulus. They did so by entrenching themselves behind a high wall of heavy mealie sacks and two-foot high biscuit boxes that weighed nearly a hundred pounds each. The hospital, a long, low building, proved most difficult to defend, but enjoyed the advantage of having only one door to the outside, which was barricaded. The Zulu main force reached Rorke's Drift around four in the afternoon, and surrounded the post. Initially they were repulsed by fierce gunfire from every available vantage point, but soon the fighting was hand to hand. The barricades held, but weight of Zulu numbers forced the defenders back from the front of the hospital. The end wall of the hospital was breached and a desperate struggle ensued, the British dragging invalids from room to room as the Zulus broke through one wall after another in pursuit. Miraculously, of the eleven hospital patients nine were pulled out alive into the protection of the defended barricades. As night fell the Zulu assault continued. They set fire to the thatched roof of the hospital, but this enabled the defenders a better sight of their attackers, and they held out successfully throughout the night. As dawn broke, it appeared that resistance was close to breaking. Less than eighty men were still on their feet behind the barricades, and they were totally exhausted. But the Zulus, under Dabulumanzi, Cetshwayo's son and heir, had exceeded their instructions by crossing the river into Natal. Once Cetshwayo learnt this he swiftly recalled them, but not before an estimated 600 Zulus had been killed at the cost of 17 defenders.

The first battle fought on Zulu territory had been an unmitigated disaster, for of the six companies of the 24th Regiment who actually took part in the battle of Isandlwana only six men survived, crossing the river to reach Natal. Historically it was one of the worst defeats ever on the British army, and psychologically sent a shock of enormous proportion through the nation. It encouraged the Zulus to believe, not only that they could defeat the British, but they could also sweep the remaining white men into the sea and regain the lands which they regarded were rightfully theirs. The subsequent defence of Rorke's Drift was merely damage limitation. The British badly needed heroes and some good news to report back in England, and the successful defence at Rorke's Drift provided that. A record eleven Victoria Crosses were awarded to the defenders.

The shock with which the news of the defeat at Isandlwana was received in England was nothing compared to the local reaction. Complacent after the successful eastern Cape campaign, the British had believed the Zulu War would be over in a few weeks. The settlers in Natal now feared the worst: provoked, there would be no way to prevent the Zulus overrunning them. Defences were hastily constructed in Pietermaritzburg and the colonists prepared for the worst.

In fact Cetshwayo was counting the cost of the encounter: at least 1,300 of his finest warriors dead and another 2,300 with serious wounds received from the soft-nosed bullets that smashed bones and tissue and which would incapacitate them. The stand at Rorke's Drift had stopped the Zulus from moving further into Natal. For the present the colony was safe.

When Frere first heard of the disaster at Isandlwana he immediately despatched a telegram requesting further reinforcements from England. The shame of defeat was such that Whitehall reacted promptly. By the end of February 6, six infantry battalions, two cavalry regiments and two artillery batteries with support staff had sailed for Durban. In total 418 officers, 9996 men, 1868 horses and 238 wagons were sent to Chelmsford's aid. Facing a delay of at least two months before they reached Natal, Frere also sent an urgent message to Cape Town for the three companies of the 4th Regiment stationed there. Sprigg responded by sending every soldier he could spare from the Cape, including those from Kingwilliamstown, leaving the defence of the colony in the hands of colonial volunteers. Further reinforcements were requested from Mauritius and St Helena. On January 26 Chelmsford returned to Pietermaritzburg in such a state of mental turmoil that Frere was worried he might collapse at any moment.

Chapter 12.

REPERCUSSIONS.

Since 1873 Disraeli's government had experienced a steady decline in popularity. An economic depression had gradually been deepening. Irish home-rulers were threatening rebellion, and there was unrest in Egypt and Afghanistan. Confrontation with the Russians loomed. The Parliamentary opposition saw an opportunity to berate the government. William Gladstone seized the opportunity to denounce the government's handling of foreign and colonial affairs. The Liberals mounted a concerted attack on the Conservatives and were rewarded with a number of by-election successes. The Russians chose this moment to send a mission to Kabul with the intention of bringing Afghanistan under Russian influence. On August 14, 1878, the British demanded that the Afghans accept a British mission too. The Amir refused to receive such a mission. Lord Lytton, the Viceroy of India, ordered a diplomatic mission to set out for Kabul but it was turned back at the eastern end of the Khyber Pass. This was unacceptable to the British, and a force of about forty thousand men in five columns entered Afghanistan at three different points. The country was soon largely under the control of the British and the Russian mission withdrew.

This turn of fortunes was a setback to the Liberals, who had banked upon embarrassment in Afghanistan to add to the government's lack of popularity. So when the news of Isandlwana broke, it provided Gladstone with a golden opportunity to attack the government on a fresh front. News of the disaster reached England on February 11, 1879. The impact on public opinion was devastating. Few people knew much about South Africa, other than that it was populated by savages and troublesome settlers, who were costing the British exchequer a great deal of money. The news that eight hundred Englishmen – members of the "invincible" British army - had died at the hands of these savages was intolerable. Who was to blame for this mess? Immediately the focus was fixed on Frere. The government, with a general election looming, was anxious to shift the burden off its own shoulders.

Conscious of the severe criticism that would be mounting in England, Frere wrote to Hicks Beach from Pietermaritzburg on January 29:

> "I need not tell you that I came out to South Africa purely on a mission of peace. Had I foreseen the warlike troubles in which I have since been involved, I should have suggested to Her Majesty's Ministers to look for some younger man…I wish you to give every weight to advice on what I believe is essential to early

and complete peace…First, as to the Zulus. When I telegraphed by last mail, I had not realized the utter prostration and demoralization of every Colonial resource, caused by our reverse on the 22nd. The Government has received a warning…that Cetshwayo was determined on a raid to destroy this town of Durban; and it is not easy for regular forces to intercept a body of thousands of naked savages travelling by bye-ways forty miles in a night, living on plunder, overwhelming by numbers any post they surprise, and then dispersing as they came by bye-paths to their own country not sixty miles off.…It will take time, some years, probably, to get over this shock and organize [the Colonial forces] so as to give the aid the regulars require. Meanwhile you must strengthen the regular force and effectually crush the Zulu King's power. This is not really so difficult as it seems. His thousands of young gladiators, so irresistible while they believe themselves invincible, will succumb when only once fairly defeated. Theirs is the courage of maniacs and drunkards, or of wild beasts infuriated and trained to destruction, and once cowed they will not rally."

He then went on to plead for further reinforcements – perhaps from the Indian regiments. Aware of the British Government's reluctance to commit more finance to South Africa, he argued:

"I do not think you need be in the least alarmed at the expense. I take it for granted that we shall not leave the country a prey to anarchy, but govern it, and make it pay for keeping it in peace and quietness through its own people.... The country [Zululand] is not difficult, and is naturally fertile, and has an outlet by water into Delagoa Bay....[and] in fact, is likely to prosper and pay its own expenses far more rapidly than Natal has done....and will add immensely to the value of Natal itself, here at present there is no such security within a hundred miles of the border."[162]

The Prime Minister, Disraeli, was very angry. Hitherto he had taken very little interest in the colonies, saying they were "millstones round our neck."[163] When he entered office he had been content to leave colonial policy to Carnarvon, who had successfully confederated Canada and felt he could apply the same formula to South Africa. Disraeli, preoccupied with problems in Afghanistan and with the Russians, had been explicit when Shepstone visited London in January 1878: "A native war is just now impossible and you must avoid it."[164] It was only in September 1878 that he finally became aware of the worsening situation in South Africa. He wrote:

"...if anything annoys me more than another, it is our Cape affairs, where every day brings forth a new blunder of Twitters [Carnarvon's nickname]. The man he swore by was Sir T. Shepstone, whom he looked upon as heaven-born for the object in view…He has managed to quarrel with Eng., Dutch and Zulus; and now he is obliged to be recalled, but not before he has brought on, I fear, a new war."[165]

The government had at its disposal an Imperial Chest of £1 million to cover minor disturbances. Unfortunately Frere had already called on a quarter of this sum to fund his suppression of rebellion in Griqualand West. It was clear that the cost of the Zulu War would far exceed the remaining funds, requiring the government to go back to Parliament for more. Disraeli felt that the need for reinforcements, whilst essential and unquestioned, threw his entire foreign policy into jeopardy, and that the cost would be a severe drain on the national finances at a time when depression threatened. Recriminations soon followed. Main criticism in London was levelled at Chelmsford for not having fortified the camp, and for faulty intelligence. Demands were made for him to be recalled. Frere's old enemy, Lord Salisbury entered the fray, calling for the Governor's head.

"Bartle Frere should have been recalled as soon as the news of the ultimatum reached London. We should then have escaped the appearance, as well as in reality, the responsibility of the Zulu War."[166]

On March 8 The Spectator published an article ridiculing Chelmsford and calling for his recall. In reference to a despatch by Chelmsford after the defeat at Isandlwana, it complained that "it is …the despatch of a man who should not be entrusted with the command of a large army, engaged on a most difficult and hazardous undertaking. He has not the primary faculty of understanding what his own subordinates and the enemy are about. He has collected no accurate idea of the country he was about to invade, saying, with a heart-breaking naivete which runs through the whole communication the country is far more difficult than I had been led to expect….Those surely were primary facts in Zululand campaigning. How is even one day's work to be arranged when the country one mile ahead is to the general like the surface of a new planet?"

Frere had his defenders however. The Queen caused the government some dismay by sending a telegram to Frere via Hicks Beach expressing her "deep feeling at the terrible calamity" (Isandlwana) and her "implicit confidence" in him.[167]

Hicks Beach, for various reasons, wanted Frere to remain in place for the time being. The Colonial Secretary attempted to cover himself by simultaneously reprimanding Frere and stating that he "had no desire to withdraw in the present crisis the confidence hitherto reposed in you."[168] This gave his opponent, Sir William Harcourt, an opportunity to mock his indecisiveness in the Commons by reading out an imaginary letter:

"Dear Sir Bartle Frere. I cannot think you are right. Indeed I think you are very wrong, but after all you know a great deal better than I do. I hope you won't do what you are going to do; but if you do I hope it will turn out well."[169]

The Queen's private secretary summed up an uneasy consensus thus:

"I do not understand anyone to have said Frere was incapable, but that he had unnecessarily plunged us into a war. If so the evil is done. To punish him for that by withdrawing him would be to punish ourselves, for it is against Abraham Lincoln's dictum that it is unwise to swap horses while crossing a stream."[170]

A majority of the cabinet was in favour of recalling Frere. It was evident to the cabinet that Hicks Beach had been a weak Colonial Secretary, allowing Frere far too much freedom . The government was vulnerable to accusations of incompetence or worse. But then second thoughts prevailed. They dare not sack Frere. For should he turn up in London his revelations of correspondence with Hicks Beach might be highly embarrassing. They chose to officially censure him for exceeding his orders, while confirming him in his appointment as High Commissioner. The authority of the Colonial Secretary was to be emphasised, and the instructions sent out to Frere were to be more detailed, specific and timely. The censure read:

"Her Majesty's Government….cannot but think that the forces at your disposal were adequate to protect Natal from any serious Zulu inroad…and they have been unable to find in any document you have placed before them that evidence of urgent necessity for immediate action, which alone could justify you in taking, without their full knowledge and sanction, a course almost certain to result in a war which, as I had previously impressed upon you, every effort should have been used to avoid…..Her Majesty's Government do not fail to bear in mind the unusual powers reposed in you…They cannot, however doubt that your future action will be such as to prevent a recurrence of any cause for complaint on this score; and they have no desire to withdraw, in the present crisis of affairs, the confidence hitherto reposed in you, the continuance of which is now more than ever needed to conduct our difficulties in South Africa to a successful termination."[171]

Frere had an inkling of what was coming from unconfirmed press reports, but Hicks Beach's letter of March 13, containing the censure, received by Frere on April 18, gave substance to the rumours. The censure reached Frere when he was in Pretoria, trying to placate the rebellious Boers. His first inclination was to resign his office. Hicks Beach was imploring him to stay; the situation in the Transvaal and Zululand remained extremely delicate. How could he turn his back on all this now? He commented wryly: "After a week of this uncertainty, succeeding many weeks of looking out for Zulu impis it is pleasant to find out that the government is not likely to defend me or anyone else."[172] The heated debate in London raged on. The nation remained shocked by the defeat, despite efforts to highlight Rorke's Drift as a triumph. Lord Carnarvon, although now out of office, pointed out that had Isandlwana been a success and the Zulus been defeated, Frere would have been hailed as a hero. But both government and opposition, for their own reasons, had found their scapegoat. Among the many personal letters of support he received, one from Gordon Sprigg, the Cape Prime minister, was telling:

> "If you were now to retire the consequences to South Africa would be simply disastrous….I hope you will not come to a decision adverse to the wishes of nearly every man in Africa….I do urge you not to think for a moment of giving way to public opinion in England on a question which no man who has never been in Africa is competent to understand."[173]

Hicks Beach was handed the task of persuading Frere to remain in office. He resorted to rather dubious tactics. He claimed that his (Hicks Beach's) career was at stake and argued that failure by Frere to accept the censure would put that career in jeopardy. He also implied that if this were to occur Frere would be forthwith dismissed, which was quite far from the truth. At the same time Hicks Beach ensured that Frere's correspondence with him was not made public by suppressing his replies and not allowing publication of his correspondence. Frere's formal reply to Hicks Beach, dated April 25, was very considered. As it is important in gauging his frame of mind, and defence of his actions it is worth quoting at some length:

"Some of the evidence of the urgent necessity for immediate action was not before the public, and was probably not before Her Majesty's Government when you wrote...including the evidence of Boer discontent – which weighed greatly with me in convincing me that any delay in acting would incur dangers far greater than those of a Zulu war. I do not mean merely the risk of an invasion of Natal....there could be no doubt as to the state of Boer feeling, of which at the time you had little evidence before you. I felt, however, quite certain that, even if I could postpone for a few weeks or even months the inevitable Zulu War, it would be impossible to avoid a Boer rebellion.....Some act of violence the Boers would certainly have committed – hauled down the flag, stopped the mails, put the administrator over the border, or done some other of the many acts of rebellion they have threatened ever since they knew we were fighting their inevitable enemies, the Zulus. We must have moved some of our troops from Natal to support law and order here, and some bloodshed would have been the inevitable result. What would the Zulus have done? Observed a strict armed neutrality? I doubt if all Cetshwayo's power could have enabled him to observe it. His young men would certainly have washed their spears in some white man's blood, whether Dutch or English would matter little to them. If Dutch, as is more probable, the Orange Free State would have been drawn in, and the Boer rebellion might have extended to Cape Colony ….it seems to me a simple choice between doing what I did – risking a Zulu war at once, or incurring the risk of still worse – a Zulu war a few months later, preceded by a Boer rebellion. You must not think I was insensible to your difficulties in Turkey and Asia. I doubt whether you felt them more acutely than I did; but you must remember they were not present in their late aggravated form, till we had gone too far in Zulu affairs to recede with honour or even with safety….Had things gone wrong in Turkey or Afghanistan you would not have thanked me for putting off war, when it involved both war and rebellion while you were in the midst of a European war."

He went on to point out that full discussion of the situation would, with the tedious communication system, "…have involved four or five months' delay at least. I feel quite sure we would not have kept the peace here so long."

He ended with reassurance, however:

"I need not tell you that I came here for no personal object of my own, and, had I consulted only my own ease and welfare, I should have returned in six months. But I was honoured with a charge to stand on sentry for other purposes than my own personal benefit; and whilst my strength lasts, I will not desert my post till Her Majesty's Government either relieves or removes me."[174]

Perhaps naively Frere believed that what he had done was right, and that once the full facts were understood the adverse judgement voiced against him would be reversed.

Later, from Cape Town, he was to write to Gladstone in response to scathing criticism that in

"…. the judgement of all military authorities, both before the war and since…it was absolutely impossible for Lord Chelmsford's force, acting on the defensive within the Natal boundary, to prevent a Zulu impi from entering Natal, and repeating the same indiscriminate slaughter of all ages and sexes which they boast of having effected in…Dingaan's other massacres of forty years ago, and in the inroads into the Transvaal territories…within the last two years."[175]

In the same letter he went even further. Referring to the Zulu raids on farms near Luneberg, he wrote:

"In the course of these inroads, every man, woman, and child who was not murdered (and, in two cases, burned alive in their huts), was carried off into slavery in Zululand…I would ask who was the aggressor? Who actually commenced the war by committing acts which, if no satisfaction be given for them, are acts of war? I have always maintained it was not we who made war on Cetywayo, but he who made war on us; and that Lord Chelmsford's first advance was preceded by acts by the Zulus, which, unless atoned for, were unquestionable acts of hostility and virtual declarations of war."[176]

Once the full facts of the heroic stand at Rorke's Drift were known, some of the heat went out of the debate. Chelmsford claimed, rather tenuously, that it had saved Natal from invasion. It has often been stated that Natal lay wide open to invasion, and that had the Zulus moved on the colony after the battle of Isandlwana the situation would have been desperate. It is overlooked that the Zulus had suffered heavy losses at both Isandlwana and Rorke's Drift, and that the Zulu army needed to regroup and tend to the many wounded. Lacking sophisticated medicine and surgery, the Zulus struggled to heal their casualties.

Chapter 13.

PRESS ON REGARDLESS.

Frere was becoming conscious that the powers in England had distanced themselves from him. Whilst many of his friends wrote to him in support, he received no assurances that he had the confidence of government – or the opposition for that matter. In South Africa itself, the climate of opinion was very different. A huge public meeting was called in Cape Town at which a large majority carried resolutions approving Frere's actions. Messages of support poured in from towns, villages, from informal groups and formal councils. The overwhelming opinion was that he was the one man who had understood the problems of South Africa and set about resolving them. A group from Cradock in the Cape wrote to him:

> "In the opinion of this meeting his Excellency Sir Bartle Frere is one of the best Governors, if not the best Governor, this Colony has ever had, and the disasters which have taken place since he

has held office, are not due to any fault of his, but to a shameful mismanagement of public affairs before he came to the Colony, and the state of chaos and utter confusion in which he had the misfortune to find everything on his arrival."[177]

Another, from Kimberley:

"It has been a source of much pain to us that your Excellency's policy and proceedings should have been so misunderstood and misrepresented. The people in this country knew that the Zulu War was unavoidable; and the time, we hope, is not far distant when the wisdom of your Excellency's native policy and action will be as fully recognized and appreciated by the whole British nation as it is by the colonists of South Africa."[178]

Messages of support continued to pour in. A public meeting held in Grahamstown on March 27 passed a resolution approving of Frere's policy, and another in George on April 4 expressed confidence in "the general policy of [Frere]." Graaff Reinett and Kingwilliamstown echoed these sentiments.[179]

The British Government had adopted an ambivalent attitude: it badly needed to restore British military prestige, but did not want a costly, drawn-out war. Under pressure in England to settle the whole affair at the least possible cost, Hicks Beach cabled Frere in March 1879 forbidding the annexation of Zululand, and again on April 10 pressing on him the need to bring the war to a conclusion at the earliest possible moment. Due to the communication problems and the lack of a direct telegraph link, these messages took months to arrive. Anxious to make amends for Isandlwana and achieve the success they had originally envisaged, this delay gave Frere and Chelmsford the time they needed to press home their advantage,

For the time being ignorant of the uproar in London, Frere could only sit and follow British attempts to turn the Zulu war round. There was little he could now do to influence the outcome, so he turned his attention to the Transvaal. Far from being mollified by the British action, the Boers were more disturbed than ever. Isandlwana gave them no solace, and the annexation of the Transvaal stuck in their craw. Kruger and Joubert, leading the Boers, continued to campaign actively against annexation by seeking assistance abroad and petitioning the British government. The fact that the main body of the British army in South Africa was heavily engaged in Zululand motivated them to be bellicose. Reports came in that the Boers were openly recruiting and drilling troops, but not to help the British out in Zululand, as Frere hoped.

Frere met Kruger and Joubert in Pietermaritzburg for preliminary talks. He made it plain that there could be no discussion as to the annexation, which was irrevocable. He was interested to see that the two leaders were not entirely in agreement: Kruger was all for armed resistance while Joubert believed this would be both disastrous and futile. Prepared to negotiate, Joubert argued for self-government under the Crown, and Frere seized on this, letting it be known that the Transvaal could have its own flag, its own constitution, self-rule, and civil servants fluent in Afrikaans. In return they would accept confederation within South Africa. He reminded Joubert that he had twice before told him this, and trusted that he had reported back faithfully to his countrymen. He also pointed out that while it was tempting for the Boers to wish for the defeat of the British, were they to be vanquished those whites remaining would be serfs under Zulu masters. What he did not reveal was that hours before he had received news that messengers had been intercepted on their way from the Zulu king to Kruger suggesting that this was a favourable opportunity for the Boers to rise against the British, or at least remain neutral.

Back in Pietermaritzburg, Chelmsford bided his time. After Isandlwana the war against the Zulus had stalled for a while. Understandably he was unwilling to risk another defeat, and therefore proceeded very cautiously, awaiting the promised reinforcements. The plan for three separate forces to converge on the Zulu Royal kraal remained intact, at least on paper. From the north Colonel Wood would advance into Zululand, while the main force would again attempt to approach the Zulu capital, Ulundi, across the Buffalo River from Rorke's Drift. In the south Colonel Pearson would secure Eshowe, thus sealing the southern border of Natal and containing the Zulus.

Unaware of the defeat at Isandlwana Colonel Wood had crossed the Blood River on January 10 and advanced to the White Umfolozi River. There a local chieftain surrendered, the first success of the war for the British. It was only then that Wood learnt of the disaster at Isandlwana, and realised that the Zululand invasion had stalled. He was well in advance of his main base, and somewhat exposed, as he could not rely on reinforcements. He therefore retreated to a defensive position at Kambula, 25 miles from Luneberg, and awaited news that Chelmsford was ready to advance again. This was likely to take some time. Unlike Chelmsford, Wood was a seasoned campaigner and possessed a very astute military mind. A protégé of Garnett Wolseley, he had seen action in the Crimea, India and Ashanti. At the age of twenty-one he had been awarded the Victoria Cross for rescuing an Indian merchant from bandits against heavy odds.

Wood resisted the temptation to push forward; he sat and waited. The countryside around Kambula was teeming with Zulus, led by minor chieftains anxious to score their own triumphs. To the east was the formidable high plateau of Hlobane, occupied by a local tribe and virtually impregnable. From their stronghold these warriors embarked upon a number of raids, causing disruption to supply columns and keeping Wood's men on constant alert. A major attempt to capture Hlobane ended in disaster for Wood's men, with the British surrounded before a relief force rescued them. Fifteen officers and seventy-nine British soldiers were killed along with over one hundred African auxiliaries.

Following Isandlwana the main body of the Zulu army had been moved north to confront Wood. Many carried guns captured at Isandlwana. Their success at repulsing the assault on Hlobane gave them the momentum to attack Kambula. On March 29 at eleven in the morning 11,000 Zulus came within sight of the British camp. As usual, they spread out across the horizon, forming two horns that advanced to either side of the British. Wood had chosen his spot well, on the top of a ridge, and had heeded the advice to fight the mobile impis from heavily fortified positions. So when the Zulus erupted with a roar and flung themselves at the British, they were ready. Four guns opened up with devastating effect, and those Zulus who survived were cut down by concentrated rifle fire from the laager. Four hours later the battle was over. 2,000 Zulus lay dead at the cost of 29 British.

The effect of this defeat was devastating to the Zulus. What was left of the Zulu army broke up and drifted back home to their respective kraals. The young warriors, who had by now "washed their spears," were anxious to take up domestic life again. In addition to the dead, countless thousands of Zulu warriors had suffered wounds from soft-nosed bullets, from which they would not recover. Shrewd Cetshwayo recognised that the British had learnt the lesson of Isandlwana, and would not be caught again. With reinforcements beginning to pour in, the outcome of the war was inevitable. Cetshwayo sent messengers to Chelmsford asking for peace and saying that the fighting was a mistake.

In the south Colonel Pearson's column had established itself at Eshowe. Although secure in his garrison, he was under siege and unable to make further progress, particularly once the central column had been destroyed at Isandlwana. So, like Wood, he sat and awaited developments. On March 23, two messengers from Cetshwayo approached the garrison under cover of a white flag offering Pearson a free passage back to the Tugela if the garrison went peacefully, but they were treated with disdain.

By the end of March Chelmsford had at his disposal 16,000 European troops, 7,000 armed Natal natives and appropriate back-up staff. Although London was directing that peace be agreed as soon as possible, and Cetshwayo wanted it, Chelmsford and Frere were not about to relent when they had the upper hand. Chelmsford was intent on rescuing his reputation, Frere on controlling Zululand so that the dream of confederation could be realised. Both of them were bent on successfully concluding the war. Only the destruction of the royal Zulu seat of Ulundi would do.

On the same day that Wood won his battle at Kambula, Chelmsford, taking advantage of Zulu disarray, set out across the lower Tugela to relieve Pearson in Eshowe. He took with him four infantry battalions and two detachments from the Naval Brigade. In total there were 3,390 white troops and 2,280 black auxiliaries. John Dunn, recognising the way the war was going, provided invaluable advice. By April 1 Chelmsford was within fifteen miles of Eshowe, where he was warned of a large Zulu force approaching. The next morning approximately 12,000 Zulus could be seen converging on Chelmsford's force, but this time he was ready. Fortified behind a huge laager, 130 yards square, the British opened up with Gatling machine guns and rocket tubes. The Martini-Henry rifles then joined in and finally the cavalry were released to mop up survivors. Within an hour the battle was over; one thousand Zulus lay dead at a cost of thirteen dead and forty-eight wounded. Eshowe was relieved. Chelmsford was not yet ready to advance on Ulundi. He left Major-General Henry Hope Crealock to lead a column up the coast and establish a strong permanent post on the coastal road.

Encouraging progress in the war strengthened Frere's hand in his negotiations with the Boers. It was time for him to visit the Transvaal. From the meetings he had held in Pietermaritzburg with Kruger and Joubert he had learnt that the Boers were by no means unanimous in their demands or feelings about annexation. Leaving Pietermaritzburg on March 15, travelling either on horseback or "spider" (a light four-wheeled covered wagon), he made slow progress over rough tracks through swamps and up precipitous mountain passes. His route took him through Howick and Ladysmith to Newcastle, where he stayed for several days. There he learnt of Colonel Wood's success at Kambula, affording him more negotiating influence. At each of the stopping places local Boers anxious for news and asking for advice approached him. Time and again they complained of Boer dissidents threatening them and cajoling them to resist annexation at pain of violence or even death. Many said that all they wanted was a good firm government, and that they had prospered since annexation. His promises of support and protection appear to have reassured them. Time was short: it was reported that the Boers were massing in a huge camp, reported to comprise of four thousand armed men with horses and wagons, on the road to Pretoria. Frere only had two companies of infantry and seven field guns not engaged in Zululand. Suppression by force was impossible in the short term: it would have to be by reason that he won the argument.

Leaving Newcastle Frere climbed through the Drakensberg to reach the high, open plains of the

Transvaal. Again he encountered Boers concerned at the pressure to renounce annexation, reporting threatened violence, and asking for advice. Many rode with Frere along the road. He employed the same gentle, thoughtful attitude that had made him many friends in India. His ability to listen to anyone with a view or a need, which had succeeded in giving him a close understanding of local needs and problems in India, impressed the farmers. Through Standerton and Heidelberg he reached Klipspruit on April 8. There he met Colonel Owen Lanyon, who had taken over Shepstone's post in the Transvaal on March 4, Shepstone remaining in Natal until May when he returned to England. A letter was sent to the Boers' camp agreeing to meet their representatives on neutral territory. The next morning a letter arrived from the Boer leaders saying that they had heard Frere intended passing on to Pretoria without visiting their camp. Frere was furious. When he reached Ferguson's Hotel, where the meeting had been arranged, he found members of the Boers' committee waiting for him. When the chairman, Pretorius was introduced, Frere refused to shake his hand and demanded how he could suggest that a promise given by a gentleman and in the name of the Queen, whose representative he was, could be broken. Pretorius was taken aback. He apologised, and Frere then shook hands.

The Boers maintained that they had no leaders, that "the people" would decide. Frere would have to meet the assembled throng. After breakfast Frere, his staff and the Boer committee started for the camp at the Kleinfontein farm, two miles away and plainly visible on the hillside. It was an impressive sight, made as imposing as possible to present an aggressive stance. In addition to the tents and between three and four hundred wagons there were five thousand cattle and two thousand horses. Frere deliberately drew ahead of the travelling group so that he arrived at the camp alone. This surprised his staff, for he had received several warnings that his life was in danger from the Boers. A path ran down the middle of the camp, and on either side now twelve hundred Boers stood in a row, two or three deep. Frere, still mounted, entered at a walk, raising his hand to his sun helmet in salute. He was met with silence, their eyes fixed on him. Not one man acknowledged his greeting. Around the committee's tent was grouped a couple of hundred older men, who received him with courtesy and respect, but no warmth. A table in a large tent had been set out. Frere and his staff sat at one side, the Boer committee at the other. Outside the tent onlookers crowded in, listening intently. Every word had to be translated, as Frere knew nothing of the Boer language. This made the proceedings slow and stilted.

Frere opened by explaining that he was on his way to Pretoria (thirty-six miles away) and alluded to the warnings that his life would be in danger. Nevertheless he had come without a single soldier to guard him. He repeated the assurances he had given Joubert in Pietermaritzburg, effectively offering the Transvaal self-government under the British Crown. Pretorius was stunned: "We did not understand this," he said, "we never heard of it." Frere replied: "Send and fetch Joubert." When Joubert was found he shamefacedly acknowledged that he had not delivered the message. Frere was furious. "How dare you fail to deliver the message that I gave you? You may leave the tent. I have done with you!"[180] The effect of this interchange was immediate. They recognised that Frere had come in good faith and was a straight-talking man of integrity, even if they could not agree with him. By the time the meeting ended he had won them over. As he left, many of the men who had received him in sulleness came forward to shake his hand.

There followed a series of meetings between Frere, Joubert and Kruger. Frere was adamant: the subject of annexation was not negotiable. He offered to relay to the British Government any petition the Boers may draw up, but he would not endorse it. Kruger was gradually coming to trust Frere's word. When Frere offered to draft a constitution for the Transvaal which would provide for self-government of internal affairs as they had discussed in their initial Pietermaritzburg meeting, Kruger was convinced. He declared that Frere "was the first High Official of Her Majesty who has laid bare the whole truth."

Frere remained in Pretoria until the end of April. The threat of an uprising by the Boers had not disappeared, and their demand for repeal of annexation remained a fundamental principle. However, the atmosphere of outright hostility had been replaced by a willingness of at least some of the Boer leaders to listen and negotiate. Frere, by his readiness to discuss the issues, his quiet diplomacy and straightforward integrity, had made many friends and earned the respect of the majority of Pretoria citizens. Unfortunately his courage and painstaking efforts to reach an amicable settlement were to be of no avail. The British Government was about to sow the seeds of conflict and disillusionment with both the Boers and Zulus for years to come.

Chapter 14.

ALL IN VAIN.

Frere's problems were not helped by a further disaster that occurred in May. Louis, the Prince Imperial of France, who had volunteered for action with the British in Zululand, was killed in an ambush. This received huge publicity in Europe, and affected Queen Victoria as badly as anyone. An interesting sidelight: it was mentioned in dispatches that one of the party sent out to recover the Prince's body was Frere's son, Lieutenant Bartle Compton Frere of the 2nd Battalion, the Rifle Brigade.

Back in London, Disraeli felt strongly that a change in command was essential. His choice as a replacement was Sir Garnet Wolseley, then serving as High Commissioner in Cyprus. Wolseley, back from Cyprus in May, went to see Disraeli, who asked his advice. Wolseley told him to make peace as soon as possible as nothing could be gained from sustaining such a costly war. He also confirmed that he would be ready and willing to go to South Africa. Disraeli immediately appointed him High Commissioner and Commander-in-Chief for Natal. This meant that Chelmsford and Bulwer would be superseded, and Frere's authority limited to the Cape and adjoining territories. The Queen was outraged: she was sure that both Frere and Chelmsford would have no alternative but to resign. Disraeli assured her that it was not his intention to recall them immediately, and otherwise ignored her protests, announcing the appointment of Wolseley publicly on May 26. Wolseley had a reputation as a decisive, shrewd general, and knew South Africa well from his previous time in Natal. The Queen and Prince of Wales continued to defend Frere and Chelmsford, but could only offer their opinion: they could not stop a determined Prime Minister like Disraeli exercising his authority. Cetshwayo was reported to have put out peace feelers to which Frere and Chelmsford had failed to respond despite the clear instruction that peace was to be encouraged.

Hicks Beach was desperate that Frere should not resign at this time. He was particularly concerned that Kruger would see these developments as the British reneging on what Frere had painstakingly set up. Frere, always conscious of his public duty, reluctantly agreed to stay on. He wrote:

"I have no wish to follow the dictates of Her Majesty's Opposition, of the Daily News, or of those who would wish ill to all South Africa save Cetshwayo and his Zulus. So I shall not consult my own feelings after being made a shuttlecock for party purposes. I hope to see South Africa out of the first Act, at least of her present difficulties, before thinking of rest for myself; but it is very weary work."[181]

Hicks Beach, by his next despatch, threw the confederation plans into confusion. Showing remarkable ignorance of the situation, he assumed that it was the Cape Parliament that was hampering progress, and urged Frere to press upon the Parliament the expediency of forging unity. He adopted a rather overbearing tone, and once his letter was made public the Cape Parliament reacted adversely. From being a strong supporter of confederation, it saw in this latest despatch abstract proposals that were difficult to foresee in practice, and their suspicions were raised. It was obvious that these were not Frere's ideas – and he was the one person they trusted. Frere wrote to Hicks Beach:

> "…colonists are very sensitive, and…. neither I nor Mr Sprigg are able to satisfy some of his staunchest supporters that their fears are groundless. They believe that Wolseley has secret instructions to confederate the Transvaal and Natal forcibly, and the almost universal feeling here is to wait till they can see what is done in Natal and Zululand and Transvaal, before they commit themselves. I do not think you have realised that a peremptory tone, which would be quite justifiable where nothing had been done towards Union, was not required here in the Cape Colony, where the present Ministry and Parliament were quite in accord with you, and

had been steadily working for a year and a half past in your direction."[182]

All the work Frere had put in to progressing confederation gently with the support of the settlers was thus destroyed. By forcing upon the Cape Parliament his proposals without regard for their feelings and previous support for Frere, Hicks Beach alienated the one province that could have facilitated confederation. Frere's assurances and promises, to the Cape and Transvaal, now counted for nothing. His well-laid plans were now in tatters. The Government had decided that Zululand was not to be annexed once the war was over, and that a decision on the Transvaal proposals was to be postponed until the post-Zulu war situation was clearer. His brief was to prepare for confederation. This represented to Frere the worst of all worlds. The two major issues confronting the possibility of confederation were the Zulu question and the status of the Transvaal. The settlers in the Orange Free State, Cape and Transvaal would await the outcome of the Zulu war and the position of the Transvaal before committing themselves, and both these questions were now outside Frere's control, and in the hands of Wolseley. Frere had difficulty in seeing how he could prepare for confederation without being involved in the resolution of these questions. It was evident to him that he was being sidelined. It would have been kinder (and a more sensible outcome) if he had been recalled directly. By splitting the authority in South Africa between himself and Wolseley, the image presented was the opposite of confederation and unity; it was separation and division. He was particularly angry that the arrangement would leave him little visible authority to carry forward confederation.

Frere was instructed to return immediately to Cape Town. His journey back to Cape Town became a triumphant procession. At town after town he was welcomed enthusiastically. A public dinner and reception was held in his honour. At Kimberley he was given a torchlight procession and triumphal arch.[183] The diamond mine was lit up and a banquet was thrown. The local townsfolk turned out in their hundreds to see him – even in Paarl, headquarters of the Dutch Afrikander League. Unusual among the tributes paid were those by non-whites, who recognised a sympathetic ruler who invariably treated them with courtesy and understanding. These reactions were spontaneous: nothing had been orchestrated. In an unexpected way, Frere's disgrace united a number of disparate factions within South Africa, and was to lead to a sense of nationhood that would be important when the Boer War occurred.

Wolseley maintained a journal during his visit to South Africa, which gives some insight into his thoughts. He was critical of the decision to keep Chelmsford in his post for the time being, and saw Frere as the main problem.

"the wretched Zulu affair…took all the breath away from our Cabinet. They could not say where [Frere] would stop & his recent despatches showed he was not one to be controlled by orders from home…He was too self confident & too strong for them. He had evidently marked out for himself a great career of conquest to end in a magnificent African Empire under the British flag."[184]

His antipathy was mixed with a certain admiration for Frere, though:

"Underneath that mild aspect of gold-spectacled respectability & Exeter Hall humanity there was however a man's heart full of that determination which makes heroes & great men, so he incidentally determined to brush from his path this Zulu difficulty."[185]

However he did agree that the war was probably inevitable, but felt sure it could have been postponed until a more propitious time. He could not resist the barb:

"…why pause to consider the cost or hesitate to embark in it because some piddling financial clerk tells you the cost will be enormous. What is cost to a great nation like England? His [Frere's] whole career has evinced a contempt for economy & an utter disregard for financial considerations that makes him a dangerous man in power. It was this popularity which I presume was mainly the cause that prevented his being made Governor General of India & which also pushed us into an honourless war when our Treasury is empty & when our foreign relations are unsatisfactory."[186]

It was important to Frere and Chelmsford that the war be swiftly and successfully brought to an end. In mid-April Chelmsford crossed the Blood (Ncome) River in the north-west of Zululand and marched on Ulundi. Wood supported him. At his disposal were 4,165 Europeans and 1,152 Africans. Recognising the inevitable, several chiefs yielded to the British along the way without a fight. Cetshwayo continued to send messages suing for peace, but lacked the diplomatic skills to have them heeded. Finally Ulundi was reached on July 3. Before the capital spread the vast Mahlabatini plain, a shallow sandy basin with clumps of long grass. At its far end stood Ulundi, across the White Umfolozi River. Facing them were 20,000 Zulus. This time the British force would have to fight in the open, and not from an entrenched position. Zulu hopes that this would be fatal were disappointed. Chelmsford moved out onto the plain in the famous British hollow square formation. The infantrymen advanced in line abreast, four ranks deep with two Gatling machine guns in the centre. Columns of two marched behind the left and right front corners, with two companies closing the rear. Twelve artillery pieces were deployed at the corners and middle of each side. This formation enabled the force to halt at any time and present fire to all four sides. A deliberate plan to use cavalry to draw the impis onto the infantry, succeeded. A steadily rising hum from the impi gave way to the deafening rattle of assegais against cowhide shields as the Zulus rushed forward. Biding their time, the British artillery opened up to devastating effect, to be followed by intense fire from the riflemen. The Zulus were cut to pieces at the cost of 10 British fatalities. Ulundi fell.

The war was over. Cetshwayo fled. Total casualties of the war were considerable: over 6,000 Zulus, 1,080 white soldiers and 570 Africans who fought on the side of the British. After the war Chelmsford immediately and pointedly resigned his position. Cetshwayo escaped from Ulundi and was hidden for several weeks by chiefs sympathetic to him. Wolseley made his capture a priority, and his officers treated the search as a competitive sport. The pressure on local Zulu communities finally told and he was betrayed. The hut in which he was hiding was surrounded and he was ordered to come out. At first he would not, afraid he would be shot, but once an interpreter, the son of a missionary whom Cetshwayo knew reassured him, he emerged and surrendered in a calm and regal way. On August 31 he was led back into camp and on September 4 put on a steamer at Port Durnford and sent to Cape Town, where he was given rooms in the castle. Frere gave orders that he was to be treated exactly as would any European officer of rank.

The news of Wolseley's impending arrival made Frere very angry, particularly as the first he heard of it was through the press. He railed against Hicks Beach: "….you wish to express either disapproval of what I have done in the past or distrust of what I might do in the future.…..What possible good can I retain after such a public announcement of confidence withdrawn?"[187] Hicks Beach attempted to assure him that no slight was intended, arguing that confederation, the highest priority, required Frere's constant presence in Cape Town. Frere pointed out that the Cape was the least of his worries: there the leaders required no persuasion.

He wrote scathingly:

"Wolseley is an old personal friend of mine and I have a very high opinion of his military ability; whether he possesses equal capacity for civil administration in countries like these or for framing settlements for Zululand or constitutions for Natal or Transvaal, you will soon be able to judge.....He may make a peace to the satisfaction of the penny Press and be home by Christmas, but he will not make one to quiet South Africa for ten years…nor one that will promote confederation. Nor pay for the next war, nor secure you against having to pay for South African wars hereafter."[188]

His words were to be prophetic. By blundering into a complex situation and acting swiftly to impose his own solution, Wolseley not only effectively destroyed the chance of confederation occurring, but set back the development of South Africa to before Frere's arrival.

Wolseley was anxious to go home. He wrote to Frere on July 29: "The sooner I can complete my work, the sooner I can clear out so as to leave the coast clear for your arduous task of confederation."[189] He appears not to have recognised that Frere's progress depended upon success in settling the Zulu and Transvaal questions. This was surprising, given his opinion during his previous time in Natal that the annexation of Zululand was inevitable if policy in Natal was to be unified. The remainder of South Africa was showing disturbing signs of disquiet. The myth was circulated that the entire British Army had been destroyed at Isandlwana, and that the British could no longer maintain control. One after the other, the tribes of the eastern Cape showed signs of rebellion. Frere proposed that a couple of regiments be spared to march through Basutoland, Pondoland, Tembuland and the Transvaal to demonstrate that not only was the British Army active, but continued to support colonial rule. Wolseley replied that his first aim was to cut present expense, and that the future could take care of itself.[190]

The Zulus accepted defeat with some equanimity. The pressing question was: how was Zululand to be governed? Wolseley did not consult Frere on his proposals, nor did it appear that any colonial official of weight or experience was consulted. He adopted the defence strategy that the British had applied in India. His object was to safeguard the two colonies of Natal and Transvaal by fragmenting Zululand into thirteen small independent principalities, each ruled by a local chief under British supervision. A British Resident was appointed with a supervisory brief, but express orders not to interfere actively. Missionaries who had left their posts during the war were not permitted to re-enter Zululand.

The appointment of local chiefs to the thirteen principalities did not result in major objections from the Zulus. With their homestead economies left intact, they were more intent on establishing their positions and co-operating with the British, who held the real power. The Zulu monarchy had been destroyed; the local chieftains had always enjoyed a degree of economic independence and therefore freedom. Now it was to be formalised.

We shall never know how much of the final plan was Wolseley's alone, but no one who was familiar with the country was happy with the outcome. The Daily News, Durban's newspaper, reported:

> "The aftermath ….was catastrophic, mainly due to the stupidity and arrogance of Sir Garnet Wolseley. We are still living with his mistakes and will have to do so for another hundred years before the political errors of that era will have begun to sort themselves out."[191]

There was an alternative view of the settlement. The British Government remained averse to annexing Zululand, primarily on the basis of cost. It did not wish to bear the expense of administering such a diverse and unruly territory. An historian, Leonard Thompson, argues that "no more astute device could have been found for setting Zulu against Zulu and thus consummating the military victory without further cost or responsibility."[192]

Frere was completely in the dark. In addition to not consulting him, Wolseley sent the final settlement to England and it finally reached Frere via the Colonial Office several months later. Indeed, he learnt first of the details through the newspapers. The principle of indirect rule was one that Frere agreed with, having implemented it in India. He believed that the nature of the Zulu military machine was such that it was incapable of remaining within its borders and remaining at peace with its neighbours But he did not agree with the fragmentation into small states. In vain he protested that to preserve Zululand in small states exclusively for the Zulus would be impractical. White incursion in the guise of settlers would not be long in coming. And then what would the Resident's powers be? "The only effect of discouraging the white man's entrance is to ensure all who come being of a bad stamp…but to exclude them is beyond the power of all the chiefs or Residents in South Africa combined."[193]

The Zulu constitution resolved, Wolseley moved on to the Transvaal. He reached Pretoria on September 29, and immediately made it clear that the Act of Annexation was irrevocable. Disraeli had given him virtually unlimited freedom to deal with the problems he confronted, which is interesting, given the censure of Frere for exceeding his authority. In similar circumstances Carnarvon had given Frere the same latitude. The difficulty of communicating effectively at such distance made the delegation of authority reasonable, but it seemed that it was only acceptable if the action taken locally was successful.

Frere was by now of the opinion that confederation would be next to impossible. Zululand was fragmented. No attempt was made to bring Natal in from its isolationist position. Now Wolseley was in the Transvaal making speeches and laying down commitments which were not necessarily what Frere wanted in his push towards confederation. Newspaper articles were beginning to appear in England questioning the principle of confederation, and speculating whether "divide and rule" might not be better. At a dinner in Pretoria on December 17 Wolseley unveiled a new constitution for the Transvaal based upon a nominated council instead of an elected one. Needless to say, after Frere's undertakings to Kruger this news went down very badly with the Boers. Addressing the camp which had not yet been disbanded, Wolseley said: "I think the Transvaal has never had such formidable enemies either outside or within its limits than the fifteen hundred or two thousand Boers assembled near this Town."[194] In 1880 two of the Boer leaders, Bok and Pretorius, were arrested on charges of high treason. Pretorius did not spend long in prison: Wolseley, realising that his imprisonment was adding to Pretorius' stature in the local community, changed his mind, released him and nominated him a member of the new Legislative Council.

One of Wolseley's aides, in correspondence with the Times of London on October 23, charged Frere with having been the cause of opposition to Wolseley by forwarding Kruger's memorandum to the British government, allowing the impression to be gained that restoration of the province to the settlers was under deliberation. Frere wrote to Wolseley to complain. His reply was that it was not his affair what the officers of his staff should write. So Frere called the attention of the Secretary of State to the matter. He also raised the question of what structure was to follow Wolseley's departure. He knew the general was anxious to return to England as soon as possible, and so he stressed the need for a unified command: one High Commissioner, not two. Hicks Beach ignored this advice.

Wolseley left for England on April 27, 1880, from Cape Town. True to character, he could not resist a waspish comment in his journal:

> "The Frere girls are, if possible, uglier than ever; thank heaven they don't come home in the Conway Castle."[195]

Sir George Colley assumed his position.

Increasingly it looked as though South Africa would crystallize into a number of separate Crown Colonies and some fragmented indigenous African "kingdoms." This made Frere very concerned. Not only was confederation being quietly consigned to the dustbin – and papers published in London indicated that even previous supporters of confederation were turning away from it – but the Cape would be on its own, forced to defend its extended coastline against potential raiders and invaders. He foresaw a situation where South Africa could fall under…."the influence of some great European power, possessing a navy, and appreciating as well as, or perhaps better than we do, the domination of the great Southern Ocean, of which the Cape peninsula is the key."[196]

Chapter 15.

THE END GAME.

Frere's days in South Africa were clearly numbered. Far from a reasoned debate going on in London over the events leading up to the Zulu war, he discovered that his despatch of November 8, 1878, had been excluded from the Blue Book and thus would not be open to public scrutiny. Frere then discovered the full extent of the culpability that was being loaded on him. Hicks Beach, in order to conceal his own weak leadership, insisted that all despatches between them remain confidential. Debates in Parliament held in February and July, 1879, heard a selective account of the war from Hicks Beach, who downplayed his own role and presented Frere as a maverick. It left Frere in an impossible position: anything he said or wrote would look like self-justification which, without the evidence of the correspondence between himself and Hicks Beach could not be corroborated. He was to have no opportunity to put his side of the story. Parliamentarians queued up to condemn him. Joseph

Chamberlain accused him of usurping the prerogative of the Crown; Sir Charles Dilke accused him of "outstanding rashness." Liberal backbenchers bayed for him to resign and Lord Kimberley, the new Colonial Secretary, refused to defend his actions. The Scotsman wrote that the "appropriation of the Transvaal and the settlement in Zululand are parts of the foolish and dangerous policy of Sir Bartle Frere."[197]

The problems besetting the British government on all sides led to elections in April 1880, in which the Liberals and Gladstone swept to power. Gladstone had been the major critic of the government's South African policy, and not very complimentary to Frere. In speeches during the election campaign he said of Frere that he had not "ever been in a position of real responsibility, or ever imbibed from actual acquaintance with British institutions the spirit by which British Government ought to be regulated and controlled."[198] Gladstone and his party denounced the Zulu War as wrong and unnecessary, and sections of the party called for the reversal of the annexation of the Transvaal. A group of MP's drew up a petition demanding Frere's removal.

It therefore came as a surprise to all when Gladstone, now Prime Minister, announced that the policy of confederation would continue, and that Frere would stay in his post. The Boers were taken aback. Sensing that Gladstone was the rising star, Kruger and Joubert had made it their business to court him and began to believe that the Liberals were sympathetic to the Boer arguments. But there was logic in Gladstone's action: like his predecessor he feared the revelations Frere might make once he was back in London. As the architect of confederation, he could be blamed if it went wrong. Frere immediately contacted the new Colonial Secretary, Lord Kimberley, to ascertain whether there was any change of policy regarding the Transvaal or confederation. He was told that these matters required consideration. Frere warned Kimberley that there was great uneasiness, and a change of policy could lead to civil war. Kimberley finally confirmed that the annexation must stand.

Gladstone heaped further humiliation on Frere by cutting his salary by £2,000 and raising Colley's by £2,500. Colley arrived in Cape Town on June 21, 1880, in the midst of a Confederation Conference. The news of Frere's humiliation had been made public, and he was seen to have no authority to press forward with confederation. Kruger managed to persuade some of the Dutch in the Cape to join his campaign to oppose the move towards confederation. With this, Frere's chances of achieving his aims were virtually sunk. On July 15 the Conference formally rejected the proposals, and the justification for Frere's position in South Africa was gone. He was informed of his dismissal by letter dated August 1. Lord Kimberley wrote:

> "There has been so much divergence between your views and those of Her Majesty's present Government on South African affairs, that they would not have thought it either desirable or fair towards yourself that you should remain at the Cape, had it not been for the special reason that there was a prospect of your being able materially to forward the policy of confederation. This special reason has now disappeared...

through the recent action of the Cape Parliament in refusing to take even the preliminary step of a conference, and Her Majesty's Government have therefore with regret come to the conclusion that Her Majesty should be advised to replace you by another Governor."[199]

The British government's tactics of blaming Frere for the misfortunes in South Africa had worked. Attention had been detracted from the weak, vacillating colonial policies, ignorance of the true situation in South Africa, and the peremptory decisions made by Wolseley, which were to have disastrous consequences.

On December 16, 1880, the Boers in the Transvaal rebelled against British rule and on February 27 1881 inflicted a severe defeat on the British army at Majuba Hill in northern Natal when an inadequate force was sent to confront the Boers there. Although they occupied the summit of the hill the British force brought no artillery with them nor did they form defensive entrenchments, believing themselves invulnerable to attack, and that the Boers would retreat. During the night the Boers formed a series of storming parties involving some 450 men. They were able to come close to the summit without being detected, and when day broke at 4.30 a.m. they used the brush cover and their superior marksmanship to overwhelm the British. 280 British soldiers were either killed, captured or wounded. Sir George Colley himself was killed there, having complacently gone to sleep during the night and only woken when the battle had started. The effect of this abject defeat was to encourage Boers throughout South Africa to assert their demands.

Gladstone reacted by immediately entering into discussions with the Transvaal Boers that led to all their demands being met. In January 1881 the Transvaal was granted independence although the British controlled foreign policy. Every point demanded by the Boers was yielded. The solemn pledges that Britain had given had been broken: the hundreds of Europeans who had settled there, and the thousands of Africans who depended upon the British for protection, were deserted.

Britain's policy in South Africa was now in tatters. Zululand had been fragmented into a number of local territories. Frere's careful work with the Boer leaders had been destroyed and their faith betrayed. A short war had yielded the Boers all they wanted without much effort, and in the process extinguished any hope of confederation. Bitterness and disillusionment were the prevailing sentiments. The patient work Frere had done in encouraging colonial leaders and the rural Boers to support his proposals now all counted for nothing. Not only had belief and trust in British rule been shattered, but also Frere was seen as a "dead man walking" without any power, authority or influence.

Frere felt the disgrace that was the result of Wolseley's decisions more than most. He wrote to a friend on December 10, 1881:

> "I have never been able to discover any principle in our present colonial policy except that of giving way whenever they find opposition or trouble. They seem to me to have thoroughly alienated both English and Dutch and to have irritated the natives, earning contempt from

every quarter; and the entire severance from all useful connection with South Africa seems to me only a question of time, unless we change our mode of proceeding. I should regret this less did I not feel sure that if we go, other Europeans will step in with a protectorate or alliance, which will render our retention of the Cape Peninsula a costly and difficult task."[200]

His thoughts on colonial policy were expanded in July 1881:

" I have always urged that we should protect and rule [fellow-subjects of European extraction] on the same principles which we profess here [the UK] and in Canada and Australia, and by similar machinery of self-government. Here, again, I must repeat my conviction that protection, without sovereign rule, will be found an impossibility."[201]

The Liberal Government in England had run into serious trouble. The defeat at Majuba had brought back memories of the humiliation of Isandlwana. Egypt, Ireland and Afghanistan remained unresolved problems. Britain's colonial policy appeared to be in ruins. Frere used the difficulties Gladstone was experiencing to open a correspondence with him in an attempt to clear his name. He was very bitter about the personal attacks Gladstone had made on him, calling them mischievous. He pointed out how they had weakened his negotiating position in South Africa. Gladstone responded by claiming that on the contrary he had acted as Frere's protector in Parliament, speaking out to refute accusations that Frere had been responsible for the annexation of the Transvaal. Frere was outraged, particularly as Gladstone had heaped vitriolic public criticism on his head after Isandlwana. Frere replied:

"As regards the Transvaal, to the statement that the annexation was no act of my administration might have been added the more important fact that during the short period I was connected with the administration of that province I earnestly pressed on Her Majesty's Government, both Conservative and Liberal, the necessity of redeeming the promises made at the annexation by the granting to the Transvaal…the same measure of perfect self-government which is now enjoyed by the Cape Colony, with the same guarantees for equal legislation and equal rights before the law for all colours and classes of men… and that had my advice been then followed there would have been no just cause for complaint on the Boers' part that promises made to them….at the time of annexation were unfulfilled."[202]

Frere never succeeded in clearing his name. Although he sought every opportunity to plead his case, nobody wanted to know. The politicians wanted an embarrassing episode in British colonial history to be quietly buried. Hicks Beach, now no longer Colonial Secretary, avoided him and refused to enter into correspondence on the grounds that it was no longer his responsibility. The press continued to be very hostile, The Spectator referring to him as a man with "no influence but for evil" and "fanatically blind as to the fundamental laws of political responsibility."[203]

Frere left Cape Town aboard the Royal mail ship *Pretoria* on September 15, 1880, arriving in Southampton on October 5. There was quite a welcome party to greet him. A special train brought a number of his personal friends and a deputation of Cape merchants who wished to express their regret at his recall. There was an invitation to stay with the Prince of Wales for a week in Abergildie in Scotland. There he visited the Queen on two occasions at Balmoral, and was shown much kindness and sympathy. At the Queen's bidding, while in South Africa he had kept up a steady correspondence with her, so she was well versed in what had occurred there – and indeed what Frere's views were.

Once back in London, he moved into 42 Duke Street with his wife and four daughters. It was no pleasure to him when the warnings he had given about South Africa began to be realised. Involuntarily he became a focal point for critics of government policy. Many of the leading colonialists wrote to him in the hope that he could make the true state of affairs in South Africa public. Frere remained staunchly loyal to the government, relaying these requests to the Colonial Office. He wrote letters on the subject to the newspapers and published articles in magazines, but the government publicity machine had done its work effectively, and his opinion was discounted. This disappointed him. On October 21 he wrote to R.W. Murray: "You can have little idea of the pertinacity of the ultra-Radicals and pseudo-humanitarians, or of the extent to which they have poisoned our English opinion by false statement of fact."[204] In particular, Gladstone in his infamous Midlothian speeches had deliberately sullied Frere's name and reputation by alluding to the Afghan war, the annexation of Transvaal and the Zulu war as though they were all three due to the impetuousness of Frere. Vainly he protested.

An article in The Spectator on November 13, 1880, was typical of the vilification heaped upon him:

> "As Governor of Bombay, he believed fully in that gigantic bubble – Bombay Company-making – under which the old Bank of Bombay perished and half the well-to-do men of a Presidency were ruined....At the Cape he fought a war off his own bat, laid down his own foreign policy, and carried it out in defiance of instructions when he was so wholly unready that Cetshwayo could have swept Natal, and that the British were nearly defeated, suffered a great disaster and gained absolutely nothing by the war....Sir Bartle Frere is perhaps the most conspicuous example of the class of men who will deliberately conceive and carry out an iniquitous policy, thinking all the while that they are doing God service and conferring benefits on the victims of their policy...He was allowed to remain in South Africa till the event proved that he had no influence but for evil.... The truth is Sir Bartle Frere believed that he had a mission to civilize and evangelize the Zulus... We are thankful that a man so fanatically and sincerely colour-blind as to the fundamental

laws of political morality no longer occupies a position of official responsibility."[205]

Frere's last appearance in public was on January 15, 1884, when he took the chair at a meeting of the Universities Mission to bid farewell to Bishop Smythies of Zanzibar. On January 16, he complained of chest pains and flu-like symptoms and was confined to bed. There he remained for sixteen weeks, becoming steadily weaker, and suffering a succession of complications. It seems that he either recognised that his illness was the beginning of the end, or his many tribulations had led him to lose the will to live. He started to put his affairs in order.

In March he rallied, and was well enough to see some of the many friends who called. He continued to follow colonial events keenly, and despaired of government policy. When news came of Gordon's defeat at Khartoum, he exclaimed: "Oh, this disgraced country!"[206] On May 26 he suffered a relapse, and his mind began to wander. Despite his troubles and the despair he felt, he never lost his Christian faith. "I have looked down into the great abyss," he said, "but God has never left me through it all."[207] The end came on May 29, when he died peacefully in his sleep.

A proposal that he should be buried in Westminster Abbey alongside Pollock, Lawrence and Outram was turned down, and he lies in the crypt of St Paul's. The accolades poured in until they became a torrent. Typical was the comment: "I have never known his like; it was impossible to talk with him for a few minutes without being the better for it."[208] The contrast between the esteem and affection in which he was held by so many, and the decline of his public reputation after the Zulu War, is stark.

Epilogue.

The story of Sir Bartle Frere is a strange one. Regarded as a great hero of the British Empire on his return from India, showered with honours and seen as the ideal person to make sense of the troublesome minor colonies in South Africa, he succeeded only in presiding over a disastrous war started at his instigation without approval from London. In three short years he went from hero to villain, from great honour to disgrace. His career was ruined by the decisions taken over the Zulu War. Indeed it can be argued that had the British succeeded in defeating the Zulus without the disaster of Isandlwana, Frere would have achieved all his aims and would have been acclaimed for it.

Frere was the model Colonial civil servant. His life was devoted to the service of the Crown. Personal gain does not appear to have featured highly in his motivation. His letters are full of thoughtful concern for the best interests of rulers and ruled. In India he followed in the great liberal tradition of Metcalf, Mountstuart Elphinstone and Outram. Ahead of his time, he believed that indigenous people should be included in the administration and command of India. He was convinced, as was Elphinstone before him, that the time would come when Indians would rule India. Under his administration the Sind was given roads, irrigation systems, a postal service, education and hygiene. Its economy was developed, and law and order established. His reforms and innovations in the Bombay Presidency were imaginative and important. He developed the economy, built roads and bridges, created ports that facilitated trade, and improved communications. He brought the railway to the Bombay Presidency. He played a major part in improving hygiene in Bombay. The infrastructure that is modern India – and Pakistan - still bears his imprint. Towards the people of India he was generous, understanding and inclusive. They loved him for it.

Why, therefore, when he went to South Africa, did it all go so desperately wrong? Why did a man, so thoughtful, so humane, so convinced of the need to involve local peoples in the administration, behave so ruthlessly, so disastrously? We can see in his spell in India some of the seeds of his misfortune. A man who thought deeply about his job, who understood his environment so well, became very impatient with central interference. By the time he arrived in India the East India Company's administration had become all embracing. Bureaucracy prevailed. The important decisions were all taken centrally, and local administrators were frustrated by the lack of initiative granted them. None was more frustrated than Frere. Whilst in the Sind he fretted at having to refer everything back to Bombay, frequently to receive the wrong answer. When he did take the initiative and act on his own authority – in defiance to Bombay – he proved to be right. The vital decision to send support to the Punjab during the Indian Mutiny, and the move to establish a postal service, are merely two examples of this. Later, his conviction that decisions should be taken locally was reinforced when his blockade of Zanzibar resulted in the reduction of the slave trade there.

On reaching South Africa he found much needed to be done, and his ability to communicate in a timely manner with London was hampered by the very slow communications. Without a direct telecommunications link he had either to cable via Cape Verde or write letters. Either way it was weeks, even months, before he received a response. Whilst Lord Carnarvon was Colonial Secretary this was not critical. In framing the terms of his post in South Africa, Carnarvon gave him a very wide brief. He trusted Frere and gave him free rein, supporting the decisions he took. By and large the moves Frere made were good ones. He was able to establish trust among local leaders, and gain approval for the decisions he took. Confederation appeared to be a real possibility. Even the recalcitrant Boers in the Transvaal recognised him to be honourable and honest. Although he would not concede to them what they wanted – an autonomous republic – they were willing to negotiate with him. It was just possible that the outcome could have established a lasting peace. An agreement over the future of the Transvaal was key to the formation of a stable confederation.

The succession to Colonial Secretary of Hicks Beach proved disastrous. He was inexperienced and ignorant of conditions in South Africa. Like Carnarvon, he allowed Frere plenty of scope, but failed to recognise what was happening in South Africa. The British Government, which had never valued their South African colonies highly, was distracted by challenges from a unified Germany and an expansion-minded Russia. It wished the South African problems would go away. There was no clear overriding policy or objective. Confederation remained on the agenda without any understanding of what would be required to achieve it. Above all, it was not prepared to devote valuable resources to South Africa, and certainly did not want a local war there.

The threat supposedly posed by the Zulus came at precisely the wrong time for both Frere and Hicks Beach. It could be said that Frere was taken in by the advice of experienced administrators such as Shepstone, who was regarded as the leading expert on the Zulus. Shepstone believed that war with the Zulus was inevitable. He could see that the goals of the settlers and the territorial needs of the Zulus were bound to clash. He had experience of the proud tradition and warlike past of the Zulus, and whilst sympathetic to their cause he recognised that any attempt to appropriate Zulu land would result in conflict. As the Boer farmers in the Transvaal were intent on expanding their domain, that conflict was bound to occur..

Frere was concerned that the settlers in Natal had opted for peaceful co-existence with the Zulus. With such a long border between the two territories, the settlers would not be able to resist a Zulu attack. If conflict with the Zulus *was* inevitable, it was essential that the British struck first.

There was a hidden agenda as well. Frere had gone to South Africa to effect confederation, and in his eyes that would only be possible with the inclusion of Zululand.

Without it, the largest and most warlike tribe in Southern Africa would be sitting, free, on its borders. To Frere the solution was both simple and inevitable: Zululand must be a part of the confederation. That would not come about without the Zulu army being neutralised. The ultimatum he issued to the Zulu king, Cetshwayo, was in his eyes a win-win situation. It required the Zulus to disband their army and submit to a British Resident in Zululand. This would have been annexation in all but name. To reject these terms would lead to war, the outcome of which, Frere was advised, would be a certain and swift victory for the British. In all probability Frere must have known enough about Cetshwayo and his generals to realise that the choice would be war.

With the best will in the world it would have been impossible for a sensible dialogue between Frere and Hicks Beach to take place before war was declared on Cetshwayo: communications were too extended. It can be argued that Hicks Beach should have seen the way Frere was going long before the ultimatum was declared, and steered him away from it. Equally, Frere should have seen the warning signs he was being given from London in time to pull back. No doubt he did: he chose not to recognise them. The frustration with central decision taking he had experienced in India came to inform his actions. He saw politicians as being motivated by short-term interests, whereas he believed his service was to the long-term benefit of the Empire. He had no confidence in Hicks Beach, whom he believed to be weak, and this sentiment no doubt influenced his thinking and actions. As in India, he believed that it was necessary for decisions to be taken locally and not at the centre. He had been sent to South Africa by Carnarvon with very wide powers to act on his own initiative, and failed to recognise that when it came to waging war on the Zulus his duty was to listen to his masters in London.

History is written by the victors. Had the disaster at Isandlwana not occurred and the British Army swept to victory in Zululand in a few short weeks, Frere may well have retained his hero status. The successes that followed Rorke's Drift suggest a rapid victory was probable: the Zulus had not adapted their successful fighting methods to modern warfare. But Isandlwana caused shock waves so profound back in England that Frere was doomed. From that moment on his career was in tatters.

There is another dimension to all this: colonial rule. Victorian Britain was riding the crest of a wave in the first half of the nineteenth century, supremely confident of its might, and that it was right. India was hugely successful as a contributor to the strength and wealth of Britain. It was to be the model for colonisation elsewhere. The decision taken to outlaw slavery led to a focus on Africa, and the need to "civilise" its peoples. This frequently meant attempting to convert them to Christianity. Frere's strongly held religious views chimed with this. In a speech which he gave to the Christian Evidence Society in London on July 2, 1872, he set out his beliefs:

"The principles on which the wild tribes of India have been, and are being, civilized, are identical with those which guide the teachers of our ragged and Sunday schools for the poor neglected children of this great metropolis. They are Christian principles, and are, as far as I know, to be found formulated nowhere save in the Christian

Scriptures, wherein they are laid down as imperative rules of action in our dealings with our weaker and less civilised fellow men…..it has been a feeling of duty towards the conquered – a conviction that we could not recede without abdicating the power of doing good to great masses of mankind, and thus permitting the existence of much preventable evil. No lower motive would, I feel sure, have sufficed to make the English nation at large approve the action of her children in India in time past, or would now induce Englishmen at large to continue to sustain the burdens and responsibilities of such a charge… the duty of doing good to your neighbour – which the nation at large recognises as the rule of action, and it has a very important bearing on the value of Christianity as a civilizing agent….The earnest Christian is irresistibly impelled by the spirit of his religion to communicate its benefits to others. He may not rest whilst any remain in misery or darkness. This aggressive spirit is of wonderful power as a civilizing agency…Christian toleration… seems to me an equally distinctive feature of Christianity, and a most potent element of civilizing energy."[209]

The rulers in Britain never lost sight of commercial opportunities, and exploitation of undeveloped countries remained a central theme to empire. With the discovery of diamonds and gold in the 1870's, the prospects for South Africa were transformed. From being a very distant, outlying collection of British possessions confronting warlike African tribes and a large, dissident, farming community of mainly Dutch descent, it became a magnet for prospectors from all over the world. The British government, which had regarded it as an expensive nuisance, began to take a serious interest in its future. The Boers, whose finances were in a parlous state and who could see the newcomers being more of an asset than a threat, welcomed foreigners who moved into the Transvaal in search of gold.

The Boers soon changed their minds. Faced on the one hand by a British government unwilling to grant them independence, and on the other by commercial men of fortune whose ethics and morals clashed with their conservative, Calvinistic beliefs, they became alarmed. The skirmish at Majuba and the subsequent independence they gained encouraged them to believe that the Transvaal Republic had an autonomous future. European governments such as Germany supported their ambitions.

In retrospect the presence of gold in the Transvaal and diamonds in the Orange Free State was always going to shape the responses of the colonial powers, and Britain was the most confident and ambitious of them all. With the continuing influx of foreigners and the growing realisation in London of what South Africa had to offer, the Boers were right to be concerned at Britain's attitude. This is not the place to examine at length the causes of the Boer War, but enough of the frictions that existed can be seen to understand why it occurred. The war was in fact started by the Boers, who saw their ideas and ambitions being thwarted. They believed, probably rightly, that it was simply a matter of time before Britain sought to recover the Transvaal for itself. Thus, the Boers reasoned, better to take the initiative and fight for what they wanted now, hoping that they would thereby surprise the British and take the upper hand.

It was a false hope. The might of the British Empire was never going to allow a small, dissident group to resist for long. It could not afford to ignore the Boer threat if its reputation for dominance as a colonial power was to be maintained. By the end of the war there were 448,715 British troops in South Africa, outnumbering the Boers by 5 to 1. The story of the Boer War is a painful one. The war lasted two and a half years before Britain triumphed. In the process there were atrocities on both sides. British military tactics were exposed as being outdated and inappropriate to the terrain and the fast-moving, sharp-shooting Boer commandos. There were thousands of deaths on both sides. The surrender of the Boers led, in 1910, to the formation of the Union of South Africa, confederating the Cape, Transvaal, Orange Free State and Natal (including Zululand) into one nation. Carnarvon and Frere's aim had been achieved.

The story of Britain's involvement in South Africa is not a savoury one. Greed, arrogance, ignorance of local peoples, intolerance of other races, all played their part. There remains today a bitter legacy of the struggle between Boers and British. The history of the Union has been a stormy one. At the insistence of the Boers, black people were not given the vote when the Union was formed. The Africans became marginalised by successive governments who saw them as a convenient, cheap source of labour. Only with the abolition of apartheid and the freeing of Nelson Mandela have these injustices begun to be redressed. If we examine British motives during this time we are more than a little uneasy about the morality of what was decided and acted upon.

Bartle Frere was extremely unfortunate to become caught up in these sordid manoeuvres. Doubtless he contributed to his own downfall, but in all his correspondence there is not a trace of self-interest or cynicism. Frere was a deeply religious man who believed implacably that what he was doing was right: right for his country, right for the future of the colonies over which he presided. An eminent archaeologist, G.T.Clark, wrote of him:

> "His religious convictions were strong. He was a Churchman of the old school, untroubled by doubts or theological difficulties. His faith was firm and simple, and though very tolerant of other opinions, and a liberal donor to many societies outside the Church of England, his attachment to her was affectionate. He was, I believe, a man of great personal piety, living ever under the great Taskmaster's eye, and carrying his conscience into every act of his life. So pure and simple was he, that I doubt whether he ever did an act that he thought wrong."[210]

At all times he remained faithful to his country of birth, and to what he saw as its principles and ideals. He would argue that everything he did was in keeping with this.

It is therefore tempting to speculate on what would have happened had Frere's dream of confederation succeeded during his administration. Many of the pillars were already standing. The Cape Colony was supportive of his plans. Natal, threatened by the large, warlike Zulu nation, would have willingly joined. The Transvaal was divided between the republican Boers and those who saw no future for it outside confederation. The rebellious Boers tend to get the headlines, but there were many farmers who prospered under the Transvaal annexation, and could see the benefits that the stability and protection gave them. The Orange Free State, the first state to strike for independence, never supported confederation, but faced by the other three provinces' assent to it, would have had little option but to acquiesce.

It can be argued that Frere came close to realising confederation. Once Zululand was conquered, the settlers in Natal and the Transvaal felt more secure. The Transvaal was prepared to negotiate with him. If London had kept faith with him and allowed him to persist in his plans after the Zulu war, he would undoubtedly have been more painstaking than the hasty Wolseley, anxious to settle affairs and return to England. If Frere had been successful in achieving his model of confederation in the 1880's, it is unlikely that the Boer War would have occurred. Development of the gold and diamond fields would have been more orderly and disciplined, resistant to adventurers such as Cecil Rhodes. An abundance of natural resources would have ensured that the new, united South Africa would have been self-supporting, and an asset to the British Empire. An orderly process towards confederation overseen by Frere would have been fair, decent and humane. As the first Governor-General of united South Africa he would have ordered the administration very differently. Perhaps the African peoples of that country would have had the vote, in which case who knows what the twentieth century in South Africa would have brought?

There remains the thorny question of the Zulus. Clearly Frere saw them as a threat to colonialism, and a constant menace to Natal, and perhaps the Transvaal. He was surely right to maintain that without their inclusion there could be no safe and sensible confederation. Cetshwayo was indeed ambitious and warlike, but also shrewd. He was well aware of the might of the British Empire, and the impossibility of resisting it forever. His people did not always go along with his thinking; he was constantly faced with young warriors anxious to demonstrate their skills and bravery on the battlefield. It is not unreasonable, however, to think that good sense would have prevailed. If Frere, that skilled, experienced statesman had been able to negotiate a settlement with Cetshwayo that preserved an element of freedom and independence for the Zulus within confederation, it is tempting to believe that his dream could have been realised.

Having said all that, Frere chose to provoke a war with the Zulus that changed the equation forever and led to his disgrace. It also caused the dismantling of the proud Zulu nation, the reinstatement of Transvaal independence followed by the Boer War, and a less than satisfactory Act of Union. It seemed so unnecessary. In so many ways the story of Frere in South Africa is at the core of how the future of that country was shaped.

This book has attempted to analyse why Frere declared war on the Zulus, why he was prepared to risk everything on such an aggressive stance. Perhaps the answer lies in his personality and strongly held beliefs. For all his liberalism and commitment to local rule inclusive of the indigenous people, he was an imperialist in the main stream of British Victorian thinking. He honestly believed that the world would be a better place if British rule prevailed.

Bibliography.

Blake, Robert: *Disraeli;* Methuen, London; 1966.

Cain, P.J. and Hopkins, A.G.: *British Imperialism;* Longman; 1993.

Carter, Thomas Fortescue: *A Narrative of the Boer War;* John Macqueen, London;

Chesson, F.W.: *The War in Zululand;* F.S.King, Westminster; 1879.

Cope, Richard: *Ploughshare of War;* University of Natal Press, Pietermaritzburg; 1999.

David, Saul: *Victoria's Wars;* Viking, 2006.

David, Saul: *Zulu;* Viking; 2004.

Duminy and Ballard: *The Anglo-Zulu War; New Perspectives;* Un. of Natal Press; 1981.

Frere, Bartle: *Afghanistan and South Africa;* John Murray, London; 1881.

Frere, Bartle: *Christianity Suited to all Forms of Civilization.*

Greaves, Adrian: *Crossing the Buffalo;* Cassell, London; 2005.

Guy, Jeff: *The Destruction of the Zulu Kingdom;* Longman, London; 1979.

Hopkirk, Peter: *The Great Game;* Oxford University Press, 1990.

James, Lawrence: *Raj: The Making of British India;* Little, Brown and Co. 1997.

Keay, John: *The Honourable Company;* Harper Collins, London; 1991.

Laband, John and Thompson, Paul: *Kingdom and Colony at War;* University of Natal

Laband, John: *The Rise and Fall of the Zulu Nation;* Arms and Armour, London, 1997.

Maclagan, Michael: *Clemency Canning;* Macmillan, London; 1962.

Macmillan, W.M.: *Bantu, Boer and Briton;* Clarendon Press, 1963.

Martineau, John: *The Life and Correspondence of Sir Bartle Frere;* John Murray; 1895.

Mason, Philip: *A Matter of Honour;* Jonathan Cape, London; 1974.

Mason, Philip: *The Men Who Ruled India;* W.W. Norton, London; 1953.

Meredith M.: *Diamonds, Gold and War;* Public Affairs, 2007.

Morris, Donald R.: *The Washing of the Spears;* Jonathan Cape, London; 1966.

O'Connor, Damian P.: *The Zulu and the Raj;* Able Publishing, Knebworth; 2002.

Outram, James: *The Conquest of Scinde;* Gosha-e Adab, Quetta.

Parr, H.H.: *A Sketch of the Kafir and the Zulu War;* London 1880.

Ranade, Rekha; *Sir Bartle Frere and His Times.*

Rees, Wyn: *Colenso Letters from Natal;* Shuter and Shooter, Pietermaritzburg; 1957.

Shand, Alexander Innes: *General John Jacob;* Seeley and Co., London; 1901.

Sultana, Donald: *The Journey of William Frere to Malta;* Progress Press, Malta.

Taylor, Stephen: *Shaka's Children;* Harper Collins, London; 1994.

Thomas, Roy Digby: *Outram in India;* Authorhouse, Milton Keynes; 2007.

Thompson, Leonard: *Oxford History of South Africa;* Cape Town, 1971

Worsfold, Basil: *Sir Bartle Frere;* Thornton Butterworth; 1923.

Journals And Newspapers.

Anglo Zulu War Historical Society Journal.

C.C.Saunders: The Annexation of the Transkei

Territories in the Archives Year Book 1976.

Cologne Gazette.

International History Review.

Journal of Imperial and Commonwealth History.

Journal of Natal and Zulu History.

Journal of the Society for Army Historical Research.

Journal of African History

Natal Daily News

South African History Journal.

The Spectator
.

Original Papers Consulted.

Talana Museum, Dundee, South Africa: Frere
Correspondence

Wolseley Journals

Royal Historical Society: The Rt Hon. Sir Bartle Frere
by Mary E.I.Frere.

British Library: Frere Papers and Correspondence

Killie-Campbell Museum, Durban: Colenso Papers

Frere Correspondence

Natal Archives, Pietermaritzburg

Public Record Office, London (Kew) – (PRO)

British Parliamentary Papers (BPP)

Index

Endnotes

1   The Spectator, November 1 q3, 1880
2   Duminy and Ballard: The Anglo-Zulu War; New Perspectives. Lecture by Etherington P13
3   Frere Pedigree P2
4   Royal Historical Society (RHS) Vol. 3 1886; P163
5   RHS P164
6   RHS P168
7   RHS P169
8   Life of Sir B. Frere, Martineau Vol.I P23
9   RHS P172
10   Martineau Vol.I P7
11   RHS P176
12   Martineau; Vol.I P11
13   Martineau Vol.I P12
14   The Men Who Ruled India, Philip Mason; P95
15   Ibid P28
16   Ibid P29
17   Martineau Vol.I P34
18   Ibid P35
19   Ibid P43/44
20   Ibid P45/46
21   Ibid P53
22   Ibid P64

23 Ibid P64
24 Ibid P69
25 Ibid P64
26 Ibid P84/85
27 Ibid P93
28 Sir Bartle Frere, W. Basil Worsfold; P19
29 Ibid P18
30 Martineau Vol.I P100
31 Ibid P111
32 Frere quoted in Martineau P111
33 Martineau P123
34 Worsfold P19
35 Mason P33
36 Ibid P150
37 Martineau P126
38 Quoted in General John Jacob P234
39 Idem P243
40 Martineau P128
41 Martineau P185
42 Ibid P211
43 Ibid P260
44 Ibid P262
45 Ibid P254
46 Quoted in Worsfold P24
47 Martineau Vol.I P289/90
48 Ibid
49 Martineau P269
50 Frere to Wood in Marrtineau P380/381
51 Martineau P317/318
52 British Library. Bombay, May 8, 1858
53 Martineau Vol.I P395
54 Martineau Vol.I P458
55 Mason P40
56 Frere to Wood in Martineau P441

57   Letter to Sir Charles Trevelyan in Martineau Vol.I, P422

58   Wood Papers in British Library: Wood to Trevelyan, February 17, 1863

59   Worsfold P35

60   Martineau Vol.II P36

61   Ibid P41

62   PRO Foreign Office papers FO 881/2270; Frere to Granville, May 24, 1873

63   Ibid P66

64   Ibid P67

65   Ibid P75

66   Ibid P86

67   Ibid P88

68   Ibid P97/98

69   FO 84/1391; April 17, 1873. Quoted in Labour Supply…

70   Martineau Vol. II, P115

71   Ibid P116

72   Martineau Vol. II, P126

73   Ibid P126

74   Ibid P145

75   M. Meredith: Diamonds, Gold and War P3/4

76   Ibid P5

77   Quoted in Zulu, Saul David P26

78   Martineau Vol. II, P161/2

79   Ibid P163

80   Ibid P163

81   Saul David: Zulu P29

82   Ibid P35

83   C1748, P103

84   Carnarvon Papers, PRO No 82

85   C10179/11; Lucas to Carnarvon, Minutes of 9,16 and 18 Sept.

86   Quoted in Meredith P69

87   Ibid P164
88   Frere to Hicks Beach, April 30, 1878; quoted in Worsfold pp 72-74
89   Shepstone Papers in Natal Archives; Frere to Shepstone, October 20, 1877
90   Martineau Vol.II P180
91   Ibid P181
92   Martineau P179
93   Frere to Carnarvon, April 4, 1877; quoted in Martineau Vol.II P180
94   Martineau Vol.II P182/3
95   Ibid P183
96   Ibid P183/4
97   Ibid P186
98   Ibid P193
99   Ibid P199
100   Ibid P202: Frere to Carnarvon, November 21, 1877
101   Ibid
102   Ibid P213
103   Ibid P216
104   Ibid P217/8
105   Ibid P220
106   Ibid P224/5
107   Laband P124
108   Wolseley's Journal, P2 in Talana Museum; W.O.147/5
109   Martineau Vol. II P231
110   Richard Cope: The Ploughshare of War P133
111   Martineau Vol.II P229/30
112   Ibid P230
113   BPP C2079; 39
114   Ibid P219
115   Frere on Colonial Defence, Cape Town 1878; British Library CSD papers 66/6 P7
116   Ibid P9
117   Quoted in David P35

118 Meredith P90

119 Jeff Guy: The Destruction of the Zulu Kingdom P48

120 Quoted in Worsfold P82

121 Quoted in Worsfold P66

122 Hicks Beach to Frere, July 11, 1878. Quoted in Worsfold P75

123 Hicks Beach to Frere, July 25, 1878. Quoted in Worsfold P79

124 JSA Vol. 3 P179; James Stuart Archive – see Stephen Taylor: Shaka's Children

125 Bartle Frere: Afghanistan and South Africa P74

126 David P41

127 United Society for the Propagation of Gospel Archives; Robertson to Moore, July 2, 1877

128 Government House Papers, Natal Archives

129 Ibid, July 11, 1878. Quoted in Worsfold P75

130 Ibid

131 Martineau Vol.II P241

132 Talana Museum: Frere to Hicks Beach Sept. 30, 1878

133 Martineau P244

134 Ibid P245

135 Talana Museum

136 Cope P224

137 Frere to Hicks Beach, October 7, 1878; quoted in Worsfold P96/97

138 Hicks Beach to Frere, October 2, 1878; quoted in Worsfold P103/4

139 Martineau P260

140 Ibid P261; C2222 P8

141 Meredith P83; Official Report

142 Ibid

143 BPP LIII of 1879, C2316, pp 17 to 21; Frere to Hicks Beach March 1 1879

144 Hicks Beach to Frere, October 17, 1878; quoted in Martineau Vol.II P261

145 CD2454 P133, quoted in Worsfold

146 David P45

147 Frere to Herbert, November 10, 1878; quoted in Worsfold pp131/2

148 Colenso Papers 28 No. 2294

149 John Laband: The Rise and Fall of the Zulu Nation P196

150 Frere Record P49

151 Ibid P493/4; quoted in Daniel O'Connor: The Zulu and the Raj P149

152 Worsfold P137

153 Martineau P263

154 Ibid P264

155 Laband: Cohesion of the Zulu Policy P6

156 Duminy and Ballard: The Anglo Zulu War, New Perspectives P62

157 David P82

158 Morris: The Washing of the Spears P140

159 Idem P142

160 Laband and Thompson P143

161 H.H.Parr, A Sketch of the Kafir and Zulu Wars P247

162 Martineau Pp277/279

163 Blake: Disraeli P665

164 Ibid P668

165 Blake P668/9

166 David P224

167 Quoted in Worsfold P244

168 Martineau Vol.II P323

169 Blake P671

170 David P226

171 Martineau P315/6

172 Frere to Herbert, April 15, 1879. Quoted in Worsfold P231

173 Martineau P322

174 Ibid P321-323

175 Afghanistan and South Africa P12/13; letter dated
    January 13, 1880
176 Ibid P14
177 Ibid P332
178 Ibid
179 Talana AZW 16200/178
180 Martineau Vol.II P296
181 Martineau P340; Frere to Herbert, June 23, 1879
182 Ibid P343; Frere to Hicks Beach, July 12, 1879
183 Ibid P333
184 Talana: Wolseley's Journal 1879; W.O.147/7
185 Ibid
186 Ibid
187 Worsfold P260; June 24, 1879
188 Frere to Hicks Beach, August 26 and September 22
    1879; Worsfold pp292 and 302
189 Martineau P345
190 Ibid P348
191 Natal Daily News: Ian Player, Senior Ranger in
    Zululand
192 Thompson: Oxford History of South Africa, Vol.II,
    P264
193 Ibid P356
194 C2505 P112
195 Wolseley Journal W.O.147/7 in Talana Museum
196 Frere to Hicks Beach Janauary 17, 1880; quoted in
    Martineau Vol.II P371
197 Ibid P389
198 Ibid P390; Midlothian Speeches Vol. I P209
199 Ibid P395
200 Ibid P420/1
201 Afghanistan and South Africa P25
202 Ibid. Letters to Gladstone. Frere to Gladstone October
    20, 1881
203 Spectator, November 18801q3

204 Martineau Vol.II P435

205 Ibid P447

206 Ibid P450

207 Ibid

208 Ibid P452

209 Frere: Christianity Suited to All Forms of Civilization
     pp28-47

210 Quoted in Martineau Vol.I P46